JOURNEY TO JUSTICE

A LINDA AND SCOTT TALE OF INTRIGUE

LAWRENCE SHIMKETS

Journey to Justice
All rights reserved.
Copyright © 2020 Lawrence Shimkets

ISBN 978-1-7345697-2-8 (paperback)

ISBN 978-1-7345697-3-5 (e-book)

Library of Congress Control Number: 2020901806

Cover Image by Driven Digital Services https://www.drivends.com

Journey to Justice is dedicated to my mother, Dotte. When I retreated to the top of the cherry tree, disheartened by primary school teachers, you encouraged me to create my own path in life with reading, writing, and music. You deserve a large share of the credit for my research award from the president of the United States and my success as a novelist. Love you!

PROLOGUE

JUAREZ, MEXICO

G lowing raindrops fell from the Guatemalan sky, intensifying the colors and sounds of Catalina's dream world. The raindrops produced harmony in the world and love for her home. The bright flowers embedded in the fabric of her yellow dress radiated beyond their natural hues. The trees were awash in vibrant greens, flooding her eyes in ethereal bliss. She felt ravishing and projected a sultry air. Juan was thrumming out a steady rhythm on his drum while Catalina and other villagers in the market moved sensuously to the beat. Juan cast her the lust-filled look of an adolescent. He accelerated the seductive beat. His stare made her look away in shy anticipation of what she dared not encourage. Her body gyrated provocatively to the music as she held his gaze and urged him on with unspoken, coquettish charm. Their amorous stares increased the flirtatious intensity as the colors and sounds spiraled ever upward in a joy and peace she had never known.

"I've got to tell Mama what a beautiful world we live in. Mama. Mama . . ."

Sadness crept in, slowly at first, but unrelenting in its push to the surface. This was a drug-enhanced version of the world she had abandoned when she left Guatemala with Bella for a journey that was supposed to end in Hollywood—where, she believed, all dreams come true. She left because her mother would die from cancer without money for a doctor. The sadness overwhelmed her. Real raindrops began to replace the glowing ones. They hurt when they hit her tender skin. Her soaked dress lost its ethereal glow. The wet fabric clung to her skin and sapped the warmth from it. She shivered. The good feelings edged toward desperation. The drumbeats faded and were replaced by a new sound, one that was less familiar. What was it, and why was it there?

Catalina awoke to the scream of a siren. Panic washed over her. Was it the police? Did they know she was an illegal immigrant? Did they know about the drugs and the men? She pulled the sheets around her naked body and noticed that flashing red and blue lights illuminated the buildings outside. She crept to the window and cast a cautious gaze on the street below. No one seemed to take an interest in her room. Someone was on a stretcher being loaded into an ambulance. The police were speaking with Rubio, the owner of her building. Who was in the ambulance? Her curiosity faded as the ambulance drove off and the wail of the siren faded into the distance. There were more urgent matters. She rummaged around the room, hoping to discover a stash for her next fix. Nothing. She became frantic. Where was Bella? She was always here to get her ready for the night. She'd never been this late before. She'd never let the bad dreams creep in.

It wouldn't be this way much longer, she told herself. Soon she would walk away from the heroin and the men. She paused to look at her trembling hands. Strange. Her hands never used to tremble. Had the drug use morphed into something out of control? Something she couldn't walk away from, even when she had enough money for Mama? She wanted to believe she was too strong to let that happen. She shivered, this time in real life.

She slid into her dress and staggered barefoot to the downstairs bar.

"Rubio, where is Bella?" she demanded, more sharply than necessary since the bar was deserted. It was rarely empty. The police must have scared the patrons off by asking questions.

Rubio had been studying stacks of receipts and was startled by the insistent tone. He stared at tormented eyes and took a deep breath. "Bella died. The ambulance carted her off moments ago."

Catalina's eyes grew wide. "Bella's dead?" She gasped in horror as she covered her mouth with one hand and made the sign of the cross with the other. "How?"

"Bad dope. That's what the police think anyway. That stuff is poison. It'll kill you sure as I'm standing here."

Catalina collapsed onto the barstool opposite him and fidgeted. "Bella's dead. Now what am I going to do?"

Rubio pushed the papers aside and took her trembling hand. "I'll tell you what you're going to do. You are going back to Guatemala. Spend some time with your sick mama. Find a boy. You told me about that guy you liked named Juan. This is no place for you."

Catalina shook her head and cast him a pleading look. "I need my fix. The men will be coming soon. I need to . . ." Her voice trailed off in desperation.

Rubio shook his head firmly, then spoke in a kind but insistent tone. "No men ever again. When did you start using?"

"When I first got here. Bella told me not to let you know. She said you'd kick me out."

Rubio cast her a mournful gaze. "I had no idea. You were always so quiet. I never took the time to understand what was going on with you. You seemed happy enough. How bad is it?"

Catalina shrugged. "Bad enough, I guess. I feel shaky." She began to cry and blurted out, "Bella was going to take me to Hollywood. She told me I would be in the movies."

Rubio rubbed his thumb across a tear rolling down her cheek. He caught her gaze and spoke in a loving, paternal tone. "Listen, forget what Bella told you. She's never been to Hollywood. She's never even crossed the border to El Paso. It was nothing but lies. Through the grace of God, you are free now. Go back to Guatemala and enjoy what's left of your childhood."

Catalina became incensed. "How could you let her lie to me, Rubio?"

"I honestly didn't know. I guess I'm too caught up in my business to pay attention." Rubio's face turned red from embarrassment, and his eyes watered up. "I—I never intended anything bad to happen to you, Catalina. Bella is—*was*, that is—my younger sister. I loved her and wanted the best for her. I paid for a trip through rehab for her. Rehab is expensive. That's why I own this dump instead of something nicer. In the end, the drugs were stronger than her. Quit while you still can."

He reached into the cash register and pulled out crisp bills. "Here, this should be enough money to get home."

Catalina started to stand, but the resolve that flashed across her face diminished quickly. "I need a fix."

Rubio shook his head. "You don't need a fix; you want a fix. The lesson from Bella is that there is nothing but pain and death down that path."

"Just one more. It will be the very last."

Rubio grew agitated. "Look, Catalina, I don't know where you can get it. I don't live in that world. Go up to your room. Lock the door and sleep it off. In a few days, you'll be fine again. Can I give you a beer? It might help."

Catalina nodded. She stared at the money laying on the counter. "Rubio," she said softly when he returned with a beer. "Am I pretty? I mean, pretty enough to make it in Hollywood?"

"No. You look like a strung-out drug addict who needs a bath, clean clothes, and two days' sleep. Look at yourself in a mirror."

Catalina drew back. "That bad?" She patted her hair enough to know that it needed a good brushing.

"That bad. Look, when I first saw you, I thought that you were the most beautiful woman I had ever seen. What happened since then? I believe you can reclaim that beauty if you quit the drugs and start taking care of yourself. You're what, sixteen? It's not too late."

Catalina staggered over to a mirror in the bar. She shook her head in disbelief as she tried to tease color into the dark circles under her eyes. She turned her head left, then right, grimacing at it from all angles.

Rubio's appeal to Catalina's vanity got her attention. There was a glimmer of resolve. "I don't want to be a call girl anymore. What else can I do?"

Rubio thought for a while. "I have a friend named Efrain Hernandez. He owns a couple of *maquiladoras*. I'll see if he can give you a job. He has a good heart. The job won't pay much, but it will be honest work. You'll be able to send some money home."

Catalina sipped her beer and smiled weakly at Rubio. "What will I be doing?"

"They make things and ship them to the US. Car parts, I think. Whatever they have orders for. It changes from time to time. I'll give Efrain a ca—Oh my god, look at your arm."

Catalina's right arm had red tracks. "Efrain doesn't hire junkies. Put on something with long sleeves and keep your arms covered until they heal. No more drugs."

Catalina stared at the crook of her arm in horror and rubbed it as if the marks would go away. When it didn't improve, she covered her arm self-consciously and retreated from the room with her beer. Hollywood wasn't out of the question if she could make herself beautiful again. Until then, she had no clear idea how to earn money for Mama. Efrain seemed the only possibility, especially if he was wealthy. Perhaps he could take her to Hollywood.

CHAPTER 1

JUAREZ, MEXICO—FOUR YEARS LATER

M y hand trembled as I lit a candle and knelt in homage to Nuestra Señora de Guadalupe, the patroness of Mexico. The brightly colored glass of the candleholder bathed my office in luminous colors that waxed and waned at the whim of the flickering wick. Red replaced blue, then faded into white across the sacred image. The resilience of her spirit buoyed my own. I would need this strength to survive what might be a dreadful day.

I knocked on Marina's office door, casting surreptitious glances up and down the hallway. The building was largely deserted due to a downturn in the Juarez economy, but I feared that one of our malevolent clients would be on the prowl. This was the day I promised the test results. I saw no one in either direction, so I entered Marina's office quickly and closed the door. Determined that this would be the last discussion of the matter, I screwed up my courage and prepared to deliver a soliloquy that would decide our conflict once and for all. I glanced around the room for a place to sit but found stacks of paper on every chair.

"Need help with the paperwork?" I asked in my most sympathetic voice.

After a spate of resignations, the GenWiz genetic testing facility was reduced to just two full-time employees. It had proven impossible to fill the vacant positions, despite the fact that the volume of business could support a half-dozen employees. GenWiz was blacklisted because the correct results of a murder, rape, or paternity case could result in a ticket to the afterlife by lawless perps.

Marina, who handled the paperwork, cast a discouraged glance at the piles of paper.

"Anna, you're far more valuable collecting and processing the samples. Few people have your technical training. Fewer still have your gift in analysis. It took a long time to find you, and I hope to keep you until I retire. Then maybe you can have my job."

I shook my head. "When you retire, I'm moving on. I've lived in this dusty city long enough."

It was true that few people in Juarez had my training. The city had the highest murder rate in all of North America, and with the *maquiladoras* sputtering due to a stagnant economy, families with talented children chose options in safer cities. I longed to move to the US because I was trained in genetic fingerprinting and DNA sequencing, desirable new technologies that could snag me a green card and a better job. My family was the only reason I lingered. My parents were underemployed *maquiladora* workers. My salary at GenWiz barely fed our family of four. Fortunately, my beloved cousin, Carlos Alvarez, sent money from El Paso. He tried to coax Mama and Papa out of Juarez by offering to buy them a house in El Paso, but my parents clung to their ancestral city with unreasonable stubbornness. I came to understand that they lacked enough courage for change.

"Marina, I was hoping to speak with you about the Hernandez case."

The air stilled. A pained expression and a flying pen suggested another grueling confrontation. Neither of us had budged from the positions we held a week ago. I cleared my throat as if to brush away unspoken objections and began in a lively voice I hoped would elicit a decisive conclusion.

"You may remember that Mr. Hernandez was one of the wealthiest men in Juarez. He died unmarried and without any legitimate children. Four people stepped forward claiming to be blood relatives and submitted samples for DNA testing. There are twin girls, Maribel and Guadalupe, whose mother is a Guatemalan immigrant named Catalina. Then there is Alejandro Martinez-Peralta with the Juarez cartel and Francisco Avila Guevara with the Sinaloa cartel."

I paused as I shuddered. Marina took off her glasses and rubbed her eyes with her middle finger and thumb as if trying to suffuse them with enough energy to endure the ordeal. "Yes, yes, I remember all that. The relationship between an older multimillionaire and a penniless immigrant of astonishing beauty has captured the interest of the entire city. Seems like news outlets left no stone unturned in delving into Catalina's sordid past. Better than reality TV. As I understand it, birth certificates for the two girls have not turned up?"

"Correct. The birth certificates are inexplicably missing. There is no written record of the girls' births, despite the fact that a hospital nurse said she helped deliver the girls."

"No doubt one of the cartel men stole them. So the last option is a DNA test. And what of Francisco and Alejandro?"

I fidgeted uncomfortably. "They were born in the same neighborhood and went to the same school but seem not to be friends. In fact, they work for different cartels and could be enemies."

Marina sighed. "With our other cases, people may not be happy to learn their spouse had an illegitimate child or their unborn child has a genetic deficiency, but they move forward in a civilized manner. This case will only result in murder."

I nodded. Marina shot me a look of foreboding. Her voice was edgy. "The results, please."

I shuffled my feet uncomfortably, forcing words through lips that didn't want to say them. "The twins are his daughters. The other two are not related."

Marina stared as if looking for some flaw in the genetic data from the angle of my head or the set of my eyes. Then she snapped. "You have repeated the tests?"

"Yes. I repeated the polymerase chain reaction from samples I personally collected. I'm one hundred percent certain of the results."

Marina squinted as if trying to collect a thought that fled as quickly as the last two GenWiz employees. "These men, Alejandro and Francisco, threatened your life if the tests revealed they were not blood relatives of the deceased?"

I gulped uncomfortably, then muttered, "Yes." My voice trailed off. Tears welled up in my eyes as I flashed back to each encounter. Alejandro had pulled out a knife and mimed cutting off body parts.

Francisco had rubbed the barrel of his gun along the side of my cheek, then slid his body next to mine as if he might rape me. Their eyes were filled with such menace. "They said I would wish I were dead. I know they meant what they said."

"I see," said Marina, a look of grave concern passing over her eyes, clouded with what could have been thoughts of her own survival. She spoke louder than necessary, as if emphasizing the point. "I'm certain they mean it. They are among the most ruthless men in a city filled with evil people. Rumor has it that Francisco kills one person a week. I know less about the other, but I'm sure he has blood on his hands."

My knees buckled, and I leaned against the doorway. Marina stood abruptly and motioned for me to sit in her chair. When I shook my head, she thrust me into it with a swift but gentle motion. I collapsed in the chair, grateful for the courtesy. The water in my eyes rolled down my cheeks as I stared expectantly at Marina. The blurry eyes that returned my stare did not offer encouragement. Marina's face was awash in hopelessness. People vanished every day from the streets of Juarez, never to be seen again. Sometimes unmarked graves were found. More typically, women of my age were forced to work as prostitutes in distant cities. The police didn't care about murder and human trafficking. In fact, inquiring about a lost loved one just might prove fatal.

I chose to learn genetic technology because it was a field that promised unambiguous answers to questions involving paternity, rape, or murder. If the crime involved blood, semen, or saliva, I could identify the guilty party. My career choice in an emerging field was well thought out. The choice of location to practice my art was not. People who expect to collect retirement benefits do not resolve these questions in the murder capital of Mexico.

Tears continued to meander down my cheeks. I tried to stem the flow with a snuffle, but my effort proved inadequate. After a moment, I blinked, then wiped a hand across my eyes. Marina handed me a tissue.

"Sorry you had to endure that," said Marina sheepishly, shuffling her feet while staring at them. Nevertheless, she pressed on with characteristic candor. "Last time you said you wanted to record the correct results and trust in God. I would argue that a god who leaves the world in such a sorry state cannot be trusted to protect us."

I became incensed. "A woman who thinks she is better than God needs to show that she can champion the innocent at the expense of the wicked."

Marina cast me a withering gaze. "Look around you, Anna. Your god does not champion the innocent. Murder happens every day in this godforsaken city." She softened her tone. "We both know that murder lies at the end of this case. The question is, whose murder? If you record the correct results, one or the other man will kill you, or worse."

Marina shuddered. I was half her age. In my early twenties and older than most prostitutes, I was still attractive enough to be sold into that dark enterprise. At her age, it was more likely Marina would face a torturous death.

Marina offered a hopeful possibility. "You could say that all four were blood relatives. The twins would get a share of money that is rightfully theirs, and everyone walks away with something."

I shook my head dismissively. "I've never recorded results that weren't completely truthful. Why would I do that?"

Marina raised her voice. "Because if you don't, you won't live long enough to enjoy your clear conscience."

I pondered whether a lie of this scope was a venial or mortal sin. It was probably only a venial sin, since I did not stand to benefit financially from the lie. My face must have brightened a bit.

Marina responded to that spark and continued with more mettle. "That's the spirit, Anna. We may lose a battle, but you and I survive to fight another day. Hernandez owned a couple of *maquiladoras*. His estate is worth over thirty million. Even after a four-way split, legal fees, and taxes, the twins stand to inherit more than you and I will make in a lifetime."

I evaluated the statement in the fullness of its long-term consequences. Relief poured through me for the first time since walking through the door. "Perhaps the cartel men kill each other and the twins get all of the money. That would be perfect justice."

Marina nodded, her face erupting into bliss. "See?" she announced proudly. "The twins can win two different ways." She shrugged with both palms facing up as if the problem was solved. "Now, let's sign the paper saying that all four are related to Hernandez."

My smile faded at a different thought. "Alejandro or Francisco could also kill the twins. If the twins die before the will is executed, the cartel men stand to make millions more. I think your solution will lead to the twins' murders."

Marina blanched, seeming to realize that this was going to be more of an uphill battle than she expected only a moment ago. Her voice developed an edge of frustration. "Okay, Anna. Why don't we leave the twins out of it? We'll declare that the two cartel men are the heirs and be done with it. We live and the twins live. Maybe the cartel men kill each other and the money goes to the government. I don't care. This idea makes the most sense. No innocent blood is shed."

Tears started rolling down my face again. "The twins have nothing going for them. Their mother is a junkie and a prostitute. They can look forward to the same unless we help them."

Marina's eyes flushed with anger. "Look, money alone will not solve their problems. Why do you feel the need to save everyone in this world? Why don't you start by saving yourself? You know the cartel men mean what they say. This document"—she waved the paper in the air for emphasis—"is a warrant for your death. For God's sake, use some common sense. Your family will never find your body to give it a proper burial. The right thing is not the best thing."

At one level, she was right. But I couldn't bring myself to agree. "I have no right to play God. I want to sign my name to the correct results. I want to be proud of doing my job well."

Marina gulped, her brown eyes growing ever larger as the color drained from her face. She seemed to sense that any opportunity to change my mind was lost. She placed her hand over her heart as if expecting a heart attack. Resignation in her voice, she muttered, "Someone is going to die over this money. I would prefer it not be you or me."

I sobbed a response. "I don't want anyone to die. I need to have the courage to do what is right. God will protect us."

Marina sighed and cast me a distressed look as I unrolled the signature page certifying the results of my test. I snatched a pen from Marina's desk, scratched my signature on the paper, then handed it to

Marina. She studied it carefully, shaking her head in disapproval. Hardness in her eyes, she spoke crossly. "Why don't you think about it overnight? There's no reason to risk your life . . ."

"Yes, there is," I said as I pushed past her. "It's called truth and justice." I slammed the door behind me.

I didn't go far after my dramatic exit. I stood in the hallway, gasping for breath between sobs, wondering what to do next. When the sobs abated, I texted my cousin Carlos. He was the one who solved my most perplexing problems. He was my last hope.

Made a mess. The cartels will kill me. Please help.

Carlos was never far away from the internet because he made a personal fortune hacking websites with his cyber gang. He loved me dearly. My parents took him in after his parents were murdered in Juarez. He assumed the protective role of older brother. Times were tough, though. Feeling guilty about being another mouth to feed in a family that was slowly starving, he left our home and went on to a lucrative career as a self-made hacker. I was saddened when he moved out, but I could at least visit him a few miles away. I was devastated when he left Juarez for El Paso because I had no passport. He visited us every once in a while. Not often enough to suit me, but he sent money to help the family survive. As his business ventures began to pay off, he sent larger amounts to fund my education and then my brother Antonio's. Carlos never had the opportunity to attend college and thought an education might help us develop more ethical careers. I didn't see anything wrong with being the Robin Hood of cyberspace, but he recommended different career paths. My phone buzzed.

In El Paso now. Can be there tomorrow morning. Get passports. Pack suitcases.

We have no passports, I typed.

Get passport photos. I'll do rest.

Can't wait.

I needed to vanish. My report on the DNA test results on the Hernandez case would not escape the notice of the cartel men for long. I placed a few things from my office into a small box. I fondly studied a long row of pictures on the windowsill. I picked up each picture, replaying key moments in my relationship with the person. Some pictures I placed in the box. I paused over a picture of me with Carlos, a personal favorite even though Carlos was not quite facing the camera. He was not naturally photogenic. This was, unfortunately, the only photo I had with just the two of us. He was a loving presence for me. Others did not share my opinion. Wanted by the Juarez police for his hacks, he left for El Paso about a year ago. Carlos would not want to risk returning to Juarez, but he could be counted on to save me.

As I reminisced over the memories generated by each photo that lingered in my hands, my wandering mind was jolted to reality by a deep voice.

"I've been trying to decide whether you're packing or unpacking."

The voice was behind me in the doorway. Panic washed over me as the hairs on the back of my neck stood up.

The voice continued, "You see, if you're unpacking, then you must have decided that I am the sole heir to the Hernandez fortune. But if you're packing, well . . ." His voice trailed off with a threatening intonation. I turned around.

Alejandro Martinez-Peralta wore a tailored linen suit. Were he a random man on the street, I would have found him devilishly handsome. Knowing his evil temperament, the sight of him soured my stomach.

He nodded to my box, polite but distant. "Well, I know it's silly, but I feel as if you didn't think I loved my dear cousin Efrain. I'm still overcome with grief, you know."

He slapped himself on the side of the head in a playful way as if to emphasize a point. "I'd think maybe you were leaving town without saying goodbye, without taking care of the little item we discussed. I say to myself, 'Now why would such a pretty young woman want to throw her life away over a matter of little consequence to her? She is young and has her whole life before her. Why would she risk death?' Then it hit me. Perhaps the padres have made you feel as if eternal salvation hangs in the balance of your decision. Do you really think the santo will protect you?" he said, pointing to the statue of Nuestra Señora de Guadalupe.

He pulled out a switchblade. With a deft flourish that was little more than a blur to my eyes, he stepped over to the santo and sliced through it twice. The candle flickered, but nothing out of the ordinary happened in consequence. Alejandro stepped back in front of the door to block my retreat. He gave me a haughty smile that exposed a gold tooth.

"If they don't protect their statues, they won't protect you. Me, I never cared for the padres. I am too busy in this life to worry about the next one. Thirty million can keep a lot of worries out of your mind. Thirty million can keep you focused on the present."

My feet were frozen in place. My body quivered. I hoped he didn't know my decision on the DNA tests. I hoped to delay him finding out long enough to escape. Alejandro seemed to revel in my fear. Sneering, he took a step forward. He raised a bloody paper. My eyes bulged.

He tossed the paper onto my desk. I blanched in recognition of the name on the top and my signature on the bottom. The timing could not have been worse. I was mere minutes between signing the paper and making a clean escape.

Alejandro seemed to enjoy watching my nervous gestures. My face must have been awash with anxiety. "I found this in an office down the hall with a woman named Marina. Her luck ran out because she happened to possess a forged document saying that I am not an heir. Look at the signature. Wouldn't you agree, Anna, that this is a forged document?"

I stared in horror at wet blood covering the lettering but refused to acknowledge the question. Alejandro studied the expression on my face, content that my silence indicated eroding confidence. Then he continued in a voice filled with mockery.

"I can see by your shocked expression that it is forged. That's exactly why I took her life. She won't be taking advantage of you again. See, no one treats my friend Anna like that and lives to brag about it."

I stared at blood, too shaken to lift my eyes or respond. Alejandro continued in a smug tone. "I'm certain you want to replace the forged document with the correct one. Let's fill it out together. I have a few milnutes to spare."

The sight of blood, the smell of cigarettes on his breath, and the threat of violence were too much. I was unable to contain my breakfast and bolted for the restroom across the hall. Alejandro blocked my way with his left arm, and I barfed on my blouse and the arm of his tailored suit. He cuffed my head with his right arm, knocking me to the ground. Then he kicked me in the ribs with a pointed boot. He wiped the vomit off his suit with a handful of Kleenex from my desk, then threw the soiled Kleenex on top of me. "I'm getting the impression that you don't want my help, Anna. I'm getting the impression you would rather die than correct this clerical error. It is a dangerous impression to give a deadly man."

My mind gained focus with the realization that my life could end here. I willed my trembling to abate while taking deep breaths. The oxygen brought renewed strength. It was an adrenaline-laced fight-or-flight response, the most primitive of survival instincts. I embraced it, drew strength from it, and then dismissed the edges of doubt in my mind. I rolled on my back and stared up at the figure over me. I brazenly held Alejandro's eyes and glowered at him. He returned my stare with the eyes of a greedy soul about to lose something valuable. I understood then that he considered me more valuable alive than dead. I gained strength from his fear. Thirty million dollars was at stake, and I was now certain Alejandro wanted it all. I pulled myself to my feet, hunching a bit from the pain in my ribs. I found my voice. "Kill me and you lose it all. I'm the last person alive in this office. I'm not going to sign your papers until you apologize and let me get cleaned up."

There was a confused stare as Alejandro considered my ultimatum. Then his right hand flashed a knife and pinned my blouse sleeve to the wall. With his hand still on the handle, he brought his face so close to mine our noses touched.

"There are few truly brave people in this world, Anna. Do not pretend to be one of them."

Alejandro gently brushed my hair away from my cheek and glared. "You have beautiful eyes. In less than a second, I can make them useless. It's a tough world for a woman with no sight. It might be better to die. This blade has taken many lives. This blade has no regret for any of them."

An involuntary shudder coursed through my body as my determination vanished. I tried my best to reply with unconcerned eyes but could see by Alejandro's glowing expression that the balance had tipped firmly to his side. My knees quivered on the edge of collapse. The corners of his lips curled upward into a sneer. He pulled the knife out of the wall, releasing my arm, but kept his face close to mine. He brushed my long hair back a bit more. "You and I will sit down and fill out the form. You will do it quickly, or I will start cutting you. And when I am done with you, I will start on your family. Your brother, Antonio, is a good-looking fellow, a couple of years younger than you, I would guess. It's up to you to keep him healthy. After all, who will support your parents? They don't seem to be working."

At the mention of Antonio and my parents, I drew back.

"That's right. I know where they live. I can have them any day. Think about it."

I pulled back on wobbly legs, then collapsed into my chair. I stared at the form soaked with Marina's blood. She was dead because of my pride. Confession may bring pardon from God, but it does not revive the dead. I could suffer most burdens, but I could not risk harming Antonio or my parents. I took a deep, trembling breath. My resolve for justice was gone. I sat at my desk and pulled a fresh form out of a manila folder. I stared at the blank page, knowing that the task ahead drew me away from all my moral principles. The great martyrs of my faith would never have capitulated. That's exactly why they were remembered in prayer while people like me were forgotten. Slowly, I copied the document word for word, changing only the names. They were words of deceit, printed by one who lacked personal courage. They tarnished my virtue and marred my sense of justice. But they were the only words that could save the lives of my family. Marina was dead. That would be my cross to bear the rest of my life, but I might be able to save the others. Alejandro studied me intently with a playful look in his eyes. He pushed all the other papers cluttering my desk to the floor. I labored under the weight of his stare. I wanted to change some technical component that he could not possibly understand that would change the meaning of the whole. Then I thought of my family. I couldn't risk their lives.

After I signed the document, I glanced up at Alejandro and then caught movement beyond him in the hallway. I gulped. Just when it seemed things couldn't possibly get worse, it appeared my life was about to shatter.

CHAPTER 2

JUAREZ

I handed the signed document to Alejandro. He greedily snatched it from my outstretched hand. As my eyes cast a glance beyond him, he must have suspected that trouble loomed. Alejandro motioned for me to stand with a nod. "Up now. We'll be leaving together."

A cold, raspy voice interrupted. It was one Alejandro seemed to recognize, but not place. "Alejandro Martinez-Peralta, I have a gun on you. Don't move or you'll have so many holes that your father will be able to use you for a fishing net."

Alejandro's face blanched. He remained perfectly motionless as he whispered, "Who is it, Anna?"

The raspy voice snickered. "Ah, you don't remember me, do you? The last time we met, you and your brothers trapped me in an alley and beat the hell out of me. You broke my leg and damaged my throat so badly my voice is raspy to this day. That was what, fifth grade? But now, now it seems as if revenge is mine. There is nothing sweeter than revenge, especially after so many years."

Alejandro's face twitched as he studied me for some clue to the owner of the raspy voice. My terror faded to amusement as I realized the men were adversaries, not partners. I relished the helplessness on Alejandro's face. There was a desperate look in the set of his eyes. The corners of my lips curled upward, even though the new man terrified me more.

I cleared my throat. "Alejandro, this is your *cousin* Francisco Avila

Guevara. I believe the document you are holding proves you were trying to cheat Francisco out of his share of Mr. Hernandez's inheritance. He will, no doubt, be angry."

Alejandro closed his eyes, a defeated look washing over his face. As quickly as they closed, his eyes popped open with new resolve. He spoke in a confident cadence. "Anna, you did not tell me my dear cousin Francisco was entitled to an equal share of the money. Had you mentioned such an important point, I would have gladly split the money with him. Fifteen million apiece sounds fair to me. What do you think, Francisco?"

The raspy voice replied, "I've hated your guts since grade school. Every time I speak to a pretty girl and she turns away, I say to myself, 'Alejandro did this to my voice. What am I going to do to him?' Thirty is a nice round number. I'd rather get thirty million. Frankly, I don't see how you can object. Alejandro, would you hand Anna the document you are holding? Slowly, please, unless you want a hole in the back of your head."

Francisco kept his hand on the trigger in case Alejandro attempted to use me as a hostage. "Good. Now, Anna, please bring the document to me. Stay clear of Alejandro, so he doesn't grab you."

I rose, walked cautiously around the desk, and handed the document to Francisco. Then I implored, "May I use the restroom? It's right behind you. I'll only be a moment."

Francisco began shaking his head, then made an ugly face. "What did you do to her, Alejandro? She smells of vomit." He nodded toward the restroom with a look of reluctance. "Do not lock the door, or you'll get what Alejandro has coming. Hurry back. We have another form to fill out."

He stepped aside as I slipped by. The door to the bathroom creaked open, then shut with a thud that might have been a prelude to the trouble brewing in my office.

CHAPTER 3

JUAREZ

A lejandro stammered, "I tried to tell her we should split the money between you and me, but she insisted I get it all. I think she wants to marry me. Women . . ." He shrugged. "They get attached so easily. I promised her nothing, of course. I know what is right in this world, and the right thing is to split the money with my childhood friend."

Francisco shook his head. "You never could tell the truth, even as a kid. You are a pathetic excuse for an adult."

"Not true. I may have done some bad things to you in school, but all boys go through stages. I have a strong moral fiber now. I'll do what is right in the eyes of God, and that is giving you your share of the money. I have tremendous admiration for the way you managed your career. You are a self-made man and a very important one. I appreciate that about you. So how about if I give you sixty percent and take forty percent for myself? That seems more than fair. What do you say?"

Francisco took a step back to listen to the restroom. The commode flushed. He relaxed a bit and stepped forward to focus on his prey. "Don't make me laugh with such a pathetic offer."

Alejandro squinted out the window at the gray sky as Francisco stepped forward, gun in hand. Then Alejandro noticed a reflection of his adversary in the window.

Francisco continued. "Your whole life has been nothing but bull-shit. I'm surprised you got as far as you did. You must work for some really stupid people. Someone should have put a *bala* in you years ago. You surrounded yourself with tough guys and discarded your friends as soon as they were no longer useful. I have no respect for you. In a fair fight, I could kick your ass twice over. But then again, you never fight fair. You like to stack the odds in your favor."

Alejandro began pleading. "Of course, there is no need for a fight of any sort. I'll gladly take less. Let's say I take five million."

Francisco snickered, then released a hearty belly laugh. "You amuse me. It seems the only way I can trust you is to kill you."

Francisco took a step backward to listen for Anna in the bathroom. Water ran in the sink. A flash of movement alerted Francisco, and he turned as Alejandro whirled around and hurled his knife in one fluid motion. Francisco raised his gun and fired. The bullet hit Alejandro in the chest. The blade struck Francisco in the shoulder, though it didn't go deep. He staggered back, then pulled the double-edged knife from his shoulder with a grunt. Blood began to soak his shirt. Alejandro slumped to the floor, gasping for breath.

Francisco winced and swore, but kept the gun trained on Alejandro. He moved cautiously to inspect the prone figure. Alejandro stared blankly at him, his hands clutching his chest to no avail as blood spurted out. Alejandro muttered something in a feeble voice, but Francisco didn't care to listen. Francisco fired once more, the bullet striking his nemesis square in the forehead.

Francisco stormed to the restroom and kicked the door open. The water in the sink was still running, but there was no sign of Anna. He glanced through the open bathroom window as he grabbed some paper towels to stem the flow of blood. He had to admit that the girl had more spunk than most men. She picked herself up from the ground just below the window. He raised his gun to shoot, then thought, *I don't want to kill her just yet. I want her to make me rich.*

She fled in the direction of a parking lot. On unsteady legs, Francisco made his way out the front door. There was only a smattering of cars in the lot. He was certain one held his prey. Could he get there before she drove off?

CHAPTER 4

JUAREZ

ead lowered, I ran in the direction of the parking lot, suspecting that one of the men would give chase. Not knowing where else to hide, I crawled underneath the most beat-up car I could find, hoping it would not belong to either man. I texted Carlos.

Gunman after me.

Go to Misión de Nuestra Señora de Guadalupe. Hide in confessional. Leaving now.

Hurry.

I could hear a raspy voice swearing and someone slamming against cars in the parking lot. A pair of cowboy boots appeared only a few feet away from my face. One boot kicked furiously at the door of the car I was under. A wad of bloody paper towels fell on the ground within reach of me. Francisco yelled, "Come out now, bitch, or I'll put bullets in the heads of your mama and papa."

I suspected he didn't know how close he was to me, but I was terrified just the same. I closed my eyes and prayed silently. *God, spare my family from this madman, and I promise to help the less fortunate, regardless of the cost to me.*

The voice and the boots drifted away. I dared not make a sound that would give me away. I lay still, frozen in terror. I continued praying until an engine started and tires squealed.

Slowly, I crawled out from under the car, wary of the possibility that Alejandro was nearby. Was he still alive? I peered over the hood.

All seemed quiet. I needed my purse and the identification documents it contained if I was to get a passport. I stepped slowly and cautiously through the front door and made my way to my office where Alejandro lay in a pool of blood. I found his bloody knife by the bathroom door and reached an understanding of the final struggle. I picked up my purse and left my office for the last time.

On my way out, I stopped by Marina's office. I stared at the woman whose life I could have saved. "I'm sorry, Marina. It may have ended badly no matter what we did. But I am truly sorry it cost your life. I will pray for our souls."

I took a bus to the church and cowered in the confessional, praying that no more blood would be shed over the money. I fell asleep. I woke at a sound from the opposite side of the confessional. At first I thought it was the priest and welcomed the opportunity to confess my sins.

"Bless me, father," I began, interrupted by a voice no louder than a whisper.

"It's Carlos."

"Mama and Papa?"

"They're fine," Carlos interrupted. "Angel has them and Antonio in a motel near the bridge. They got passport photos, and we'll keep them safe until the passports are ready. Angel has a friend who does fake passports. He made me one that worked fine. Hoping we can get them across the river within a week."

Angel Morales was a member of Carlos's cyber gang. Lately, their friendship had blossomed into romance. Angel was cute and spunky. I was confident she was blessed with enough street smarts to keep the family safe until the border crossing.

"I'll take you to the motel. We'll wait this out together. But first, I have a present for you."

He slid open the window separating priest from penitent and handed me a large bracelet. "It's a GPS tracker. Place it around your ankle. Do not take it off until you are safe in the US. That way, if we get separated, I can find you. Cool, huh?"

It was bulky and unattractive, but I did as I was told, delighted he cared enough to protect me. I cinched it tight around my ankle with a Velcro strap and slid my pant leg over the top of it. Things seemed to be going remarkably well. "Which motel?"

Carlos whispered as if the confessional was bugged.

I said, "Good choice. How about if I meet you there?"

"No, let's stay together."

I shook my head. "I have to check on Catalina first."

Carlos gave me an irritated look. "Who's Catalina?"

"Francisco's next victim. The man who is trying to kill me, the cartel man I texted you about, he wants to kill Catalina and her girls. Her girls are heirs to thirty million, and he wants the money for himself. He already killed once today."

"All the more reason for you to come with me straight to the motel."

"No, no, Carlos. I need to warn them. It won't take long. Besides, you have this tracker on me."

"It's a tracker, not a magic amulet."

"Oh, he won't kill me just yet. He wants me to sign some papers saying he is the sole heir to the thirty million."

Carlos raised his arms in frustration. "Anna, you're too damn stubborn for your own good. I traveled all this way to help you, and you better start appreciating it."

I gave him a loving smile and placed my hand on his. "I love you. But I have to save this woman and her kids if I can. I just promised God I would help the less fortunate."

"Fine," he said sharply. "We'll both go. But this has to end quickly. There's a big blow on the way. It's predicted to be a real monster. The dust storm of the century."

I rolled my eyes reluctantly. I didn't want to endanger Carlos, but I didn't want to seem ungrateful either. "Let's go together. Tell me about the blow."

"Sixty-mile-an-hour winds. Works in our favor because no one will be out looking for us. We'll lay low and wait for the passports."

"The blow is a bit out of season, isn't it? Aren't there more during the spring months?"

"On the average, yes. But they can happen any time of year. You know, global climate change."

When I exited the confessional, the church was quiet. A single elderly lady knelt in front of flickering candles before a painting of Nuestra Señora de Guadalupe. We walked to the back of the church where Carlos peered out the door. He let it close immediately, a look of panic on his face. "When I came, there was a car in the parking lot with a well-dressed man sitting inside. The same guy is still there, sitting in his car. Do you think it's Francisco? Do you think he followed you here?"

I shook my head. "Francisco left before me, driving his own car. I took the bus. He couldn't possibly know I'm here. Mind if I look?"

I opened the large door the barest crack, then gasped as it closed. "It's him. We're trapped."

We backed away from the door and sat in the last pew, pondering what to do. I was stunned. "This doesn't make sense. He couldn't know I'm here unless he circled around and followed the bus from GenWiz. He could have snatched me as I walked from the bus stop to the church. Why is he just sitting there? I think we should leave through the rectory, though that door tends to be locked on weekdays."

Carlos said, "Good idea. If it is locked, we could move to the sacristy. If we see him coming, we could hide in the closet with the vestments. That's as far from here as we can get."

The elderly lady rose, made the sign of the cross, and hobbled to the back of the church on arthritic legs.

She nodded to me. "Did you just get here?"

Before I could respond, she said, "Did you see a handsome young man in a brown car in the parking lot? He's my son. He's waiting to give me a ride home." Then her eyes twinkled and she added in a teasing voice. "He's single. He needs to find a nice, churchgoing girl like you. He needs a godly woman to settle him down. He can get a little wild."

I was stunned. By pure coincidence, Francisco had come here to pick up his mother. He likely didn't know I was in the church. I shook my head at the old lady. "Thanks, but I have a boyfriend." I nodded toward Carlos and snuggled close. He wrapped an arm around me.

The woman studied Carlos for the first time and seemed to find him wanting. My cousin was one of the wealthiest men around, but dressed as he was in jeans, T-shirt, and sneakers, he didn't look impressive. He was also overweight and hadn't shaved for days.

"Oh, I see," the woman answered as politely as possible in her disappointment. "It's too bad. Francisco makes a good living. He has a fancy car, a convertible. He has a good heart. He drives me home from church every day at this time." Then she cast a sad smile at Carlos and nodded to the candles in the front of the church. "People who pray together stay together. My husband believed that, God rest his soul." She smiled at me as she toddled out the back door. I held my breath, hoping to hear the car start and drive off. Didn't happen. We ducked into a dark corner of the church just as the front door swung open. The old lady said, "There's a lovely young lady I want you to meet, Francisco." She stared around the empty church. "That's strange; she was just here a moment ago."

"Come on, Mama. I cut my shoulder and need stiches," the raspy voice replied impatiently.

Just before the front door banged shut she said, "That's really strange. She was just there. Perhaps she was an angel."

In a minute made longer by our anxiety, the car started and the transmission engaged. I exhaled sharply. "That was close. It's just a matter of time until he finds us."

CHAPTER 5

JUAREZ

W e stopped at a drugstore to get a passport photo for me, and I gave it to Carlos. Then we walked in the direction of Catalina's apartment, hoping to flag down a cab. No cabs and forty-five minutes later, we rounded the corner in time to see Francisco's car cruising slowly ahead of us as if he was looking for house numbers. He hit the brakes hard in front of Catalina's apartment complex. I cringed behind Carlos, hoping his full figure hid me from a glance in the rearview mirror.

"His mama isn't in the car," I whispered.

"No, he probably dropped her off first. This means he's up to no good."

"Stall him, Carlos. He doesn't know who you are. I'll get Catalina out of there."

Carlos sauntered up to Francisco, who had backed into a parking space and was just getting out of his car with a sling cradling his left arm. Carlos stood between Francisco and Catalina's apartment so that I could sneak by unnoticed.

It worked. I crouched furtively in front of Catalina's door. I tried to knock loudly enough to be heard but softly enough to escape Francisco's notice. Below, I could hear the men talking.

"You must be Francisco," Carlos began in a voice filled with apprehension. He wasn't normally good at spontaneous conversations.

"Who wants to know?" the younger man challenged belligerently.

Carlos ignored the question. "Say, what happened to your shoulder, man?"

No one answered my knock. I knocked again a bit louder and continued to listen in on Carlos in case trouble ensued.

"The guy who did this to me died this afternoon," Francisco said, almost daring a confrontation.

Carlos spoke with sympathy. "True justice, no doubt."

Irritated, Francisco blurted out, "Do I know you?"

His raised voice put me on full alert. I was trapped between the front door and the car. If Catalina wasn't home, I'd be discovered. Then what? I knocked again.

Carlos continued to stall for me. "Spoke with your mama at church earlier. Saw you drive away with her. She says you take good care of her. She's a nice person, though a bit lonely since your papa died."

Francisco's response was louder, as if he'd pulled himself up to his full height. "You seem to know more about my family than you should."

Things were getting ugly. As I tested the doorknob again, the door swung open. Catalina gave me a startled look. She must have recognized me from when I took samples of her girls' DNA for testing. I pushed her inside and locked the door behind us.

Breathless from anxiety, I panted, "We have to leave right now. Francisco is outside. He intends to kill all of us. He wants the whole inheritance for himself."

Catalina remained surprisingly composed despite a brief flash of fear in her eyes. "We were just leaving. Out the back door," she ordered in a commanding voice that left no doubt as to her resolve. She put a large new pack on her back and picked up Maribel. I instinctively hefted Guadalupe to my hip. Catalina locked the back door behind us. She led the way down the back steps and an alley clearly having some destination in mind. We slunk furtively behind signs and parked cars at intersections, hoping to avoid Francisco's notice.

"How did you know?" I asked. "You were already packed and ready to go."

"He would come sooner or later. I hired a coyote to take us across the border tonight. Thirty million isn't worth the lives of my girls. I'll be in the US in a few hours and then make my way to Hollywood."

I noticed Catalina's eyes light up at her mention of Hollywood. I slowed suddenly. "You have friends in Hollywood?"

She shook her head, a touch of sadness on her face.

"El Paso, then?"

Catalina shook her head again.

I quit walking, and this caused her to stop. "You can't carry two three-year-olds across the border. There's a water crossing. There will be miles of walking in rough desert terrain with loose sand and rattlesnakes. And there's a blow coming tonight."

Catalina shrugged, selfless in her maternal instincts. "I can't stay here. My girls are too precious. I have to try. Want to come along?"

I shook my head firmly. "I have a better idea. My cousin Carlos can get you passports. We can hide in a motel until they are ready. He'll bring us food and supplies."

Catalina stared at me intently. "How long will that take?"

I shrugged. "A week, maybe."

Catalina started walking again, more briskly than before. "I can't wait that long. I'm leaving tonight. It's a matter of life and death. It's all arranged. I—we—can't live in fear of Francisco and Alejandro any longer."

"Good news there," I muttered. "We're down to just Francisco."

Catalina stopped at a bus stop. She blinked hard as tears welled up in her eyes. "One is more than I care to worry about. My life has been nothing but trouble since I arrived in Juarez. I just lost the only man I ever loved, and now . . ." Her voice trembled as it faded out but came back, resolute. "This place is cursed for me. I need to get my girls to safety, no matter the sacrifice."

My heart ached for her. Catalina seemed stoic and selfless, a far cry from the woman she was rumored to be. News travels fast when thirty million dollars is involved, and there was endless speculation on TV about her unsavory past. Most people thought the rumors of drugs and prostitution must be true if the twins' father Efrain didn't marry her. Instead, I found a noble mother before me, though understandably one on the verge of a breakdown.

Catalina collapsed onto the bench at the bus stop. Tears trickled in waves down her face. "I want a better life for my girls. There is nothing for us here, and there never will be. I have to leave for them."

Maribel began to cry softly, probably recognizing her mother's distress. Her crying grew louder despite Catalina's attempts to soothe her between her own sobs. Guadalupe followed suit. Helplessly, I attempted to soothe all three, but the tears kept coming. I thought about my promise to God to help the less fortunate. Before I had time to check myself with a reasoned response, I blurted out, "Okay, I'll go with you. My cousin can meet us in El Paso."

Maribel had a soulful expression in her tired eyes. "Francisco is bad. He has a gun."

I nodded. "That sums it up."

"He wants to kill us." She studied me for confirmation.

"But we escaped."

Catalina's lips tightened. "The good guys don't always win, honey. We escaped this time, but that doesn't mean we will always escape. That's why we have to run as fast as the wind."

"Fast as the wind," Maribel sighed.

"Fast as wind," Guadalupe mimicked.

My thoughts suddenly turned to Carlos. We were about a block away from each other, separated by the bulky apartment complex, and I hadn't heard a gunshot. That was a good sign, but it didn't mean he was clear of trouble. I texted him about my change in plans. He wouldn't be pleased.

CHAPTER 6

JUAREZ

C arlos Alvarez gave Francisco a blank stare, having run out of things to say. Francisco cast an angry glance at him. "How do you know my mom?"

Alvarez became flustered and began stammering. "I—I mean we—I mean from church."

Francisco lost all patience. "Out of my way. I have some business to attend to."

He paused to check the apartment numbers, then stormed up to Catalina's second-floor apartment and tested the knob. When it didn't give, he pounded on the door. Alvarez ducked out of view beside the car and let air out of one of the front tires. Francisco was too enraged to notice as he kicked the front door open and barreled inside. Alvarez emptied his water bottle into the gas tank, then melted into the shadows of a clump of bushes across the street with anxious concern. Francisco emerged from the house a few minutes later. He kicked the railing on the way down the steps. He winced then grabbed his shoulder. Clearly, he had found no one in there. Alvarez exhaled a sigh of relief.

Francisco stormed back to his car and started the engine. As he pulled forward, the car wobbled on the flat tire. He put the car in park with the engine running. He kicked his flat tire and cursed. He opened the trunk, cursed again, then drove half a block before the engine died.

Alvarez chuckled as Francisco tried to start it over and over but got only a grinding noise.

Alvarez slipped away with a grin on his face as the shadows lengthened in the late afternoon light. He hadn't expected water to enter the fuel line so quickly. The car must have been low on gas. Now he just needed to find Anna and head to the motel.

He studied the western sky, which was the odd shade of orange that preludes a dust storm. He hated blows, but they passed. He hoped that the wrench in the pit of his stomach was not an omen of something far worse. Then his phone vibrated.

CHAPTER 7

JUAREZ

After getting off the bus at the edge of town and walking for over a mile, we arrived at an attractive house whose number matched the address on a scrap of paper Catalina held in her hand. The sky darkened prematurely as a swirling breeze kicked up sand. In the northwest, an orange cloud of dust reddened with the late afternoon sun. It did not look like a good night to travel. I started to make that point to Catalina when a young man came out of the house. Catalina handed him a wad of US dollars, and he counted them.

"There are only three thousand dollars here. There are four of you. I charge three thousand per person."

Catalina said, "You told me I could bring my girls for free."

"Yes," the man named Mateo said. "But you have another woman with you. She costs three thousand dollars too." He held out his empty hand expextantly.

"I don't have the money," I stammered defensively.

He emphasized his point by shrugging. "Three thousand if you want to go."

Catalina pleaded with him. "I need her help to carry my girls. I can't do it alone."

The man lifted her backpack with his free hand, then shifted his gaze to the twins but still shook his head. While he was off-balance holding the backpack with one hand, I snatched the bills from his other hand and gave Catalina a smug smile. "It's not a good night to travel anyway. There's a dust storm coming. It looks like a big one."

Mateo dropped the backpack and tried to grab the money back. Mouth agape and eyes wide, he seemed startled at my speed. I was good in soccer. I could hold my own with quick moves. "No, no. It is a good night to travel," he insisted.

He tried to reach around me, but I kept twisting and turning, the money tantalizing but just out of reach. He stammered, "The US Border Patrol will not be out tonight because of the storm. It is the safest time to travel."

I repeated firmly, "I don't have the money." Turning to Catalina, I said, "Let's go back. We can have passports in two days and cross safely and for free after the dust storm has passed."

I grabbed Catalina's arm and pulled her away. To my surprise, she followed. Perhaps she thought I was being coy. Perhaps she was worried I couldn't go and she would have to do it all on her own. Mateo tailed us. Now there was a pleading tone in his voice. "Okay, you can all go for three thousand. But we need to leave quickly because the storm will be here in a few hours."

Catalina stopped despite my gentle tugging, which became more insistent as she resisted. I winced at her words. "Let's go, Anna. We can make it before the storm hits."

We both turned to look at the angry sky. The storm was larger than Juarez and seemed to be swallowing the city. The sun was barely discernible in the dust. The blowing sand pricked my skin like needles.

I tried again to deter Catalina. "I'm worried the blowing sand will hurt the girls' delicate skin and eyes."

Catalina righted the backpack and pulled out two sweaters with hoods. "I can cover them."

My mouth went dry. I started to object but then let it pass. It seemed to make Catalina happy to leave. I remembered my promise to God to help the less fortunate. Who could be less fortunate than Catalina? She lost her lover, and now a madman was threatening her and her children. She was truly alone. What would be the harm in helping her across the river? Carlos could always find me in El Paso with the anklet.

"Let's go," I said as I texted Carlos yet again.

CHAPTER 8

JUAREZ

A lvarez texted Anna repeatedly. In her first reply, she said she was all right and was helping Catalina flee with her children to someplace safe. In her second reply, she said she would meet him at the motel. Alvarez was nearly back to the motel when he received a text from Anna saying she would help Catalina cross the Rio Grande tonight and meet him in El Paso.

Alvarez balled his fist in frustration. Anna didn't use common sense. She always placed the needs of others before her own safety. He had gone to considerable effort to put everything in place to move the entire family quickly and efficiently across the Rio Grande. And now she had abandoned the plan for something where the outcome was anything but certain.

Alvarez called again and again, pleading with her to use common sense. Coyotes were expensive. Coyotes couldn't be trusted. A major dust storm was approaching. There were rattlers, scorpions, tarantulas, and Gila monsters that couldn't be seen in the dark. They were risking the lives of the girls. She was risking her life for people she didn't really know. His reasoned arguments were ignored. The woman could be madly stubborn when she was taking the righteous path. His impassioned calls went to voicemail.

Alvarez stopped by the motel to fill in Angel and Anna's family. He was near tears, explaining that Anna had trusted her life to a coyote she didn't know on a journey of unlikely success. He drew solace in the only way he could, by tracking her movements on his computer with the GPS transmitter around her ankle. If he could find her, he might be able to rescue her. He tried to allay the tension by showing her parents how he was tracking her movement. The blinking dot on the screen was reassuring and calmed the group, but it didn't guarantee rescue. At that moment, she was traveling east of Juarez along a desolate stretch of the Rio Grande bordering Hudspeth County, Texas. He spoke with confidence about rescuing her, if only to relieve his own anxiety.

Then Alvarez left the motel and headed northeast to the only people he trusted with this problem—Scott and Linda Williams. He had met the couple nearly a year ago when he showed up at their ranch looking for his Cessna and his friend Bushwhacker. His plane had been shot down by a Pentagon black op and his friend murdered at their place, Setting Sun Ranch. As luck would have it, they were former FBI agents with considerable talent. Together with the Williamses, he had unraveled an assassination plot of historical proportions and saved the US president's life. Alvarez became a national hero in the US. For his part, Alvarez was granted US citizenship and awarded the Presidential Medal of Freedom. This was his ticket between the sister cities of El Paso and Juarez, a ticket most Mexicans, including his family, couldn't buy. Nevertheless, he had powerful enemies in Juarez and preferred anonymity. So he handed the agent a passport for Jorge Rodriguez, which he'd used to enter the country earlier in the day. The passport was the work of Angel Morales's friend and scanned clean.

Setting Sun Ranch was located near Sierra Blanca, a town off I-10 about eighty-five miles from El Paso. Sierra Blanca was named for the nearby mountain. The mountain was named for the white poppies that bloomed in profusion during the spring. Alvarez could barely see the outline of the mountain in the dust storm. He was herded into a US Customs and Border Protection checkpoint that searched for contraband and illegal immigrants. His scruffy appearance and Latino heritage inclined the agents to take a closer look. The checkpoint had gained notoriety with the arrests of singer Willie Nelson, rapper Snoop Dogg, and actor Armie Hammer for possession of pot. The agents took a quick peek in the back windows but didn't search Alvarez's vehicle.

He inquired about Hudspeth County Sheriff Office's celebrity deputy, action star Steven Seagal, who patrolled the area a few days each month, but he learned Seagal wasn't on duty.

It was near midnight when he arrived at Setting Sun Ranch to a warm cup of coffee. Linda Williams was both beautiful and deadly. In her early forties with long dark hair and sapphire eyes, she spoke and acted like a Southern belle. All eyes turned to stare when she entered a room, some from lust and others from jealousy. In the martial arts, she was the match of anyone, male or female. Her athletic prowess astonished all because she seemed so helpless in pumps and makeup. On the shooting range, she could hold her own with a pistol. She and Alvarez had bonded when she cracked his computer code.

Scott was tall, dark, and handsome, the masculine complement to Linda's femininity. His brash style alienated many, especially those with lesser abilities. Scott had an exemplary record in solving cold cases. With unparalleled observation skills, some likened him to the mythical Sherlock Holmes. He was a crack shot with a long-range rifle, trained to be on a SWAT team, but ultimately preferred to be a detective. He had saved the president's life when he killed a sniper.

When they first met as newcomers at the FBI, Linda found Scott to be self-absorbed. He was fast-talking and easily provoked. Though strikingly handsome, she dismissed him immediately and resisted his efforts to date. When she finally relented, the hug at the end of her first date with Scott was a rush she hadn't expected. She relished the passion in their relationship. His hugs came to be moments of inspiring calm in a whirlwind of FBI turmoil. After twenty years in the FBI, Linda and Scott retired to Sierra Blanca so Scott could try his hand at ranching. Scott had wanted to be a cowboy since he was a kid. Though he wasn't very good at it, he was enjoying the challenge. Linda, not so much. She missed the malls, museums, and big-city life. It was an ongoing source of tension between them, especially since the ranch netted red ink.

Alvarez arrived at Setting Sun Ranch feeling sandblasted, and the blow wasn't over yet. He fired up his computer and pointed to the major problem, a blinking light on a map that had remained stationary for over an hour. His voice was laced with anxiety.

"Anna crossed the Rio Grande almost directly south of here. She isn't far from here as the crow flies, but there are few roads, and I don't have four-wheel drive. The thing that worries me most is that their progress suddenly stopped. They've been at this same spot for over an hour. If they are moving, at least I know they're alive. Now, I don't know."

He wrung his hands in anguish.

Linda intervened. "They've probably holed up from the sandstorm. I was just looking at the weather forecast. The storm will probably blow for a few more hours. We know exactly where she is, and we can be there at the crack of dawn with horses and a four-by-four truck."

Reassured, Alvarez relaxed his grip. But the tension didn't diminish entirely. For all the genius that trickled through his body, his life was little more than a continuum of anxious moments. He was not particularly social or adventurous, and the past year had tested his mettle beyond what he thought he could bear. Now they were talking about horses. He hoped he wouldn't have to ride a horse across sand dunes in the desert. That would be an extraordinary challenge to one more academic than athletic.

He smiled at Linda as he gazed into her eyes. He was drawn to the brilliant blue color of her eyes. It seemed as if they held honesty and assurance. He didn't have the courage to hold the gaze very long for fear something tender would break.

Scott could do little more than stand back and watch things play out between Linda and Alvarez. It was difficult to communicate since the two men operated on different frequencies. So while Linda and Alvarez talked, Scott packed. Hard to know exactly what was needed. None of them could imagine the consequences of the storm.

CHAPTER 9

RIO GRANDE, MEXICO

W e were nearing Hudspeth County, which had a porous and desolate border that kept life interesting for the ranchers. The paved road became a dirt road, then the dirt road became a rutted mess. Mateo negotiated his way around, or more often through, deep holes. The jostling was entertaining at first, but soon deteriorated into an unwelcome chore fighting for purchase in the bed of a shifting truck. When Guadalupe began whimpering, Catalina beat on the back window. "Can you slow down? We're taking a beating back here."

Mateo didn't slow down. "Storm's coming fast."

Finally, I turned my phone off and placed it in my pocket. It was getting low on juice. Catalina reached out and touched my hand. "I'm so grateful you are here, Anna. You give me confidence. Thank you."

I nodded but couldn't bring myself to say, "You're welcome." Carlos had so unnerved me that I was now certain I had made the wrong decision and our lives were about to be forfeit. Catalina sat with an arm around Maribel, staring into the darkness at an uncertain future. Above us, billions of twinkling lights winked out in the gathering dust cloud. Behind us, the swirling dust engulfed Juarez, nearly blotting out the city lights. It was clear that the dust would pass directly over us, and I hoped it wouldn't consume us like a swarm of locusts.

Mateo turned the headlights off, navigating the pitted road with only the amber running lights. I suspected he did this to avoid being seen by Border Patrol agents on the other side of the river. He called the crossing point Javelina Hill. I hoped there were no javelinas. They had scary tusks. I glanced over at Catalina, who seemed calm. Unexpectedly, Mateo veered sharply left into a thick clump of river cane, throwing us to the side of the pickup bed. He turned off the engine and sat, listening to the night sounds. After a brief pause, the frogs and birds resumed their ancient choruses as if there were no humans around.

"Looks good," Mateo whispered. "This is where we cross."

The temperature was in the mid-sixties. The wind kicked up sand that swirled in gusts, offering a gentle reminder of what was bearing down on us. Catalina lifted Guadalupe out of the truck and then Maribel. She offered me a hand, but I leapt into the soft sand unassisted. The river gurgled where the wind made waves that lapped at the shore or against submerged branches. The river looked broad but didn't seem very deep from the branches protruding above the surface. The prolonged drought left the farmers in the area desperate. Local Juarez news stations had reported that Elephant Butte Lake was down ninety-six percent, and wells were being dug in a feeble attempt to save the agriculture industries. As a result, the Rio Grande was reduced to a trickle.

Clutching both of her daughters, Catalina stared across the water and announced to them with perfect confidence, "Across the river is the US. We'll leave Mexico forever."

Guadalupe tugged her mother's arm. "It's dark and scary."

Catalina bent down and pulled her girls close. "There is nothing to fear. Francisco will stay on this side of the river. Once we cross, there will be no more bad guys."

In her eyes, all opportunity lay to the north, where the disadvantaged could become movie stars or presidents. But all that was academic as we stared across the gurgling river into a dark void. I came up behind her and touched her softly on the shoulder. It was meant to be reassuring. She gripped my hand firmly in her uncertainty and need. A quiet determination welled up inside me to do right by her girls. I would gift her the same determination I received from Carlos. Three people needed me. I couldn't let them down.

What was Carlos so paranoid about? The man was infuriating. It was part of his psyche to reduce choices to a series of equations and follow the safest path. I understood that this crossing was not as safe as passport control, but what harm would come from it? Perched above the eroded riverbank, the United States seemed so close. It didn't seem difficult to get there. Wade across the river, walk a mile through the desert, then meet a pickup going to El Paso. What could go wrong?

As Mateo scouted for the best path across, Maribel sat down and began playing in the warm sand. Guadalupe followed suit. It was past their bedtime, but some children shed the bondage of routine more easily than adults. Their innocence was infectious. I dropped to the ground and shoveled sand on Guadalupe's legs. She giggled as Maribel did the same. Surely the best was yet to come. In a few hours, we would be sleeping in a motel in El Paso, reveling in the adventure of a lifetime.

Mateo hoisted the pack onto Catalina's back and another onto his own. "Quickly. We have a ride waiting and a sandstorm to beat."

The urgency in his voice snapped me to attention. I scooped up Maribel while Catalina grabbed Guadalupe. We kicked our shoes off, and before long, mud was squishing between our toes. The water was colder than I expected, numbing my feet by the time I made it across. Fortunately, the river wasn't deep, coming no higher than my thighs. Now we were in the United States! The land of the free. Slipping my shoes back on while balancing Maribel on one hip, I scrambled up the steep riverbank and through the cane to the desert. There was a worn trail, and I recognized it for what it was—Mateo's private path into the land of opportunity.

As soon as I burst through the protective cloak of the river valley and surrounding giant cane, I was nearly blown off my feet by the force of the wind. The barren floodplain offered no respite from the sand blowing across the desert. Plant debris blew across the trail before us. Maribel started to cry. Catalina stopped Mateo. She unloaded blankets for the girls. We covered all our exposed skin. While it helped for a while, we soon found ourselves choking on the sand. Even Mateo seemed to be laboring against winds that threatened to blow us sideward at a misstep.

Catalina tripped and fell in a spot of sand that was much softer than the rest. She screamed in surprise. On the way down, she had the presence of mind to twist so that she landed on her backpack instead of Guadalupe. A mournful groan echoed in the wind. I rushed over to help Catalina up, thinking she might have twisted an ankle.

Catalina's eyes grew wide. "Someone's under me!"

She recoiled and reached into the side pocket of her backpack for a flashlight. The sand formed a raised surface the size and shape of a man. There was another groan. I set Maribel down and dug furiously. In a few minutes, we uncovered the man's head. I cradled it in my lap, gently brushing the sand off his face. Who was he? How did he come to be here? What was wrong with him?

Mateo snapped at us. "Turn the light off. The Border Patrol will see it."

Still cradling the man's head, I asked for some water. Mateo said he had none to spare, but Catalina pulled out a water bottle. She pulled a blanket out of her pack and propped it up as a lean-to in order to block the swirling sand. Everyone huddled under the blanket, studying the man. Catalina turned on her flashlight again in our makeshift tent and unburied his legs. Mateo said, "Snakebite. A sidewinder. See how swollen one calf is?"

I studied Mateo. "We need to take him to the hospital."

Mateo gave me a hard stare. "There is no way we can carry him a mile or more to the nearest road. If we called the authorities to pick him up, they would know we were here, and before long, we'd be in jail and then on our way back to Mexico. Crossing the desert is never easy, especially at night. Some don't make it."

I snapped at him. "Is this your doing? Did you leave him here to die?"

Mateo shook his head. I wanted to believe him but wasn't convinced by his body language.

Mateo continued, "You can't risk the lives of all for one unlucky person. This," he said, pointing to the man's leg that had a horrid, gangrenous odor, "is bad luck. It's an act of God."

Eyes still closed, the man tried to speak but was too feeble. I slowly poured some water down his throat, and he swallowed it. I boldly announced, "Well, this one is going to make it if I have to drag him."

I recognized my folly as soon as I spoke. We were already burdened beyond capacity with two children and backpacks. Outside the makeshift tent, the wind howled ever louder. Wind gusts ripped violently at the blanket and wailed off into the darkness. It seemed as if the storm would either sweep us away or bury us under feet of sand.

Mateo pulled a blanket out of his backpack to increase the size of the lean-to. Catalina's back supported one side and her backpack the other. Sand drifts were already forming around it as the temperature fell. There was no choice but to huddle in the piercing sand until the storm blew over.

After Mateo wrapped the other blanket around us, he ducked out of sight. I thought I heard Mateo speaking on a phone. When Mateo came back to the lean-to, his phone was in his hand. He must have come here often to learn where in this barren landscape he could get phone reception. This maneuver required help from others, and a phone was necessary.

As he put the phone away, I asked, "We're going to miss the pickup, aren't we?"

Mateo shook his head. "They're delayed too. The storm is slowing everyone. We'll have to stay here for a few hours. Get some rest. We have nearly a mile to walk to the road."

I gave the snakebit man some more water. He swallowed it gratefully, this time opening his eyes and studying me. His eyes drifted toward the others, seeming to understand that this was another desperate family on an uncertain journey. His eyes focused on our leader. "Mateo, did my wife and children make it?"

Mateo nodded weakly, then turned and left. "He lied to us, Catalina. He left this man to die. I don't trust him."

Sick as he was, the man understood and whispered. "Most of them can't be trusted. It's not like the old days."

I ripped his pant leg, nearly gagging from the smell. The tissue was black and swollen. The poison or an infection from the poison had spread up his calf into his thigh. I suspected immediately that the leg would have to be amputated soon for the man to live.

The man spoke again. "My leg was not Mateo's fault. Rattler. Stay close to Mateo when you cross the desert. He'll listen for snakes. With the wind and the cold, I doubt they'll be out."

I started to question the man about his circumstances, but he drifted back into unconsciousness. I spoke to him as tenderly as a mother, even though I suspected he couldn't hear me. "I'm going to help you." I took the GPS ankle bracelet off and put it in the man's pants pocket. "This is so I can find you after we get picked up. We'll get you to a hospital."

Despite the howling wind, the girls fell asleep with their heads on Catalina's lap. Catalina's back was supporting part of the blanket, and occasionally debris hit it with a dull thud. It was a thick wool blanket, though, and provided excellent protection. Soon a sand drift built up that strengthened the lean-to. The other end of the lean-to was supported by Catalina's backpack, which stood upright in the sand. I sat in the center, providing a third support. Mateo was gone. Did he desert us, now that we had discovered his dirty lie? Catalina seemed to be crying softly.

"Mateo may leave us here to die too," said Catalina. "He has our money and no reason to stay. For all we know, he's already on his way back to Juarez. I'm so sorry, Anna. You've done so much for me. You don't deserve this."

I touched her arm gently to encourage her. "Don't worry. Carlos knows exactly where we are. He will find us in the morning." My answer seemed to reassure her, and she stopped crying.

Mateo came back when the wind began to abate. He ignored me and sat next to Catalina. "Catalina, you are a pretty woman, and I could use you for a wife. Why don't you come back to Mexico with me? I make a lot of money and will take care of you and your girls. And we'll have other kids. Boys."

Catalina pulled away. "I have friends in the US. I think we have a better future there."

Mateo continued, "Think about it. We could live in a fine house with servants. You would never have to work again."

Catalina became angry. "And when you tire of me, you will abandon me like the man with the snake bite."

Her words angered Mateo. He was apparently not used to women in this delicate position scorning his advances. Their lives were entirely at his mercy. Mateo pulled Catalina close. He groped her breasts. Catalina turned to defend herself, waking Guadalupe in the process. However, Mateo's grip was strong, and she couldn't break it. He tried

44

to kiss her, but she turned her head. Guadalupe began to cry, and soon Maribel was crying too.

I lunged at Mateo and slapped him across the face as hard as I could. "Release her, or I'll kick you so hard you'll turn from a rooster to a hen."

Mateo punched me, and I sprawled on the sand, gasping for breath. Mateo's head caught the top of the blanket and pulled it up, destroying the makeshift shelter. The blanket unfurled in the wind. Sand covered us. Mateo snatched his blanket in disgust and stuffed it in his backpack.

"Let's go," he ordered. "They'll be here soon."

Catalina picked up her blanket. Mateo bristled. "Come on, or you'll end up like him," Mateo said, pointing to the man lying prostrate.

We had no choice but to follow. I whispered to the sick man, "I'll be back soon." The man was unconscious and didn't seem to hear me. I placed a cloth over his face to keep the sand from blocking his breathing. I picked up Maribel and followed Catalina, who was carrying her backpack and Guadalupe.

The wind had died down considerably. Mateo led the way with a small flashlight trained on the ground. Catalina was next, then me, forming a tight caravan. We each tried to step into Mateo's footprints, though that wasn't always possible. We sometimes sank ankle deep in the soft sand. There was no obvious path, so we sometimes circled around clumps of brush. I picked up some thorns when I brushed against a cactus. Even Mateo yelped once or twice.

Given the many obstacles in our path, I had no idea how Mateo knew which way to go. There were no stars to navigate by, no city lights, no moon, and no sunrise. In little over an hour, we came to an SUV parked at the end of a dirt road facing the north. Two white men came out to meet us. The smaller one opened the door for us. The cab light did not come on. I imagined the light was off so they wouldn't alert the Border Patrol. He inspected us carefully with a flashlight as we got in the car. The larger one grabbed Catalina's pack and placed it in the back of the SUV. Then they closed the doors. There was some discussion, at one point loud and bitter, but I could not make out what they were saying. I couldn't see what they were doing either in the dark. This made me uncomfortable. I didn't think there was need for a lengthy discussion. We only needed a lift to El Paso to finish the journey. I turned on my phone to text Carlos. No service. Then I opened the door a crack to listen to the men, but the conversation was over.

Without saying a word, the driver started the SUV and began to drive away. When he turned right onto a main road, I suspected it was the wrong direction. Then I caught sight of a digital compass in the rearview mirror that said *E*. I panicked, because we should be going west. I checked my phone again. Still no service. My anxiety rose. Having given my GPS tracker to the snakebit man, there was no way Carlos could track me if I was being abducted. I began to worry. Did I make a hasty mistake? Once again, I ignored sound advice from Carlos, and this time it could prove fatal. I fidgeted uncomfortably, hoping for any clue that my suspicions were incorrect.

The sky was beginning to lighten in the east, confirming the accuracy of the digital compass. After twenty minutes of steady eastward progress, I spoke.

"Excuse me. We seem to be going east and should be going west. We are going to El Paso, right?"

The two men in the front seat exchanged uneasy glances. An awkward silence ensued as neither one answered the question. Finally, the large man in the front passenger seat spoke. He had an unusual accent that I wasn't familiar with. "We are going to El Paso, but we need to avoid the Border Patrol checkpoints and the roads that are closed from sand drifts. We'll turn west shortly. You can take a nap. We'll be in El Paso in two to three hours."

He spoke words I wanted to hear, but I suspected he was lying. Fifteen minutes later, I still had no phone service and asked in an insistent manner, "We're still going east. When are we going to turn west?"

The man in the front passenger seat turned around, frustration evident in his dark face. He lunged for my phone, ripping it out of my hand despite my scream of protest. The man spoke angrily. "We are not going to El Paso. We're going to New Orleans." He flicked open a switchblade. "If you don't quiet down, I'll do something desperate."

My whining gave way to stunned silence. I reviewed my options. There didn't seem to be any. Finally, I spoke in a meek voice. "What will we be doing in New Orleans?"

The man ignored me and studied the phone. He scrolled through the text messages, but nothing interested him.

"Huh, Anna," he said to his companion, shrugging. "Nice name." He opened the car window and flung the phone into a desert that seemed so vast it was difficult to believe it didn't comprise the whole world. It was the only way I had to contact Carlos.

I wailed, "Not my phone. Go back and get it right now."

The car didn't stop. I continued to lament my loss with great vigor. The man pulled out the switchblade and flicked it open again. I shut up. Then he answered my question. "Men will be visiting for the Super Bowl and then for Mardi Gras. You'll show them a good time. Boss will give you fancy clothes, a nice apartment, food, jewelry, school for the girls, whatever you need. In return, you will treat these men well. Smile, talk to them, make them feel important. If they ask you for more, you do that too. You'll do whatever they ask. You may even get tickets to the Super Bowl. Now that's something."

"Huh. You're an idiot. What makes you think I care about the Super Bowl? What happens if we refuse?"

"Not my problem. I'm just the delivery service for Boss. To be frank, girls go missing when they misbehave. Children of girls go missing when their mama misbehaves. In short, you got no choice."

Catalina pulled her girls closer and cast me a pleading look.

The driver slowed down and said, "Louie, do I need to pull over for a little discipline?"

I stared at Louie with fiery brown eyes but said nothing. He fingered the blade and said absently, "Some people have to learn the hard way. Some people never learn at all. I believe you're smarter than that."

I averted my gaze. I couldn't risk harming the girls. "No need to pull over. I'll be quiet."

I cast Catalina an angry look for getting me into this. She refused to meet my eye. It wasn't her fault, of course. I made a series of bad choices all on my own. How could I be so reckless, so stupid, so naïve? The smartest man I know gave me chance after chance to pull myself out of this death spiral, and I refused his advice. I should be in a motel in Juarez with my family awaiting my passport. Instead, I was now a modern-day slave about to become a prostitute. What was next? HIV, herpes, a love child with some fat bastard? An involuntary shudder coursed through my body. My eyes welled up with tears. Without the phone or the GPS transmitter, there was no way Carlos would know I had been abducted and taken to New Orleans. I had many gifts, but it seemed like common sense was not one of them.

I relaxed a bit when the car accelerated. Confident he made his point, Louie put the blade away. He stared blankly out the windshield, though there was nothing but dust and sand as far as the eye could see. The world was bathed in monochromatic light.

Suddenly, living in Juarez didn't seem all that bad. At least I understood the rules. Here, the rules were different and needed to be learned by trial and error. I wasn't going to acquiesce without a fight and began to prioritize my options. Two things made it to the top of the list. I needed to find a way to alert Carlos to my fate. I wouldn't blame him if he chose to opt out after our fight, but he was still my best hope, perhaps my only hope. We also needed to escape before we made it to New Orleans. It could be hard with the two little ones, but maybe not impossible. I would look for opportunity and seize it.

CHAPTER 10

HUDSPETH COUNTY, TEXAS

I n the dimness of predawn, Scott was about to turn onto a road that would dead end about a mile from the Rio Grande. Suddenly, he slammed on the brakes and stopped the truck. The horse in the trailer behind the truck neighed in alarm.

"Look," Scott said excitedly, clearly disturbed. Linda, who was sitting next to him, and Alvarez, who was in the backseat, peered forward but didn't understand. They got out to inspect the tire tracks in the sand. In the fresh sand drifts were two sets of SUV tracks with precisely the same tread pattern. Linda stared at them glumly.

"Please explain," Alvarez demanded.

Scott pointed to the tracks with the flashlight. "An SUV came from the east, went down the road, turned around, and headed back the same way it came. If Anna is in the SUV, she isn't going to El Paso. She's going in the opposite direction. On the other hand, if your GPS is correct, she, or at least her transmitter, is where it has been for the past six hours next to the Rio Grande. The dilemma is whether to follow the tracks before the wind obliterates them or find the GPS transmitter."

Alvarez nodded in approval at such a succinct answer. "What do you think we should do, Scott?"

Scott didn't hesitate. "I believe Anna is in the SUV. I'd follow the tracks. Maybe we can even catch the vehicle. The tracks are still fresh. I'd be willing to drop the trailer here and have Jose pick it up later today."

"When I gave her the GPS transmitter, I told her not to remove it for any reason. I'd like to believe she heeded my advice. She should be by the Rio Grande. What do you think, Linda?"

It fell upon Linda to break the stalemate with a life-or-death decision. "I know Scott well enough to say he's probably correct. Still, with each mile I drove down the road, I'd wonder if I made the wrong choice. If nothing turned up in a couple of hours, I'd hate myself for not going to the river first. I'll side with Alvarez. I want to end one possibility so I know to focus entirely on the other."

Scott was irritated with the split vote. "Wrong plan, but majority rules. This is why I like to work alone. Before we commit, give Anna a call."

Alvarez pressed the button on his phone. "No bars."

Scott turned down the dead-end road. When the road ended, Scott led Mr. Ed out of the trailer. The sky was brightening in the east, though it was darker than usual from the retreating storm. Putting on a headlamp, Scott trotted Mr. Ed toward the river through the tangle of brush and cacti. Much of the scrub was buried in fresh sand drifts. Traces of a trail shielded from the storm by rock and debris gave way to large drifts that would have obscured the path to anyone who didn't understand that the point of the trail was to move people from the Rio Grande to the road as directly as possible. Scott read the signs in the set of the alluvial plain, descending to the river. Scott urged Mr. Ed to follow the fresh tracks toward the river.

CHAPTER 11

RIO GRANDE

L inda and Alvarez followed the GPS signal as close to the source as they could, which Alvarez estimated to be accurate at ten to twenty feet. Disappointment greeted them in the form of meandering dunes fashioned from the recent storm. Alvarez was devastated at not seeing Anna and insisted they find the ankle bracelet. He drew a large circle in the sand that he thought represented the area in which the transmitter lay. Then he started at one edge and moved toward the center while Linda started directly opposite. They kicked at the surface layer of sand, hoping the transmitter would pop through. They met in the center without any luck. Was the signal off, or had they not dug deep enough? The transmitter was small compared to the vast amount of sand before them. Standing in the center and looking ninety degrees from their last pass, Linda thought she saw something resembling the shape of a body. Maybe two bodies.

"Look. Is someone buried over there?"

Alvarez squinted as she shined her flashlight on the area. "Look. Legs, waist, arms."

Beginning with the legs, which were the most pronounced, they brushed away six inches of sand to find jeans. Alvarez brightened. "This is not Anna. She was wearing nice slacks."

Linda unearthed a leg swollen to immense proportions and wrinkled her nose at the noxious smell of decaying flesh. She pulled back in alarm. She removed the sand from around the head, which was covered in a small blanket. "The rag over the face was meant to protect it from sand. Male. Thirties, I'd guess. No pulse on the carotid. I think this man just died. The body is still warm. No sign of rigor mortis. The leg is horribly infected. He probably couldn't walk with the rest of them. Perhaps the person was still alive when Anna passed by?"

Alvarez was never good with blood and guts. He once watched a man being devoured by a great white shark. A year later, he still had nightmares. He looked away while Linda continued studying the body.

"Would you check the pockets, please?" he asked.

Linda pulled a circular object out of the pant pocket. She held the flashlight on it. "This it?"

Alvarez shook his head in mute horror as he realized that Anna had probably given this man her transmitter so she could find him later. It was just like her to put others first, to her own detriment. Now the man was a corpse, and she had been abducted. It infuriated him that she never heeded his advice. He stood and walked away. Anna was his favorite person in the whole world, and now she was gone.

"I guess I should have heeded Scott's advice." In the privacy of the desert darkness, he began to cry.

CHAPTER 12

RIO GRANDE

The tracks ended at the Rio Grande. Scott paused to look for someone on the other side. Seeing no one, he crossed over into Mexico. The river was wide but not deep, and there wasn't much of a current. Mr. Ed was not experienced with water crossings but responded to Scott's prodding with poise. On the other side, Scott found a rutted road and followed it west toward Juarez. He came to a clump of cane that had been repeatedly beat down and rutted with tire tracks. There was no truck there now, but the fact that the ruts were not filled with sand meant that the truck had left only recently. He eased Mr. Ed into a near gallop and followed the road. Drifts of sand obscured the road in places but bore fresh truck tracks. Mr. Ed was fleet and sure-footed on the rutted road. Before long, taillights appeared in the distance. In a matter of minutes, he had halved the distance.

The truck driver flashed a surprised look when an Anglo on horseback came galloping up beside him. Potholes that threatened to swallow the truck slowed his progress. A horse could jump them, but not his truck. The driver tried to outrun the horseback rider until he noticed the Glock pointed at his head. He brought the truck to a stop and put it in park. He raised his hands as he sat in the driver's seat.

Scott motioned him to turn the truck around. The driver did and retraced his exodus to the broken cane. Scott motioned him out of his truck with a flick of his weapon. The driver came out with his hands raised.

"You a coyote?" Scott barked at him. The driver shrugged.

"You see two women and two girls tonight?"

The driver was silent. Scott thought there was comprehension in the set of the man's eyes and lost patience. "The first shot goes in your tire. The next one goes in your leg. Talk before I shoot."

The man was silent, and Scott shot out the front left tire. The man jumped, then raised his arms in distress at the sound of air leaving the tire. Scott leveled the gun at the man's thigh. "Did you see two women and two girls?"

The man nodded quickly.

Scott continued. "Where are they?"

The man pointed toward the rising sun.

"What is your name?"

The man remained silent.

Scott moved the gun closer to the man's leg.

"Mateo. I'm Mateo."

"You need to be more specific about where the girls are, Mateo."

Mateo pointed again. "East. Men took them east."

Scott became impatient. "The tire tracks suggest they went east. Tell me who took them and where they are going. Otherwise . . ."

His threatening tone had no effect. Mateo returned a defiant expression.

Scott lashed his lariat around Mateo's waist and tethered the rope to the saddle horn. Pulling a piece of rope out of his saddlebag, he tied Mateo's hands behind his back. He mounted Mr. Ed and spurred him down the road faster than Mateo could go without jogging. When he came to the Rio Grande, he noted panic in Mateo's eyes. Scott prodded Mr. Ed down the muddy riverbank with the reluctant prisoner dragging his feet. In the middle of the river, Mateo lost his footing on the muddy bottom and fell. Scott didn't slow, and Mateo came up gasping for breath. "I want the Border Patrol."

"You speak English very well. No Border Patrol."

The Border Patrol did little more than send illegals and their coyotes back to Mexico. Most of the coyotes crossed the border again for the money, since there was no real punishment. Scott was determined to make this message stick. He dragged Mateo across the river and up the opposite riverbank. Mateo struggled to maintain his footing, but managed to keep his head above water with some difficulty.

"We can stop anytime you tell me where the girls are."

"*No lo sé.*"

Scott dragged Mateo along the coyote trail, occasionally losing the trail in the fresh sand drifts and traversing instead through snarly brush and thickets of cacti.

"Where are the girls?"

"*No lo sé.*"

Scott brought the bleeding and breathless prisoner to Alvarez and Linda. Scott loosened the lariat.

"Here's your coyote. Name is Mateo. He knows exactly what happened to the girls. He's not talking, though. Perhaps the walk back here changed his mind."

Mateo's clothes were torn and his arms bleeding. He was breathing hard and collapsed in the sand. He recoiled when he recognized the dead man lying next to him.

Scott spoke in a bitter voice. "It's quite a racket. He charges his clients to go across the border, then sells them to the highest bidder on the other side. I think we should kill him."

Mateo shook his head, pleading for the Border Patrol.

Scott pointed his Glock at him. "We have our own justice for scum like you, and it doesn't involve the Border Patrol."

Suddenly Mateo sprang to his feet and bolted through the brush like a jackrabbit.

Alvarez panicked. "Don't let him get away."

Scott calmly mounted Mr. Ed and pulled out his lariat.

Linda shook her head in amusement. "I've never seen Scott lasso anything. He always misses."

To their surprise, the lasso descended neatly over Mateo's head. As Scott tugged it taut, the rope pulled Mateo's feet out from under him. Mr. Ed dragged the bound coyote back to the corpse. Mateo lay gasping for breath, resigned to his capture.

Alvarez spoke to him in Spanish in a passionate tone without success.

"What are you doing with the coyote, Scott?" Linda exclaimed with genuine concern.

"I thought I'd string him up like they did in the old Westerns. Don't worry, they'll never catch us. He'll be dead by morning, and the buzzards will pick his bones clean by tomorrow."

Linda gave him an angry stare. "May I approach the bench, Your Honor?"

Scott returned a frown, dismounting. "Certainly, Counsel."

Linda shoved her face up close to his and began an angry tirade. "You are not judge and jury. You abducted him in Mexico and brought him to the US illegally. That's at least two felonies."

Scott whispered, "I didn't tell you the part where I blew out his tire, but that's probably just a misdemeanor. Look, he is our only hope. Trust me."

Scott kicked the ground fiercely, spraying sand over the coyote. He gave Linda a fiery look that the coyote was certain to see. "Well, I don't work for the FBI anymore. Stay in your lane. No one knows where I found him but you and me. He sold women into slavery. He deserves to die here and now."

"Be reasonable, Scott. If he spends half a day staring directly at the corpse, he might develop a sense of humanity."

Scott scoffed at her. "The smell might attract real coyotes that would gnaw his body until he died."

Scott threw the rope over the bough of a small tree. The bough was hardly substantial enough to support the weight of a grown man, but the effect was riveting.

Mateo pleaded, "Wait, wait. I'll tell you what you want to know. I have names. I have phone numbers. I'll help you get the women back. Please, don't kill me."

Scott placed the noose over his neck and pulled it taut enough that the Mexican needed to stand on his toes to keep from choking. "Commend your soul to your God."

The coyote broke down. "Jesus, Mary, and Joseph, I will reform my life if only you let me live. My phone is hidden under the seat of my truck. It has names. It has phone numbers. It's not too late."

"Where are they going?" asked Scott, pulling a bit harder on the rope.

The coyote gasped. "I don't know. The men had strange accents, not Mexican or American."

"How much did you make?"

"Four thousand. The money is in an envelope next to the phone. Go get it. It's yours. It's not worth dying over."

Scott relaxed the rope a bit and tied it off out of the man's reach. "I'll go check it out right now. It better be exactly as you tell me."

The man coughed. "It will be. Don't worry."

Scott pointed to the dead man partially buried in the sand. "What do you have to say about him?"

The Mexican sobbed. "I'm sorry, old man. It wasn't my fault. Snake killed you, not me."

Scott rode Mr. Ed over to the truck and retrieved the phone and four thousand dollars. Scott held the money and the phone up for Mateo to see. "Password on the phone?"

"One, two, one, two, one, two."

"These are mine now. Now tell me about the money."

The coyote sputtered. "I got a grand from Emile and three grand from Catalina. I swear to God there's no more."

"Emile? Now there's a name I'm hearing for the first time. He got a phone number?" Scott held up the phone and examined the call list. "Most recent calls were to and from this number." Scott pointed to a number. "That Emile's number?"

Mateo nodded.

"Emile have anyone with him?"

Mateo nodded.

"He have a name?"

"Louie," said Mateo, sputtering from the rope.

Scott lowered the rope a bit. "Either of them have a last name?"

"Don't know," said Mateo more comfortably as his face lost the tortured look.

"You see a license plate?"

"No."

"Well, Mateo, you gave me enough answers to spare your life. I'm gonna call the Border Patrol now to come and pick you up. I see you in this country again, and you'll be hanging from the nearest tree. I live nearby, and I'll be watching for you. What you do isn't right, and you deserve to die. It's called vigilante justice."

They placed Mateo and the dead man next to each other along the road. While Mateo's hands were secure, Scott was only able to use a small amount of duct tape on his feet since he was at the end of the roll.

Linda dialed the Border Patrol while Scott loaded Mr. Ed into the trailer. She put the phone on speaker so they could all hear. "This is Linda Williams. My husband Scott and I have a place south of Sierra Blanca called Setting Sun Ranch. We were out checking fences this morning after the blow cleared when we came across two men, one living and one deceased, just north of the Rio Grande. Good chance they're illegals."

"They on horseback?"

"Uh, no. That's our horse you hear. The men probably crossed the Rio Grande on foot. There's a truck we can see on the Mexican side. The deceased man is older. Body is still warm. One leg is badly swollen. I would guess snakebite. He looks badly dehydrated."

"How about the other man?"

"He's younger, though too old to be the son of the deceased. First name is Mateo. That's all we got out of him."

"We can be there in about an hour or so."

"We can't wait an hour. We have an urgent family matter to attend to. We're going out of town as soon as we get the horses back to the ranch. It's a bit open-ended at this point, but we'll likely be back in a few days. I'll give you the GPS coordinates, and you have my phone number. Please call if there are any problems."

Linda gave them the GPS coordinates, and they left the dead man at the end of the road along with the coyote. The Border Patrol had a full plate, but it was strictly catch and release. Mateo would probably be a free man in Mexico tomorrow, though the dead man might complicate matters a bit.

Linda cast Scott an angry glance. "You wouldn't have really strung him up, would you?"

"Of course not, Counsel. He wasn't cooperating. I needed to squeeze him. He really was our last hope."

"The anger seemed real. You were like something from a horror flick. 'Talk or you die.' I've never seen anything like it from you."

Scott blushed. "Okay. You know how I hate it when people take advantage of the less fortunate. Grabs me right here." He pointed to his chest. "Mateo took innocent girls and sold them into slavery. Little ones too."

"And what if he didn't break?"

Scott shrugged. "Come on. Everyone has a breaking point. We both knew it wouldn't come to that."

Linda nodded, but said nothing. When they reached the crossroads, Scott got out of the truck to examine the tracks. He shook his head in disappointment that the blowing sand had erased the tracks. "Gone."

Alvarez wailed, "We made the wrong choice, didn't we?"

Linda tried to console him. "I was thinking the opposite. We got lucky. Capturing the coyote was a gold mine. We have Mateo's phone and know the number of his contact. We know the contact's area code, and that should tell us what direction to take. We recovered four thousand dollars. Anna probably has a cell phone we can ping to follow. If nothing changes, we have sufficient clues to find her, hopefully by nightfall. Scott and I have solved cases with far less to go on."

CHAPTER 13

SETTING SUN RANCH

I t was late morning when Mr. Ed was returned to his stall at Setting Sun Ranch. Alvarez had tried pinging Anna's phone as a tracking strategy. The reception was poor, and the service intermittent, but he located the phone in the desert a couple of hours away. Unfortunately, the phone wasn't moving.

Linda studied the map. "Did it run out of juice?"

A look of aggravation swept across Alvarez's face.

Linda smiled thoughtfully. "Maybe they just stopped for lunch. Where is area code five-oh-four?"

"New Orleans. It's a thousand miles and a fifteen-hour drive on I-10. They could be dropping them off anywhere between here and there. I have to find her. She's family. Actually, she's my favorite family."

"We'll all go," Linda soothed. "Scott's already packing. I can be ready in twenty minutes."

Scott had caught the last bit of conversation while he packed. He was a compulsive packer. He became angry with himself when he needed something he didn't have because he wanted to be prepared for anything. He was already angry that he hadn't had have enough rope or duct tape to secure Mateo properly. "They're obviously headed east. My bet would be New Orleans, with the Super Bowl coming up. They probably want young hotties to work the French Quar . . ."

He trailed off and walked away, clearly upset with the notion he'd come to with his stream-of-consciousness thinking. For his brash attitude on many things, he was righteous when it came to protecting women. He wanted nothing more than to find these men and hang them out to dry. How many women had they abducted over the years? How much misery had they unleashed on helpless Latino aliens whose desperate act of crossing the border was forced upon them to feed a starving family? Killing went against Scott's upbringing and training with the FBI, but it wasn't entirely out of the question in the proper context.

Things had been so much more difficult when he worked for the FBI. Scott would have lost his job for lifting the four grand, even though the bulk of it belonged to Anna and her friend. He would have lost his job for crossing the border to capture the coyote. He would have been reprimanded—or worse—for the bruises Mateo suffered. The FBI worked with their hands tied behind their backs, conscious of a legal system that bent over backward to protect the guilty from the innocent. Now retired, his position was unfettered by legal complications. A bullet could serve the masters of truth and justice succinctly.

An hour later, as they were about to depart Setting Sun Ranch, Anna's phone still hadn't moved. Alvarez's frustration was evident. One more thread vanished in the shifting sands.

Linda offered hope. "Alvarez, we have the phone number of the man Mateo called. Is it possible to ping that phone to follow his movements?"

Alvarez nodded respectfully. He had been working down that pipeline for the past hour. "The police do it. It's not legal and I need a hack. I'm working on it. It's my only chance to follow them in real time."

They left Alvarez pounding away on his keyboard, anxious to leave but unwilling to sacrifice the last clue for a hasty retreat. Texas was vast. It would not be possible to get internet access in the more desolate areas west of San Antonio.

Scott and Linda walked out to the barn to look at the horses. "Mr. Ed was magnificent today," Scott noted proudly. "He was the best birthday present I ever received. Thanks, honey."

Linda smiled, grateful he acknowledged her. He had dropped a clue that he wanted a mustang for his birthday. He was thinking car.

She was thinking horse. When she gave him his birthday present, they had a good laugh. Scott quickly came to love Mr. Ed.

Pedro and Jose were brothers and competent cowhands who had been with them for a couple of years.

"Thought you'd be gone by now," said Pedro.

"Hit a snag," replied Linda. "Alvarez is working on a way to track the girls using the phone number of the men who abducted them."

Jose grinned at her. "That guy is amazing. I mean, he's kind of odd in most ways, but he's the James Bond of the internet."

"True," said Linda. "The FBI offered him a job on the spot after he uncovered the presidential assassination plot. He's not really a team player, though. He likes to do his own thing and seems to make a lot of money at it. He is absolutely brilliant."

"Why is he so odd?" inquired Pedro. "I mean, you'd never know there's genius lurking there from the way he dresses and the way he acts."

Linda nodded. "He has a touch of autism. People like that act odd because they don't see the world the same way we do. They don't study how the other people around them dress and act. Plus, they focus on tasks that others can't begin to fathom."

"Zero points for style," Pedro offered.

"But millions for substance," Linda countered defensively. "They are honest, hardworking, and brilliant. Alvarez is no exception."

"How old is his cousin Anna?" Pedro asked shyly. "He told me she is beautiful, smart, and single."

"My guess is about twenty-four," Linda answered, a sly smile growing on her face. "That would make her Jose's age, right? Perhaps we'll bring her back here for a few days. You guys haven't seen a girl your own age in a while. It'd do you good to go on a date." Linda sighed. "This area is so isolated. It's hard to have much of a social life."

Just then, Alvarez bounded out of the house, more joy in his face than was typical. "Got it. Let's go. They're almost to San Antonio."

About thirty minutes later, his mood soured. "Bad news," exclaimed Alvarez in an eerily pensive voice.

"What is it?" said Linda, startled out of the monotony of passing desert.

"The phone stopped moving in Junction. I thought they might have stopped for gas or food, but it's been about thirty minutes now, and there's no sign of movement. I think they ditched the phone. It's a smart move when you're on the run to switch phones often."

"Call the number," said Scott. Linda did so, and the phone went unanswered. The mood in the car soured quickly. This GPS trace was the very last link they had to the vehicle, and now it was gone. It had been so reassuring to watch the red dot move across the map, knowing exactly where they were heading. Now the red dot was blinking helplessly. Though Scott didn't say anything, the car accelerated as if the newfound urgency in his brain suddenly translated into movement in his foot.

Linda put her hand on Scott's leg to calm him. His leg relaxed as the speed dropped back to the cruise control setting. "This changes nothing, you know," she said. "We still know where they're going. We need to hold course and stay strong. Anna will contact you when she has a chance, Alvarez."

Alvarez's heart soared. Linda's words had a magically soothing effect. Of course she was right. For now, this changed nothing. For now, they could stay the course with confidence. But then he reasoned his way into a reality check. The longer the silence continued, the greater the uncertainty. What if Anna's final destination was San Antonio or Houston instead of New Orleans? They would blow right by them. They only assumed the destination was New Orleans because of the area code on the phone number. It was nothing worth betting a life on—or four lives, as it turned out.

CHAPTER 14

I-10

L ouie cast a searching glance in the driver's direction. He was fed up with me and had little problem airing his grievances. "The old bitch is losing it. I'm not sure she's worth the trouble. Any idea what we'll get for her, Emile?"

Emile turned his head to study Louie. "She's prettier than she looks right now. Her blouse smells like she puked on it. But she'll clean up. Problem is she's six, maybe eight years older than Boss likes 'em. Now the young one with the kids is top drawer. Best lookin' bitch I've seen. I was gonna ask twenty grand for the whole lot. Boss will counter with ten or twelve grand. We'll settle for something in the middle. We'll make our investment pay off tenfold. Not bad for two days' work. Wish I had more jobs like this."

Louie studied the finances. "How much does he make on them?"

Emile shrugged. "The hot ones can fetch a thousand an hour, maybe four grand a night. We're talking high-end stuff here for guys who wipe their asses with hundred-dollar bills. Boss can get eight years out of the young ones if they stay healthy. After expenses, he clears two million tax-free on each girl."

Louie grew more interested. "Why don't we work 'em ourselves? I mean, we did the heavy lifting. I could use a million dollars."

Emile rolled his eyes as if he'd spoken heresy. "It's about opportunity, Louie. It takes a network. Boss has the black book with the clients' names. He has the muscle to keep the girls honest. He has the guns to keep others from moving into his territory. We'd be dead if we did any more than act as mules to bring the girls in. I'm not unhappy with the deal. God bless America. We need more trips like this. By the way, did you give Mateo the new phone number?"

"Of course."

"Did you discard the old phone like Boss asked?"

"Yep."

I had been listening to this conversation with equal measures of fascination, contempt, and fear. "Excuse me, did I hear you say you were going to sell us for twenty thousand dollars?"

Louie laughed self-consciously. He hadn't realized I had been listening. "That's right," he said indifferently.

I was ready to make a deal. "I'll give you forty thousand to release us."

Louie turned around to study me with an amused look on his face. Emile snickered. "The babe's got balls, Louie. Would that be cash, check, or money order? You got some gold bars?" He began a snicker that turned into a belly laugh.

"No, really," I said defensively. "I have a wealthy cousin who could arrange payment by the time we rolled into San Antonio."

Louie's eyes grew large. "A wealthy cousin might be willing to pay a hundred thousand."

"Possibly," I offered tentatively. I had no idea how much Carlos could afford and was concerned about the number going too high.

Louie turned and caught my eyes. I held his gaze. "Emile, she's serious. I'd end this right now for a hundred grand apiece."

Emile belly laughed again. "She's bluffing, idiot. I've handled dozens of these over the years, and there ain't none of them that can buy a bus ticket back home. She's taking you for a ride, Pardner, and she's getting the better of you."

"No, seriously," I said. "I could raise that kind of cash with just a phone call."

Louie studied her. "She's wearing nice clothes. I didn't expect to find one dressed this nice. I think we should hear what she has to say."

Emile stopped laughing, and all went silent as he spoke. "Two problems with that. First, Boss expects us to show up with babes. If we don't have the goods, we don't go back to New Orleans. He might suspect we were double-crossing him. Not a problem for you. You can vanish, move to California, change your name. I have a wife and kids in New Orleans. I need to protect them. I'll take ten grand with the possibility of a steady job and a long life any day. The second problem is that her one call tells someone where we are and what we're up to. We goin' to a bank to collect the money? Busted. How you gonna arrange it so we don't risk getting nabbed by the cops? We got at least four felonies sitting in the back seat."

Louie didn't want to let go just yet. "Got to be a way. Maybe she has a suggestion. Speak, Anna. Enlighten us with a foolproof scheme."

"My cousin Carlos lives in El Paso, and he owns a jet. He could fly to San Antonio with the money. Cash. We could meet him at the airport. You get the cash. We get on the plane. You can go back to your meeting place, pick up a few more refugees, and keep your boss happy. You are two days late and a hundred thousand dollars richer. No one's talking, and there's a happy ending for everyone."

Emile studied me in the rearview mirror, seeing me for the first time as a woman and not as the goods. "She's a sly one. I'd take her up on it in a heartbeat if I knew we could show up in New Orleans with babes. What can we do?"

Louie didn't hesitate. "He owns a jet? Maybe a hundred grand isn't high enough. Maybe it should be a million? I say play it her way but with a flexible pickup. They'll be expecting us at the airport. That's where the cops will be. We change locations on them at the last minute."

Emile took a deep breath. "We'll work out the amount later. Don't get too greedy. My grandma always said, 'Don't count your chickens before they hatch.' I need to stop for gas. Let's keep discussing it. I'll pump the gas. Anna, no one goes anywhere without an escort. You sit in the car and keep your mouth shut."

Emile got out of the car to pump the gas. Louie got out of the car to stretch. Catalina spoke to me for the first time since we were abducted. "I'm so sorry. I had no idea it would end like this."

Tears streamed down her face. Nestled on her lap, her two girls became agitated. They had been asleep most of the ride, exhausted from the night's journey. "I want this nightmare to end, Anna. You have no idea what it's like to have strange men climb on top of you. I'd

66

rather die than go through that again. Please help it end, if not for me, for my girls."

I flushed with anger. "You're not the helpless woman you pretend to be. Muscle up. I can't make this happen without you. You got my back?"

Catalina drew back at the strong words. She seemed encouraged by their pluck but diminished by their chiding. Anna worried that she had given up completely and totally. Catalina ran an absent, nervous hand over Guadalupe's hair. Then, something like resolve hardened in her eyes.

She said calmly and confidently, "I have your back, Anna."

"I'm going to leave a note for the police in the restroom."

I opened her door a crack and addressed Emile. "The girls need to use the restroom. We all do."

Emile looked around. "There's one in the diner. Hey, Louie, escort them to the bathroom and keep an eye on them. I'll finish with the gas."

The diner was largely deserted. Louie knocked on the door of the woman's restroom and, when no one responded, went inside. There were two stalls and no windows. Louie parked himself in a booth in front of the woman's restroom. "Little mama, you go first and take your girls."

"She has a name," I spat.

Louie looked at Catalina expectantly and waved his hand trying to get her to speak.

"Catalina," she murmured reluctantly.

Louie nodded. "Anna, you wait here with me until Catalina is done." He pulled my arm, and I fell into the booth.

When Catalina emerged, Louie said, "Girls, come sit with me while Anna has her turn."

I entered the restroom.

Pulling a tube of lipstick from the recesses of my pocket, I ducked into a stall and scrawled a message. "Four girls kidnapped by LA VFP 982."

After five minutes, Louie barked, "Okay, out the door."

I eyed the food in the display with longing. It had been a while since we ate. I imagined the girls were hungry. "The little ones could use some food, Louie. We all could."

He ignored me and followed us to the car. Emile was finished with the gas. Louie said, "I'm going to pick up some snacks. What would you like?"

Some suggestions were offered, and he left. Once inside, he went straight to the woman's restroom, and I cringed. When Louie reemerged, he stormed back to the car.

Louie whispered something to Emile, then announced, "One of you has been naughty. I found a note in lipstick on the door of one of the stalls. We have a change of plans. We're dropping the two little ones off with ICE agents. You'll never see them again."

Catalina wailed so loudly I thought someone would surely notice, but the parking lot was empty. Even as she tried to pull her girls tighter, Louie circled behind her and wrapped his arm across her chest. He pulled her in one direction while Emile grabbed one hand of each of the girls and pulled them in the opposite direction. Agony and terror washed over Catalina's face as her girls were wrenched away, maybe forever. Catalina yelled and squirmed and kicked, but she couldn't break Louie's hold. She pitched forward as far as possible and stretched out her arms to her girls, but they didn't reach. She twisted and turned in fury, trying desperately to reach them, but she couldn't.

Louie calmly said, "It hurts to be separated from your girls, doesn't it? It hurts to know you'll never see them again. Remember this heartache. It could have been prevented."

Catalina's yells diminished into gut-wrenching sobs, and her body went limp under Louie's vice grip.

"Stop," I yelled. "I wrote the note. Punish me instead."

I lowered my eyes in defeat and stretched out my arms. "Please don't give her girls to ICE. That's as cruel as you can be to a mother."

I stepped toward Louie, arms outstretched, hoping he would break his hold on Catalina. He nodded to Emile, and the two men released their grips on their hostages. Catalina rushed to her girls and hugged them in a way that seemed to shield them from the two men. I stood resolutely still, hands up, awaiting my punishment.

Emile was the first to speak. "Remember the sense of loss, Catalina. That was just a warning. Next time they go to ICE."

Relief washed over Catalina's face. Her body quivered as she sobbed. She nodded acceptance to the dictated terms. Emile and Louie stared at me. Reluctantly, I nodded in agreement. I had no choice. In a matter of minutes, the pact I had made with Catalina was gone. I was drained and helpless.

To my surprise, Louie picked up a plastic bag he had carried out of the store, tossing me two egg-and-sausage breakfast biscuits as he cast a snobbish pout in my direction. "Don't get cute again."

Then he pulled out an ice cream bar and held it up in front of Maribel who cautiously glance at her mother. Guadalupe had no reservations and lunged for it. Louie pulled it back just before she snatched it. He laughed. "Sisters need to learn to share."

Then he produced another ice cream and handed one to each with sleight of hand that was like magic to the youngsters. I was dumbfounded by the brute. There was pleasure in his eyes at the gratitude they showed. He patted each on the head and gave them a kindly smile.

Maribel tugged on his sleeve when his gaze drifted to Catalina. "Papa buys us ice cream." Her face saddened.

He mimicked her sad expression. "Where is your papa now?"

"He died," she said without hesitation.

Louie's dark eyes clouded with sadness, probably realizing that he placed the people he trafficked on a tremulous road between forgettable pasts and difficult futures. Louie closed the door softly, lost in his own thoughts.

CHAPTER 15

FORT STOCKTON, TEXAS

S cott estimated that the kidnappers had a four-hour head start. It would be an insurmountable lead if it were a race to the finish. But there was no obvious point of victory short of recovering the girls before unspeakable things happened to them. There was only the grind of right against wrong in spinning tires and spinning thoughts.

Alvarez received a call. It was a number he didn't recognize, and he placed the call on speakerphone.

"Hello," he said in his typically dry monotone.

"Carlos, it's Anna. I've been kidnapped. They want money to ransom me."

Before he could ask whether she was being treated well, a gruff voice with a Cajun accent spoke. "We want a hundred grand. Can you pay it?"

Alvarez gulped. "Sure. I need some time. Where are you?"

The voice continued, "You got to be quick. San Antonio in one hour. Hear you got a jet."

Alvarez became flustered. Why had Anna told them lies? Perhaps she wanted to impress her captors. He did own a Cessna, a far cry from a jet, but it was tucked away in a hangar in Juarez. He spoke slowly, deliberating on each sentence. He would pay to have her back, but the timetable was outrageous. "I can't possibly be there in an hour. I'm in El Paso. The plane is in Juarez. It'll take a couple hours to fuel the plane and get it in the air. It's another two to three hours in the air.

Plus, I need to go to the bank to get the money. We're talking five hours minimum."

There was a grunt, and the phone clicked off.

Alvarez kicked the back of the seat in frustration. He was worried he had ruined their chances to ransom Anna.

One of Linda's strengths with the FBI was hostage negotiation. Her genial demeanor and soothing voice lent a steady hand toward calming desperate people. "You did the right thing, Alvarez. You told them you could come up with the money, and you gave them a reasonable timetable. They're mulling it over now. If it suits them, they'll call back with a proposition. We need to decide what we will do. Do you have access to that much money?"

Alvarez nodded. "I can wire the money to any bank. Getting that much cash won't be possible except in a major city like San Antonio. Even then, I'm sure someone will get suspicious. Can you even get that much cash at once?"

Linda nodded. "I've seen it done in ransom cases like this when I worked with the FBI. The bank will need a heads up, but a hundred thousand isn't a big deal. We'll make it happen. This is a far better situation than following them to New Orleans. Hey, are you pinging the new number?"

Alvarez allowed a tiny smile to crease his face that was otherwise rigid with tension. "They're in Boerne, about twenty miles west of San Antonio. Should I call them back?"

"No," said Linda firmly. "Calling them is bad. It will make you seem desperate. They could raise the ransom or speed up the timeframe. It may also worry them that you have their number. They have to feel like they're one hundred percent in control. If they want this, they'll call you back. If not, we'll continue tracking them. We're about four hours behind them, and the timetable you gave them was five hours. So right now, we can meet the expectations."

Scott said, "We're almost to Fort Stockton. That's our best bet for a large city. There's not much between here and San Antonio. The banks may be closed by then."

The car accelerated. This time Linda didn't put her hand on Scott's leg to calm him. Suddenly, another phone rang with an unfamiliar ringtone. Scott pulled Mateo's phone out of his jacket pocket. He looked at the number, then tossed it back to Alvarez. "It's them for Mateo. They probably want to see if more girls are available. They'll be expecting a Spanish accent. You better handle this."

Alvarez panicked. "What should I tell them?"

"If you tell them there are no girls available, they may want to hang on to Anna. Maybe there is a quota or something. If you tell them there are lots of girls, they may go for the ransom. That's probably what they're mulling over right now."

"Mateo here," Alvarez said.

"Mateo, my man. Louie. We need some more bitches. What ya got at your end?"

"Lots."

"Do they look as fine as Catalina?"

Alvarez had no idea whether Catalina was attractive but played along. "Better. I can bring them across anytime. The sooner the better."

"How many?"

"Four, maybe five."

"We'll call."

The line went dead.

Scott rocked back and forth, a thoughtful look on his face. "Let's make a deal."

CHAPTER 16

SAN ANTONIO

I clutched Catalina's hand anxiously as our captors talked. I was silently praying that they would decide to ransom us.

Emile glanced over at Louie. "You know, I turn forty today."

Louie shot him a surprised look at this most unexpected comment in the midst of high-stakes negotiations. "What, you want a birthday card or something?"

Emile continued, "What are you, about twenty?"

Louie shot him a hurt look. "I'm twenty-four."

"That's how old I was when I started working for Boss. My cousin Vinny and I started at the same time."

Louie returned a skeptical look. "Vinny? I don't know no Vinny. No one by that name works for Boss."

"My point exactly," said Emile. "Vinny was a little impulsive, high-strung. Kinda like you. We were young. Me, I just wanted a steady job. I had a wife. Vinny, he wanted more. He started working some things on the side, pulling in a little extra dough. It didn't amount to much, a few thousand here, a few thousand there. Then he bought a fancy sports car. He thought Boss wouldn't know or wouldn't care. Vinny always said, 'This country was built on free enterprise. God bless America.' One day I go to pick him up—we were partners—and Vinny wasn't home. Seemed odd 'cause his sports car was parked in front of his house. No one's seen Vinny since. Rumor has it Boss tied an anchor around his neck and tossed him in the bayou. Some fishermen found body parts downstream a few days later. Gator had its way with the body. Still don't know if it was Vinny. This was back before they did DNA tests."

"Bottom line is you're chickening out," said Louie, accusation in his voice. "Ain't nothing to be afraid of. There're more bitches where these came from. Mateo said so. We collect the ransom, go back west, pick up a few more broads, and head back to New Orleans. We're a few days late, but no one's any smarter for it."

"Until you use your money to buy a sports car. Then Boss gets curious about your personal life, maybe goes to the dealership or the bank. Before long, you're keeping Vinny company."

"I'm too smart for that. The money goes in the bank. No one knows about it."

"If you don't plan to spend the money, then why do you want it so badly?"

"I don't know. It's a once-in-a-lifetime opportunity to make a little dough. Maybe I'll move to California. Maybe I'll need it in my old age."

Emile countered matter-of-factly. "Or maybe you go out and buy that speedboat you've been talking about since I first met you."

"No, no. I wouldn't do that. That would be stupid. Boss would figure that one out."

"Exactly," said Emile. "Back to my birthday. I'm forty today. I want to retire in a few years. My kids'll be getting married. There'll be grandkids. I want to kick back and enjoy the fruits of my hard work. I've kept my nose clean with Boss. I don't want to keep looking over my shoulder, wondering if you're going to do something stupid that will turn us into gator bait."

Louie became indignant. "Dammit, you ain't got no balls, man. No guts, no glory. It's a simple thing. Meet the jet at the airport and make a trade. Wham, bam, we're out of there in five minutes."

Emile studied him, a look of disbelief on his face. "I've been in this business nearly twenty years. You're just startin'. Ain't nothin' that simple. You ain't thought this through. We have to count on Mateo to fix us up with more girls."

Louie became indignant. "I thought this through. Mateo says he has girls. You heard him. He said that the girls are just as pretty as Catalina. You heard him say that too."

Emile interrupted, "I don't give a damn what he said. That doesn't make it so. In the years I've been doing this, I've not seen another girl as pretty as little mama. Most of them are dogs. And to tell us he has four or five of them is flat-out unbelievable. I doubt if he has any. Fewer and fewer have been coming into the country since the economy turned bad. We've been waiting two weeks for these two. That tells me he's lying. We can't go back to New Orleans with no girls. We can't go back empty-handed."

There was silence for nearly a mile as Louie mulled this over.

Before he could reply, Emile started up again. "Even if we had more girls, we have to count on this guy with the jet to go easy on us. What if he brings bodyguards? What if he brings the heat? No one parts with a hundred grand that easy. A guy with a jet is no fool."

Louie turned back and stared at Anna. "What's your cousin's name again?"

"Carlos. Carlos Alvarez." My face was devoid of expression.

Louie continued, "And what does this Carlos Alvarez do for a living that he can afford a jet? He traffic drugs out of Juarez? He have cartel connections?"

I could have told Louie that Carlos was an extraordinary computer hacker who brought down more accomplished men than him. I could have told Louie that Carlos made millions from unethical companies and sent many executives into quick retirement by threatening to bring down the law. I could have said Carlos was the Robin Hood of the cyber world and Louie was now on the radar of his cyber gang. Instead, I answered meekly, "Computers."

Louie raised his hands as if victory was assured. "We got nuttin' to worry about from a computer nerd. I flash him this"—Louie placed his hand in his coat pocket where I suspected he carried a gun—"and we're home free."

Emile shook his head in disbelief. "What if he tries to double-cross us? What if he brings some guns or the heat? What'll you do then, big man?"

Louie spoke indignantly. "I'm not afraid to shoot it out. Look, I'm tired of this what-if shit. Let's just do it."

Emile's voice was calm and measured. "I know you're a brave man. All I'm saying is we haven't studied the enemy. That name, Carlos Alvarez, has a familiar ring to it. You ever hear that name before?"

Louie shook his head, his face awash with anger. "I don't give a shit who he is. He's just one guy. The two of us can take him."

Emile kept repeating the name Carlos Alvarez over and over, trying to dredge up why it seemed familiar. Louie studied him in bemusement. Finally, Emile's eyes lit up, and he adjusted the rearview mirror to stare directly at me. When he caught my eyes, he said, "Carlos Alvarez foiled an assassination attempt on the president that left several men dead. The story goes that he fed a traitorous US general to sharks."

I fought to keep a blank face, but my cheeks quickly heated. The story was true. With Louie and Emile both staring at me, I shook my head and stammered quickly, "Don't know what you're talking about. Carlos Alvarez is a common name in Mexico, like John Smith is here."

Still staring at me, Emile continued, "You're not a very good liar, Anna. You have guilt written all over your face. He is the same Carlos Alvarez, isn't he?"

I continued to shake my head, but was silent. My gaze gradually drifted from the mirror in defeat.

Emile refused to give up. "He got some kind of medal from the president, didn't he?"

I continued shaking my head, staring out the window.

"Killed a bunch of terrorists, didn't he?"

My eyes welled up with tears. I had so hoped the ransom angle would work. Now it seemed hopeless. I would become a prostitute.

"You're a horrible liar," Emile continued, a grin emerging on his face.

Louie nodded with the unexpected turn of events. "She sure is. Her cousin fed a guy to sharks? Damn. Maybe you're on to something, Emile. He sounds like a badass dude. Let's just take the bitches to New Orleans. Sure am disappointed my payday isn't gonna happen."

I sobbed. I made a mistake telling them my cousin's real name. It was so easy to make a mistake in a game you never played before.

CHAPTER 17

FORT STOCKTON

L inda's cell phone rang.

"It's the Border Patrol," she said matter-of-factly before answering. "This is Linda."

Her face became crimson. "Gone? I warned you it could happen. We had only a little rope and duct tape. What about the truck in the grass . . . ?

"Gone too? That means he had time to change his flat tire. Did you guys stop in Sierra Blanca for a two-hour breakfast on the way . . . ?

"No, I'm not being disrespectful. I'm disappointed. There is a difference . . ."

She cringed. "No, I didn't catch the tags. I'm sure Scott did. He has a photographic memory for numbers." She handed the phone to Scott. "Mateo escaped. They want the tag numbers on his truck."

While Scott was talking to the Border Patrol, Linda leaned back to Alvarez. "Mateo's probably hiding under his bed in Mexico, but we need to be careful in case he's a vindictive person. Scott humiliated him, and sometimes those people come back with a vengeance."

When the car carrying Anna passed through San Antonio without stopping, Alvarez knew the kidnappers had gotten cold feet. He asked Linda over and over whether he should return their call. Her answer was always a firm "no." She had no idea why they changed their mind. One hundred thousand dollars was certainly more than they would make delivering the girls to New Orleans. Her experience as a hostage negotiator told her that the kidnappers would not change their minds, and a call like this could only jeopardize the situation.

When Anna's car passed through Houston three hours later, Alvarez had given up all hope of getting her back today. As the car crossed into Louisiana, Linda studied his glum face.

"You handled it beautifully. I couldn't have done better myself. It takes a lot of courage for kidnappers to try to close the deal on a hostage negotiation. They know they could get shot or arrested. They chickened out. It's not your fault. They might still change their mind, but I don't think so. The good news is that we're still following them and, if nothing changes, we can recover Anna within hours after they arrive at their final destination. The girls will be safe enough until then."

Alvarez, however, was inconsolable.

When Anna's car veered off I-10 in Lake Charles, Alvarez alerted the others. "They're off the interstate, far enough off that they're not just stopping for gas or food. In fact, they turned down a road that dead ends at the bayou. If we were closer, we could trap them. How far away are we?"

Scott answered, "We just passed through San Antonio. We have three hours to Houston, then another hour and a half to Lake Charles. If they're spending the night, we'll catch them."

Linda studied the map on her cell phone. "They wouldn't be stopping for the night already. It's not even dark. But they're definitely headed for the bayou. There's nothing but meandering watercourses. Perhaps they're not going to New Orleans after all. Perhaps they're taking a boat somewhere."

CHAPTER 18

LAKE CHARLES

Louie studied Emile. "How long it been since you had any?"

Emile rolled his eyes. "My cousin Vinny told me never to use the drugs you sell, 'cause by the end of the week, you'll be short of money and realize it all went up your nose."

"I don't want to hear any more shit about Vinny. I never heard of the guy before, and now he's all you want to talk about. I'm just saying we got two lovely women in the back seat who need some practice for when we get to New Orleans. I'll even give you first pick. I know you never had a bitch as good-lookin' as Catalina. She's as fine as they get."

Emile shook his head in disgust. "We're not gonna deliver damaged goods. When we get to New Orleans, you can take your money and buy any woman in the French Quarter. Hell, you can buy a whole brothel."

"Sounds like you forgot your Viagra, old man."

"I don't need that shit, asshole. Keep it in your pants till we get to New Orleans."

"Sorry, I was just havin' fun. Hey, my cousin has a place in Lake Charles. Want to stop for dinner? We could have some fresh catfish."

Emile was tired of driving and wanted to take a break. "How far off the road is it?"

"Five, ten miles max. It's right on the water. Think fresh catfish."

"I love catfish. Okay, give him a call. But we're not spending any more than an hour."

Louie dialed the number, but there was no answer. "Hell, let's go anyway. I know where he hides the key. We'll see what he has in the fridge. I could use a cold beer right about now."

In twenty minutes, they pulled up to a white house nestled under live oaks dripping with Spanish moss. The house needed a fresh coat of paint, but that appeared to be its only shortcoming. In the waning light, they could see a dock with a flat-bottomed boat. Louie went to the front door while Emile stayed with the girls in the car. Louie knocked first, then rummaged under a mat in front of the door. He grinned while he held up a key for Emile to admire from afar. Then he unlocked the front door and turned the lights on. He went straight to the fridge and popped himself a cold one and carried another out to Emile. "Nice place, huh? I could see myself living in a place like this someday."

Emile nodded to Louie appreciatively. "Let's get the girls inside. Lock them in a bedroom while we get dinner ready."

Then Emile cast a sidelong glance at Catalina. She was a beauty. French Creole girls, with their mix of European, African, and Native American blood, were stunning, but he thought this Latina could hold her own against any of them. Louie had a point about getting her used to life in New Orleans. It had been a while. Maybe he would have to show Louie he didn't need Viagra. He put this thought on pause for the moment. Then he studied her girls curled up next to little mama. They had been well-behaved. He thought about his daughter at the same age, and guilt welled up in him. He then hit the "delete this comparison" button in his brain.

Emile nodded at the girls. "They must be hungry. Let's see if there's milk or juice in the fridge."

Catalina nodded warily. This was the only nice thing he had said the whole trip. She had been completely ignored, which was fine, even preferred, given the circumstances.

When they entered the house, Louie was popping the top on another beer as he stared into the fridge. "There's all kinds of stuff in here. Fresh shrimp. Let's have a shrimp boil."

Emile's eyes softened. "I'd love some fresh shrimp. Why don't you get it going? I need to find something for the girls. Hey, Catalina, do they like grapes?"

Catalina nodded gratefully. He handed her a bunch of red grapes. Then his eyes drifted to Anna. "You like shrimp?"

She shrugged weakly while staring out the window, which irritated Emile. "Find something to eat. We're not stopping again until we reach New Orleans."

Anna didn't move, so Emile snapped, "Suit yourself."

Emile found some Old Bay in the cupboard and took it over to the stove. "I'll take over here, Louie, if you want to lock the girls in the bedroom."

Louie seemed irritated to be booted from the kitchen. His consolation was to pop open a third beer as he herded the girls into the bedroom. He pitched Maribel on the queen-size bed. She bounced a few times, then took to it like a trampoline. Guadalupe followed suit, but then stopped abruptly when she saw the gun protruding from Louie's jacket. "We're good guys. Mama said so. Are you bad?"

Louie shook his head defensively. "No, I'm not a bad guy. Why would you think that?"

"Good guys don't have guns."

Louie drew back with a forceful response. "No, girl. I'm not a bad guy. This is for protection from bad guys."

"Francisco tried to shoot us. Mama was crying. I was scared."

"Who's Francisco?"

"He's a bad guy. He has a gun." Guadalupe said with perfect innocence.

"Everyone who has a gun isn't a bad guy," Louie said, trying to make it seem as if it was true in his case.

"Will you protect us from bad guys?"

"Yes."

"Promise?"

"I said yes," Louie barked in frustration.

Guadalupe began jumping again and tuned Louie out.

Louie undid the latch and tried to open the only window in the room. He couldn't budge it. He locked the latch and turned away from the window. Maribel and Guadalupe bounced on the bed with pent-up energy from the eleven-hour drive. Louie left the room and closed the door behind him.

CHAPTER 19

LAKE CHARLES

As soon as the door closed, I began rummaging through drawers. No guns, but I did find a penknife. It wasn't much of a knife compared with Louie's, but I cradled it in my hand lovingly. I whispered to Catalina, "There's a boat tied up at the dock. If we can get out on the water, we're free. There's only one boat, so there's no way they can follow."

Catalina shook her head. "I can't. What about ICE?"

"We left ICE behind hours ago. There is no way they would go back. We're practically to New Orleans. It's now or never for escape."

Catalina seemed to find an inner resolve and bristled with encouragement. "I have your back."

The dock was about fifty yards away, mostly downhill. As I unlocked the window, I noticed paint around the edges that had prevented Louie from opening it. I sliced through the paint between the frame and the window. I tugged. The window creaked slightly, but didn't give. I pulled harder. Still nothing. I put a foot on the windowsill for better leverage. The window gave way suddenly with a loud bang. I closed it quickly and dropped on the bed.

Louie burst through the door, and his eyes swept the room to see what caused the noise. Catalina picked up Maribel apologetically. "Maribel fell off the bed into the dresser. She banged her knee, but she's all right."

Louie gave Maribel a fatherly look. "You okay, sweetie? We'll be eating soon. There's some ice cream in the freezer." Maribel smiled in the coy manner of a three-year-old. Louie turned his attention to Catalina. "Keep them quiet. We're watching TV out here. Dinner will be ready in twenty minutes."

When he closed the door, I sprang to my feet. I inched the window up a little at a time until I could fit through the opening. Catalina fed Maribel through the opening into my arms, then Guadalupe. I stood there, one child in each arm, until Catalina rolled out with little grace. She didn't have much athletic prowess. I thrust Maribel into her arms as we dashed to the dock in the fading light.

Though the sun had set, the moon rose in the east, nearly full as it illuminated our path. There was enough light that we could keep our footing in the sand. Across the water and upstream we could see city lights. I would call the police from the nearest house. I hoped to have these men in jail by midnight.

I was relieved to see paddles and two life jackets. Having grown up in the desert, I couldn't swim. I suspected I would drown. Priorities as they were, I was willing to take my chances with the boat rather than two malicious men and whatever lay in store for us in New Orleans.

I untied the rope securing the boat to the dock. I slipped the oars into the oarlocks. I began tentative, awkward strokes that were largely inept. Moving too far to the right, then too far to the left, our escape was more of a zigzag course than a thin line of beauty. Still, in a single stroke, the dock was five feet away, and the evil men were still clueless. In two strokes, the dock was out of reach for anyone but a strong swimmer. In five minutes, I had learned to even out the rough spots by pulling evenly right and left. I began to move more or less in a straight line. The lights in the cabin faded into the twilight.

"See if you can put the life jackets on the girls."

Catalina struggled for a few minutes. "They're way too big. Adult size, I guess."

I glanced back at the house. No sign of the men. Those men seemed really stupid. Put a beer in their hand, turn the TV on, and you could do most anything, even while caring for two three-year-olds. I was giddy with excitement. We were finally free.

CHAPTER 20

JUAREZ

The rages came easier these days. Francisco thought the hard part was over when he burned the birth certificates of the twin girls. All he needed now was a forged DNA test saying he was the Hernandez heir. But Anna of GenWiz had vanished, along with Catalina and her twin girls. Then there was the mystery of the flat tire. There was no puncture in the tire. Someone deliberately let the air out while he went looking for Catalina. It had to be the guy who stopped him in the street. The same dude probably put water in his fuel tank. And how did this guy know his mother? Francisco asked his mother about her friends at church but didn't get anywhere. He even went to mass one day to see if he could spot this guy in the crowd. The mystery man remained a mystery.

One of Francisco's jobs with the Sinaloa cartel was collecting coyote fees. The cartel charged coyotes for crossing territory they controlled. Before the downturn in the American economy and the Bush-era crackdown on illegal immigrants, it had been much easier to collect these fees. When the well was full, everyone drank their fill. These days, fewer people crossed north because it required papers or a green card to get a job. The coyotes had fewer clients and, consequently, there was less revenue for the cartels. This had led him to the outskirts of Juarez to visit Mateo, a prolific coyote he had dealt with in the past. Mateo's obvious success was manifest in a nice house, a newer-model car, and an old pickup. Nevertheless,

Mateo constantly regaled Francisco with sad stories of financial hardship.

Mateo was working on his truck when Francisco caught him by surprise. "Mateo, my man, looks like you got new wheels. I'm here to collect."

Mateo turned toward the voice and grimaced. He stood up and hobbled toward him.

Francisco drew back as he studied his face. "What's with the bruises on your face and that limp?"

"White dude from the US tied me to his horse and dragged me across the Rio Grande and through the cacti. Stole all my money. Four grand. I barely escaped with my life."

Francisco thought it more likely that the bruises came from a fight in the local bar. Mateo was known to be a mean drunk. "Why would this man do such a horrid thing?"

"Apparently my girls were special to him. He was pissed that I sold them to some dudes from out east."

Francisco's eyes lit up. "Girls?"

"Girls," Mateo said firmly. "Two young women and two little ones."

"You know their names?"

Mateo nodded. "Catalina. She's a beauty. I proposed marriage, but she blew me off. She'll be sorry when she has to become a whore. I would have treated her well. I got a nice house. Then there was Anna. She didn't like me, and she didn't want to do the border crossing. When Catalina got cold feet, I took Anna free of charge to make it work out. She repays my kindness with this," he said, pointing to his bruises. "Some dude chased me down on a mustang and beat the shit out of me. His wife called him Scott. Scott Williams, I'd guess, at least that was the name she gave the Border Patrol. Took all my money. And that's the honest truth. I got nothing from that trip, man, honest to God. Plus, he shot out my front tires. It was my only trip all month, and it ended up costing me money."

Francisco pulled out his gun. "The cartel doesn't like it when I return empty-handed."

Mateo panicked. "Look, man, search me. Search the house. I got nothing but bruises. May have some broken ribs too. I'm sorry I ever met up with them. I'd shoot this guy, Scott. Hung me by my neck from a tree on the Rio Grande. You can't make this stuff up." He pointed to dark bruises around his neck.

Francisco fumed. Mateo had always been reluctant to part with any cash for the cartel, always spewing some hard-luck story about how he got stiffed or robbed or threw one in for free out of the goodness of his heart. It didn't seem likely this story was true. On the other hand, this story held an intriguing link to Anna. "I've got a notion to shoot you here and now, Mateo. You've stiffed me time and time again. This story is bull."

Mateo became desperate. He had stiffed the cartel in the past. There was no way the cartel could determine how many people he moved across the border. His neighbors probably talked, but he tried to keep his business private. He took all his earnings and invested them in his house and car so that he had little cash on hand for visits from Francisco. However, this approach made his success all the more obvious. "No, man. Don't shoot. Scott lives near here. He has a wife named Linda Williams. They live on Setting Sun Ranch. We can find him and make him pay back the four grand. I'll split it with you."

"Where's Setting Sun Ranch?"

"Near Sierra Blanca. No more than twenty miles from the border. Nothing but wide-open space between here and there. Dude must have money if he owns a spread like that. He had a truck with a trailer and a horse. We might get more."

Francisco thought about it. "We might get picked up by the Border Patrol."

Mateo shrugged. "Not to worry. Happened to me before. All they do is send you back. They don't want you over there."

"Tell me about the girls."

"Girls?"

"The ones you sold to the slavers."

"Oh, Catalina and Anna. Yeah, this Scott dude was going to find them and bring them back. He might not be back for a few days. We could go and plunder his house while he's gone."

"Is he going to find the girls?"

"Probably. He took my phone. He has the contact numbers of the slavers, and from there he can figure out the addresses. Hey, why do you care?"

Francisco was silent.

Mateo continued. "I'll bet you want Catalina. She might like someone like you. I mean, you got nice clothes, a nice car, a steady job. She'd be worth waiting for. Best-looking woman I've ever seen."

Francisco became visibly agitated and fingered the gun more than Mateo liked. He backed up a step and raised his hands in alarm.

Francisco said, "Shut the hell up. You're not getting it. Why does Scott care about these girls?"

A puzzled look crossed Mateo's face as he shook his head. "Don't know. It seemed more to do with Anna. There was a third guy. I think he was her brother."

"What's his name?"

Mateo shook his head. "I don't remember. I think it began with an *A*."

"Antonio?" Francisco asked. He had been unable to find Antonio or Anna's parents since the shooting.

"Could have been, or it could have been Alvarez. I don't remember."

Mateo closed his eyes and was silent for a while. "I think her brother was a friend of Scott's. That's why Scott came after me. You're thinking they'll have some firepower in the house to protect Anna? I doubt they'll suspect we care. I mean, we don't care, do we? We just want some easy cash."

Francisco spoke coldly and clearly, venom hanging in every word. "Chick owes me money. I want her to know I'm hunting her. I want her to know she'll pay or die."

CHAPTER 21

LAKE CHARLES

After Emile and Louie had eaten their fill, Emile called the girls. There was no response. Louie was two sheets to the wind after six beers. Emile had restrained himself to one beer and was quite irritated with Louie. It might have been humorous if they were buddies in a bar, but with twenty grand at stake, Emile was cautious.

"Bring them out. I'm sure they're famished."

Louie had collapsed into a chair and did not respond. Emile went into the bedroom but found it empty with an open window. His voice rose in anger. "They've escaped, you idiot. I gave you a single job, and you screwed up."

Louie rose on uncertain legs. He meandered toward the bedroom with a compromised sense of urgency. He tried to focus on the window, then closed one eye and squinted at it. "I checked the window. It was painted shut."

Emile studied the edges of the window. "She used something to chip the paint away. Looks like they took the boat."

Emile crawled out the window. The bulkier Louie elected to wobble out the back door. When they reached the dock, the boat was gone.

"Where can we get a boat?" Emile cried out, imagining his money and his life vanishing into the night.

Louie pointed upstream. "There's a rental place up there with motorboats. It'll be closed, but we can borrow one if they left the keys in the ignition. They usually do. The girls have a rowboat. We'll catch them in no time."

Though he was seething with anger, Emile spoke in a tone of defeat. "To what purpose? Nothing but darkness in all directions."

"Not at all," Louie replied, nodding toward Lake Charles. "They'll be drawn like moths to a flame."

Emile realized the wisdom of his words. "Let's go."

Emile reached the SUV first as Louie tripped over a root and sprawled. He lay there for a moment, breathing hard. When he did try to rise, he had a difficult time finding his feet. He staggered to the car, barking out directions that were somewhat slurred. "Out to the road, and turn right."

Louie yanked the door open, trying to stay focused. He collapsed into the seat but had difficulty closing the door. Emile gunned the engine harder than was necessary and left a large rut in the driveway. The force of the acceleration closed the door for him.

"My cousin won't appreciate that," said Louie.

Emile spoke with a calmness that did not reflect his anger. "I don't give a damn about your cousin. If we go back to New Orleans empty-handed, our lives are over. Boss expects girls. Boss doesn't like to be disappointed. I disappointed him once, and I have a scar to prove it. Vinny disappointed him and disappeared forever."

"Sorry," was Louie's terse reply. "Turn here," he yelled suddenly as they nearly passed the entrance to the rental place.

Wheels squealed as they pulled into a dark, empty parking lot. Emile rushed onto the dock. He didn't find a key in the ignition of the first boat. He jumped in the next boat and found a key. He turned the key to no avail.

"Prime the gas," he yelled to Louie, who stumbled into the boat. Louie staggered to the engine. The starter made a grinding noise while Emile coaxed it on. "Come on, you mother. I got big bucks riding on you. Turn over." The engine roared to life in a haze of blue smoke and the smell of gas and oil. "Get the ropes," Emile yelled.

When Louie failed to respond, Emile undid the ropes and leapt back into the boat. He set a straight course for the flickering city lights of Lake Charles. The boat was fast. "We'll catch them. I'm sure girls from Juarez can't row worth a damn."

CHAPTER 22

LAKE CHARLES

The rowing seemed fun at first when every stroke spoke of freedom. I set a course for Lake Charles but found the current my master. With each stroke, Lake Charles became more distant. After twenty futile minutes, I conceded defeat. Catalina tried her hand and was far worse. She crashed into the shoreline, nearly taking everyone's heads off with a low-hanging branch. She turned the oars back over to me. I steered the boat near the center of the channel as the current carried us downstream. The lights of Lake Charles, our last hope for rescue, dimmed and then twinkled out.

"I wonder where we'll end up," I mused to no one in particular. Catalina gazed at the fading lights, then put a brave twist on things. "There'll be a dock. It doesn't matter where we go as long as they don't find us."

While I wanted to believe Catalina, no flickering lights or inviting docks were apparent along our current course. I had no idea where the water would take us, but it seemed as if a wilderness as vast as the universe had swallowed us whole.

The bayou was different from anything I had ever seen. Lit by a full moon and lingering twilight, the channels were lined with large trees whose branches spread out over the water. The branches were covered in ferns and Spanish moss that played with the light. The trip harkened back to a bygone era where pirates and pioneers plied the wilderness in search of a better life. Then the night sounds began with a chorus of frogs on both riverbanks and birds in the canopy above us. The sounds were loud yet soothing in their repetition. The moist air and the fresh breeze became intoxicating. The night creatures that called so fervently and were answered so immediately spoke of devotion to castes and mates and children.

"Girls, do you want to hear a story Grandma Josephina told me about Coyote?"

The girls nodded.

"I love Coyote stories," said Maribel.

"One day," Catalina began, "Rabbit was sitting in the shade underneath a big rock. He was feeling perky when Coyote came along.

"'What are you doing, brother?' the coyote asked the rabbit.

"There was a twinkle in his eye, but the rabbit spoke in a panic. 'Come here quickly, Brother Coyote. The sky is falling. It will crush us all. Push against this rock to hold the sky up while I go for a stick. We'll prop the sky up with the stick.'

"The coyote looked at the vast sky and cringed. 'All right,' said the coyote, terror in his voice. He began pushing with all his might. Since the coyote was stupid, he did exactly what the rabbit told him. After an hour, his arms grew tired, but the thought of being crushed by the sky made him try even harder.

"'Brother Rabbit, bring the stick quickly. My arms are so tired that I can't hold up the sky much longer.'

"But the rabbit didn't return. The coyote shouted in desperation, 'Come back, Brother Rabbit! The weight of the rock has made me tired.'

"Still, the rabbit didn't return.

"Finally, weary from pushing so hard, he stepped back from the rock. 'Brother Rabbit, I'm going to leave, even though the sky will crush us,' said the coyote. But as he backed away from the rock, he fell into a ravine and disappeared."

"Mama, does the sky fall?" Maribel asked while staring at the moon.

"No, it doesn't, sweetheart."

Maribel nodded. "Coyote's stupid."

Catalina stroked her head. "Coyote is like many people, too gullible to think for himself. Some people tell lies. Learn to think for yourself."

"Is Señor Louie a bad guy?"

"Definitely a bad guy."

Maribel nodded in agreement. "He has a gun. He said he was a good guy. The gun was for protection."

"He's not telling the truth, like Rabbit. Hopefully we'll never see him again."

"Because we're as fast as the wind, right?"

"Tonight, we're even faster than the wind. Now, get some sleep."

I sang to keep our spirits high. Catalina followed suit to help Maribel and Guadalupe fall asleep. When our voices gave out, we hummed bedtime songs. Eventually the humming was drowned out by the night sounds. While the desert quieted down after sunset, the bayou crawled with creatures of the night—humming, chirping, and occasionally screaming. At first, the eerie sounds unsettled us. But when nothing bad happened, the girls made their peace with the night sounds and fell asleep.

The boat drifted forward as if both will and purpose forged a destiny bereft of unholy trespassers. Clothed in darkness and surrounded by sounds I hoped were friendly, we meandered ever southward, driven forward by physical forces beyond our control. Contrary as a child, the channel widened then constricted then widened as it meandered east, then west, but ever southward. I learned how to steer the boat with the paddle held behind the stern like a rudder. I tried to keep the boat in the middle of the channel where the light was brightest and the chance of brushing a tree with unwanted visitors like snakes and spiders was minimal. It was a dangerous ploy. If a house or a dock without lights were spotted, the current might carry us past before we could make a landing. With the gentle rocking of the boat, Catalina's head began nodding.

"How did you find your way from Guatemala to Juarez?" I asked to keep Catalina from dozing off.

"Sad story. I was sixteen and as gullible as Coyote. Mama had cancer and needed a doctor. We were poor and couldn't afford one. All my life, people had told me how beautiful I was. It seemed like my only virtue. I wasn't smart. I wasn't a good athlete. I couldn't sing or dance. I couldn't do much of anything. So I decided to go to Hollywood, hoping I could become a movie star and give Mama the money she needed to get well. A woman named Bella offered to take me for free if I worked a bit in Juarez to earn some money. Bella lied to me about what type of work I would be doing and nearly ruined my life with drugs. Fortunately for me, she died one night. I never made it to Hollywood, but I did meet a wonderful man."

"How did you and Efrain meet?" I asked. I needed her company to keep another set of eyes looking for a dock.

"I was working at a bar in Juarez. It wasn't good work. I was doing things nice girls don't do. The guy who owned the building and bar, Rubio, invited Efrain to stop by and meet me. Efrain offered me a job in his factory. It didn't pay well, but it was honest work. One day at work, he noticed I had a drug problem. He could have fired me then and there. I told him I left Guatemala to raise some money for Mama, who was desperately ill. He surprised me and told me that he would send money home for Mama if I cleaned myself up. It was hard to kick the habit at first, but I did because I loved Mama, and there was no other way. He was a generous man and expected nothing in return. He kept his promise and sent her money. My mama died, despite the help of doctors. It was a sad time, because I never had a chance to say good-bye. Efrain recognized my sadness and comforted me. He was much older than me. Sometimes he acted like a father, other times like a friend. I grew to love him. He saved my life, and he was all I had in the world. He worked constantly to make his businesses successful and never had fun. I became the fun he had missed all his life. We went places together, enjoyed each other's company. Most people thought I was his daughter, but it didn't matter to me. One thing led to another, and before long, I was pregnant. I was afraid to tell him for fear he would abandon me. It was an honest accident. I was taking the pill and don't know how I got pregnant. This is why I love Efrain. He rescued me again. He came over frequently to help me out. He bought baby furniture. He was happy he was going to be a father. He was at the hospital when the girls were born. The happiest day of my life was at the christening. We were all dressed up and so loving. After the christening, we went to dinner together and back to my place. We put the girls in their cribs and sat on the couch together, enjoying each other's company. I thought he might ask me to marry him. I wondered if he was trying to propose, because he was nervous and fumbled for words, despite being such an articulate person. I would have accepted instantly and been the happiest girl in the world. Then one baby started crying, then the other, and before long, we were sitting on the couch with a baby on each lap instead of in each other's arms. That broke the spell forever. I think Efrain was afraid to get married because it might have pulled him away from his businesses. He spent most of his time at work. When he wasn't working, he spent time with us. He loved his girls, and they loved him. I have two empty spots now, one for my mother and one for Efrain. His heart just gave out one day. Odd for someone so young. It was such a sad day. The girls will grow up without knowing what a fine man he was."

Tears came to my eyes as she spoke lovingly about Efrain. Her voice cracked with emotion. "I loved him because he was the only man who loved me. My father wanted a son and was angry at getting me instead. We were never close. I loved Efrain because he accepted me for who I was and helped me to be a better person. He gave me much more than I gave him. I loved him most of all because he loved our girls. He wasn't angry that they weren't sons. He was my father and my boyfriend and my girls' father rolled into one. That's the end of the story."

"But not all there is to be told," I added wistfully. "Perhaps Efrain is guiding us now. I think the dead can still care for the living in ways we don't understand. Hopefully in the morning we'll be on our way back west, you to Hollywood and me to El Paso. Do you really want to go to Hollywood when your girls are heirs to so much money? I mean, you paid a lot of money to have the DNA tests done. Don't you want to try to reap the benefits?"

"I had the DNA tests done because Efrain's lawyer said that's what Efrain would have wanted. He knew that Efrain loved his girls, and the lawyer wanted them to get the money. He was mystified about why the birth certificates were missing. He told me that copies might be among Efrain's papers, but to be on the safe side, the DNA tests needed to be done. Right now, I have a bad taste in my mouth for this country. It hasn't been kind to us since we crossed the border. If I could go back to Juarez and get the money without risking the lives of my girls, I'd do it. Then I might go to Hollywood. I'm only twenty. I could still become a movie star. Wouldn't that be cool? But as long as Francisco is alive, I won't go back to Juarez."

"Don't blame you in the least. But what if Francisco died?"

"If Francisco died, I'd go back and collect the money. But what are the chances? He's not much older than me."

I pondered this statement in silence. There must be a way to rid ourselves of Francisco. He was a threat to me as well. I expected a Mexican passport soon, but that only entitled me to visit the US for a short time as a tourist. Sooner or later I would have to deal with him again.

My silence must have disturbed Catalina. "What about you, Anna? Do you have a boyfriend?"

"I never found a boy I couldn't live without. I was more interested in a career and hoped I would find someone who shared my interest along the way. In the end, I found an interesting job but no man to share my life with."

Catalina tried to be reassuring. "You are young and pretty and brilliant. I'm sure the right man will come along. Come to Hollywood with me. Maybe you'll meet a handsome actor or a marvelous writer."

My thoughts drifted to the one man in my life I loved the most, my cousin Carlos. There was an abiding love that a sister and brother might share. I wasn't as close to my brother, Antonio. What was Carlos doing? Was he panicked while waiting for me to call? Did he know where I was? Did he even care anymore? I had been so stupid. He asked me not to cross the Rio Grande with a coyote. I did anyway. He asked me to wear the GPS tracking device. I took it off. My last hope of being followed was my cell phone, but Louie threw it out the car window in West Texas. For a moment around San Antonio, it had seemed as if we might be ransomed, but that hope vanished over a matter of hours. Now we were hopelessly lost in the Louisiana bayou. The last town of any note faded into darkness hours ago. We needed food and water. We needed assurance that this meandering waterway would touch civilization again. I thought it possible that, after drifting for days, we would wither up and die. Someday, someone would find our boat floating with four skeletons in it.

Catalina's head began nodding again.

"Why don't you snuggle with your girls in the bottom of the boat to keep them warm?"

Catalina put her head down. The wind blew from the north and chilled me. I pressed onward, hoping to secure a landing. I longed for someplace warm and safe to spend the night.

I had never been in a boat before. There was something peaceful about the gentle rocking. I was dozing when something thumped the bottom of the boat. I startled awake and centered the boat in the channel. I thought I might have hit a submerged log or a sand bar, and the thought panicked me. What would I do if the boat ran aground in this desolate place? I couldn't face the thought of having to get out of the boat to push. The boat slid forward in the current with casual grace.

Another thump, and this time the bow lifted out of the water enough to awaken Catalina. The boat drifted sideways again. Could it be a fish? It would have to be fairly big to raise the bow of a boat with four people in it, bigger than any fish I had seen. When I straightened the boat again, two large eyes peered at me from just above the surface of the water. The reflection of the moon captured the shape of a knotted reptilian head. I tried to judge the size of the alligator from the reflection of light off the exposed head. The distance between the eyes might be over a foot. I imagined he was longer than the boat. The gator moved toward the boat again. And then I understood. He hadn't casually brushed against us on a night swim. He was hunting dinner.

CHAPTER 23

LAKE CHARLES

The boat was in full throttle as Emile passed under I-210, past the Contraband Bayou Golf Club, and shot across Lake Charles to the town by the same name. He paused briefly at a broad succession of docks stretching far into the night upstream, and let out a curse when he did not see the rowboat. He continued upstream one dock at a time until he noticed a man on a dock tending his boat.

"Good fellow," he yelled, with more politeness than usually expected.

The French Creole man glanced up and smiled with unusual friendliness. "Can I help you?"

"I'm looking for two ladies in a rowboat with two little girls. Have you seen them?"

Louie stood and stumbled to the front end of the boat, eager to hear the conversation. The man shook his head, a sad expression washing over his face. "Been out on the water all evening. No ladies. Where did you last see them?"

"Across the lake and downstream a bit."

The man peered downstream as if expecting to see them emerging from the inky blackness. "It rained the past couple days. Current is strong. If they had a rowboat, I think they would be downstream from where you last saw them. It's hard to row against this current." He scrunched his shoulders. "Not many people strong enough to deal with this current. Stay close to shore. You'll see 'em before too long."

Emile berated himself for not thinking of the current. He had driven the boat at least a mile, much of it upstream. Four females in a rowboat couldn't have done that. "What's downstream?"

"Nothin' but trouble. Gators and snakes for miles. There's moccasins as long as your boat and even longer gators. If the girls are lucky enough to make it through the bayou, there's the Calcasieu."

"Calcasieu?" Emile inquired cautiously.

The Creole man blinked at Emile as if he were completely ignorant. "If they survive the night in the bayou, there's Lake Calcasieu with big sharks. God help them. I believe the bayou will have its way with them and they'll be pulled up on the first dock they find. Course there aren't many docks till da Calcasieu. God help 'em. Not a place for ladies with youngins."

Emile nodded, not wishing to have his ignorance thrown back in his face again. He turned the boat sharply and accelerated. The turn came without warning and was a little too sharp for the tipsy Louie, who was flung overboard. Emile cursed at his incompetent partner, but stopped all the same. He circled round and thrust the boat into neutral. Emile stretched his strong right arm over the rail and hauled a gasping Louie on board. Emile closed his eyes, a look of despair washing across his face. It was no longer about getting a bonus. It was about surviving the wrath of Boss, who was expecting girls. A calmer voice prevailed inside him. Despite his anger, he was mostly to blame for Louie's soaking and helped him to his seat.

Louie took off his sopping coat. He pulled his gun out of one pocket and sat it on the seat. It would need to be cleaned. He pulled his phone out of his other pocket and tried to turn it on. "Dead," he scowled.

He threw it toward the shore. The phone skidded across the dock near the Creole man.

As gently as his frayed temper would allow, Emile said, "Louie, sit down. We have to go. I think we've come the wrong way."

Louie did as he was told. The swim in the cold water seemed to sober him up. As Emile left Lake Charles, he made a sharp left on a waterway. "No, not that way," barked Louie, who was huddled tightly to stay warm in the stiff breeze.

Emile turned right and then banked left as another channel opened up. "Not that way," barked Louie again.

Emile banked right and, when another waterway appeared, stayed left, only to have Louie correct him again. Emile would have become hopelessly lost in the myriad of meandering channels if not for Louie. It was one thing to move toward Lake Charles's city lights. It was quite another to make choices by moonlight. "Where to now?" he yelled over the engine noise.

"Hug the shore to your right. There will be a long stretch of bayou. Then there'll be fishing shacks with docks. Pass each slowly and look for the rowboat."

CHAPTER 24

HOUSTON

S cott was irritated that Alvarez stopped at a toy store and an electronics store. He made good use of the time getting gas, groceries, and fast food, but the stops cost them nearly two hours. Alvarez and Linda were less concerned. The vehicle with the girls had stopped west of Lake Charles and might be settled in for the night at the edge of the bayou. Earlier, Alvarez even called up an old satellite image. Trees hid the house, but they could see the bayou, a dock, and small boat. They were only five hours away, nothing if the other party had stopped for the night.

Alvarez met them outside the electronics shop with a cart containing four large bags. Scott helped load them in the trunk, peeking into one long enough to suppose they had no practical purpose.

As Scott pulled out of the parking lot, Linda offered Alvarez a burger. "Did you find everything you wanted?"

"I purchased things every spy needs. I need to do a little soldering, but I think I have enough."

Back on the freeway, Alvarez turned his computer on to continue following the GPS signal. It was still where they left it. Or was it? At first glance, he thought it moved a little further upstream, though still on the edge of the bayou. And then the unexpected happened. He cried out in alarm. "They're crossing the water."

Linda's first instinct as an FBI agent was to challenge the data. "Are you sure? What's your resolution?"

"Resolution is not a problem. I have enough satellites locked in," Alvarez replied, referring to triangulation. At least three satellites were needed to unambiguously mark the location, and more satellites improved the resolution to a few yards or even a few feet. "They are clearly out on the water headed toward Lake Charles. And they are moving pretty fast."

Linda puzzled over the data. "It's a curious move. Why Lake Charles and why by boat? They could drive there in a similar amount of time. Why would they abandon the SUV?"

Scott offered a hypothesis. "I have no doubt they will return to the SUV. You don't abandon a thirty-thousand-dollar vehicle. This is a temporary excursion."

"For what purpose?" Linda challenged.

"Something subversive. Drugs. More girls. Maybe they split up. I doubt they are dropping the girls off there. What's in Lake Charles? Hey, Alvarez, did you make a clear notation of the location of the SUV?"

Scott referred to the fact that they were tracking the kidnapper's phone and could no longer monitor the location of the SUV.

"Yes, we need to swing by there at some point. Maybe the SUV will be there, maybe not. Hey, the boat seems to have stopped in Lake Charles. I have a good location on it."

Alvarez called up an old satellite image. "It's a residential area with docks. I think I can pinpoint the exact house." Then he groaned. "The phone just stopped transmitting."

Linda cast him an anxious glance. "Maybe the battery went dead. We may get a signal as soon as they charge it."

Five hours later, the phone was still not broadcasting a location. They bypassed the last location of the SUV and headed directly to the last location of the phone. The SUV might be gone, but it was a virtual certainty that the owner of the house would know something about the visitors. Road-worn and bedraggled, Scott knocked on the door of a shabby home with a dock in Lake Charles. The lights were out, and no one answered the door. He pounded more urgently.

Linda stood in the front yard. "Light just came on upstairs. Someone will be down shortly."

A man answered, a groggy look on his face. Scott jumped right in. "Excuse me, we're looking for two women in their twenties and two three-year-olds."

The Creole man gave them a confused look as he stepped onto the porch. "Two men stopped by in a boat 'bout, oh, five hours ago looking for four girls in a rowboat. I haven't seen them."

Scott cast Linda a hopeful look, then turned back to the man. "They weren't with the men then?"

"No, sir. In fact, I told the men they most likely went downstream. They said the girls had a rowboat. It's hard to row against the current. I hope they all right."

Scott scratched his chin. "Did one of the men leave his phone behind?"

The Creole man looked ashamed. "He did. He fell in the water and he left it on my dock. It don't work. Here, let me get it."

The man went inside to get the phone. Scott had a broad grin as he shouted toward Alvarez, who was standing beside the car. "Seems like the girls escaped. It's just a matter of time before Anna finds a phone and calls you."

The man came back with the phone in a mason jar half full of rice. "I was dryin' it out. Sometimes they work again after you do that. Here, you take it."

The man handed the jar to Scott, who eagerly accepted it. "Tell me again, what's downstream?"

"Bayou for a long ways, then the Calcasieu, then the Gulf." He glanced at his watch. "They be most ways to the Calcasieu by now. Not a place for girls. There's gators and snakes along the way and big waves on the Calcasieu."

"Any place to pull off along the way? You know, docks, houses, towns?"

The Creole man shook his head. "There's miles of twisting channels in the bayou. They some docks in a small town and later a bridge. Lot of bayou between here and there. Best go by boat if you want to go lookin'."

Scott nodded appreciatively. "We'll do that. Did you ever see these men before?"

"No, sir. One was Creole, about forty. Spoke like he was from New Orleans. The other was a big strappin' guy about twenty. He's the one what belongs to this phone."

Scott handed the man a business card with his number on it. The card read *Linda and Scott Williams, Setting Sun Ranch, Sierra Blanca, Texas*. "If you see the men again or find the girls, please call."

The man studied the card carefully, a confused expression washing over his face. "Why a rancher from Texas come to bayou country?"

"The girls were abducted in Texas. They seem to have escaped, but to what end if they die in the bayou?"

The man's face became serious. "That be wild country down there. If they stay close to shore and find a dock, they be all right, except for gators. There's gators as big as cars."

Linda studied the phone in the mason jar. Then she flashed the man her most charming smile. "Thanks. I know exactly what to do with this."

CHAPTER 25

THE BAYOU

Moonlight glistened off the reptilian head as I cinched the oar closer to my body. The smooth wooden handle was comforting but provided little protection against the large beast. I felt the urge to lash out at the gator, to strike it with the full force of the oar, to reclaim my territory. Yet when that effort was spent, I might have nothing left to protect the children. Better to wait in case the need became urgent.

The boat drifted with the current, lost to purpose in everything but the push to the sea. The gator followed just off one side, quiet but relentless in pursuit. Occasionally, the moonlight would reveal ripples in the water where the tail beat out a steady rhythm. A creature of the night called out in a piercing voice that sliced through the chilly night air. Whether the call was in pain or in ecstasy was never clear, but the noise rattled my calm and sent shivers down my spine. This was a wild world. The stakes were life and death of a different sort. Here I was, trying to avoid becoming part of a food chain. It struck me that there must be a part of the brain that remembers the pursuit of predators from the caves of ancient man and guards the tribe. I became that guard, the last bastion between life and death. Catalina was snuggled in the center of the boat with the girls, her eyes closed. She was unaware of the danger, and I thought it best to keep it that way.

I touched the oar to the water to straighten the boat. The boat picked up speed in the more streamlined position. I peered back. The gator followed, accelerating the beat of his tail to match the speed of the boat. He hovered far enough back that I couldn't reach him with the oar, but close enough to appear ever menacing. I thought about pulling the boat toward shore, but the brush was a thick tangle. I doubted I could even reach the shore through the tangle, and even if I did, would it be solid ground? Would the gator pursue us onto shore, attack us in a beached boat? Moving in that direction might trap us and leave us even more vulnerable. At least this way we were going somewhere. I had no idea where, but at least it was away from the men who kidnapped us. Maybe the gator would tire.

A screech from the shore pierced my ears, a feral sound of an animal being killed by a stronger foe. I shuddered as I pulled the oar close. In the direction of the sound, I could see only blackness. I glanced back at the gator. It was gone. I relaxed a bit. Perhaps the eerie noise had driven it off.

Suddenly, the left side of the boat lifted out of the water. Water breached the gunwale on the right and began flooding the boat. But the gator was unable to lift the broad craft high enough to flip it over. I thrust my weight to the left as the boat collapsed back onto the water surface. The girls, now wet, began wailing. Catalina sat up helplessly in the center of the boat in a puddle of water several inches deep, holding one girl in each arm.

I called out in desperation. "An alligator is trying to flip the boat. Stay in the center and hold your girls tight. He doesn't have to flip the boat to get us; he just needs to flood it enough to sink it."

I repositioned myself near the back where the gator was watching and waiting. Suddenly he was gone again, and I prepared myself for another attack. Ripples from the powerful tail fanned out near the underbelly of the boat. I struck something solid with the oar. I stabbed again and again, but it was like striking rock. My cold hands ached from the force of the blows, but each blow could be the difference between life and death.

The boat lifted in the air again, this time from the right side. Water slogged over the left gunwale, adding to the load. The boat collapsed back onto the water, now riding deeper and looking more like a wading pool. I tossed a plastic bucket to Catalina. "Bail before we sink. One more pass, and we're done for."

Catalina snapped to attention despite the wailing girls. She was quicker than I imagined, pitching bucketful after bucketful overboard. I studied the head of the gator. I reared back and came overhead with the full weight of the oar. The blade shattered. The head submerged, and the tail pushed the creature toward the underbelly of the boat. Now the oar was more like a harpoon. I thrust the point over and over at the submerged body, hitting home every time. The animal was protected by a suit of armor. My hands were raw and began to blister.

Now the gator tried to lift the back, which could finish the boat off for good. That kept the gator's neck within my reach. I stabbed repeatedly as the animal rose. My hands ached, but I dared not let up. The back started to rise. I put my whole effort into one final strike. Miraculously, the animal yielded under the force of my blow and the boat fell back into the water. I was stunned at my success. I thwarted a creature much longer and stronger than me. A second gator of similar size approached the boat, cutting my revelry short. I sank back as hopelessness washed over me. My hands were bleeding, and my energy was tapped. I may have won the battle, but it seemed as if the war was lost. How many of those things were there?

CHAPTER 26

THE BAYOU

The bayou was a morass of interconnected channels separated by islands and sandbars. Without Louie's directions, Emile was certain he would have been hopelessly lost. But he learned to keep the houses close on his right. Emile recognized the boat rental place where they had borrowed their boat and, a bit later, the house they stayed at. Further south, the last vestiges of civilization melted into the bayou. For a couple hours, he held the boat in the middle of the channel, scanning for a boat or a dock or any sign of the missing girls. Nothing. His anger with Louie continued to mount as he mulled over the consequences. None of the options were attractive.

They could call off the search and return to New Orleans empty-handed. That would invite certain disaster with Boss. Perhaps if he threw himself at Boss's mercy and blamed Louie, Boss would let him slide. Perhaps. He had been a loyal employee for twenty years. However, Boss was so volatile, there was no predicting the extent of his rage.

They could call Mateo and pick up more girls. That would add a few more days to the trip but was probably better than returning empty-handed. What if Mateo was lying and he had no girls? That could add several days to the trip, and he would still return empty-handed. The situation was so complicated; Emile didn't know what to do. It was not his fault the girls had escaped. It was all on Louie, who had paid more attention to his beer. As he pondered his choices, he believed Louie needed a reprimand.

Emile spoke in a firm voice as if to a son who disappointed his father. "Look, Louie, we've been partners for a few months now. You screw up all the time, locking keys in cars, losing luggage, forgetting important dates and times. You've been completely unreliable. Now you've lost our girls. I'm having a difficult time dealing with this. This one's gonna cost both of us, and it could be bad."

Louie sat in the bow, sulking. He made no sign that he heard Emile and offered no apology. He picked up his wet gun from the seat, pulled a rag out of the dry box, and began breaking the gun down and drying off the parts. Emile, steering the boat from his seat in the stern, watched Louie handle the gun with some apprehension. The man had a lot to drink earlier, though he did appear to have sobered up in the cool air.

Emile's voice developed an angry edge when he was ignored. "I get the impression you're not listening to me. You know, I don't like it when my ass is on the line for another person's screwup. I got a family in New Orleans. Boss has been known to take things out on the family."

Louie reassembled the gun. His speed in the darkness was astonishing and should have given Emile a warning. Had Emile thought about an angry man with a loaded gun, he might have backed off. Instead, his anger continued to surface. "Boss could take things out on my family. I need to keep them safe. I don't want them to end up like Vinny."

Louie snapped a round in the chamber and lashed back. "I'm goddamned tired of hearing about Vinny. Vinny this, Vinny that. Leave Vinny the hell out of it."

Emile flinched at Louie's retort. The fact that Louie now had a round chambered gave him pause. "I'm sorry. Vinny and I were very close. He's my favorite cousin. Was my favorite cousin, that is. It's tragic what happened to him. Tragic to me, anyway."

Louie picked up the gun. He pointed it in various directions, pretending he was aiming. "Well, I don't give a shit about Vinny."

Emile raised his voice a notch. "You should give a shit about him, because you have a lot of Vinny in you. You're both impulsive and reckless."

Louie pointed his gun in Emile's direction, then fired a single shot.

CHAPTER 27

THE BAYOU

W ith two gators in pursuit, a swamped boat, and little energy left, all hope was fading. Catalina continued to bail the boat, but I didn't believe we could survive another attack. My hands were blistered from pounding the gator with the broken oar. His armor-plated body barely noticed my pummeling. My arms ached. I was drenched in sweat despite the cool temperatures. My eyes drifted back and forth between the two creatures stalking the boat. One more pass by either gator, and we were done for.

"Catalina, can you swim?"

Catalina answered in a terrified whisper. "No."

"Me neither. I think our only hope is to make a run for it. I'm going to maneuver the boat close to shore where it will be difficult for them to sink the boat. If I can get it near solid ground, perhaps we can run to high ground."

Catalina drew her girls closer. The girls were wet and cold, sobbing quietly. "Would you take one in case I trip and fall? You are more athletic and have a better chance of making it. That way at least one girl will survive."

"Sure," I answered quickly. "But we're all gonna make it. Gators can't run on land, can they?"

As if reading my mind, one of the gators pulled between me and shore, cutting off our escape route. My heart sank. Still, an opportunity might present itself. I traded my broken oar for the good one and readied myself for the right moment.

One of the gators lifted its head out of the water and emitted a low, rumbling bellow that stilled all the other night sounds. The other pursuing gator also raised its head. It let out a bellow of its own.

"What is it?" Catalina cried in alarm. "Is this what they do before they eat you?"

"Maybe. It might be a war cry."

Each gator bellowed again. I shook my head, mystified and horrified. The gators suddenly became more interested in each other. The boat drifted forward without the armored guard. I could hardly believe our luck. The bellowing continued, but lagged further and further behind.

"Good news, I think," I replied with a hopeful twinge to my voice. "They'll either mate or fight to the death, but either way, they've lost interest in us."

I sat the oar down and wiped my bleeding hands on my sweaty shirt. The salt stung the raw wounds. As the bellowing receded upstream, we rounded bend after bend of heavy canopy and found no potential landing spots. Catalina had bailed out most of the water. She cuddled with her girls, who settled down. I was exhausted. All I could do was keep the bow pointed downstream and let the current do the rest. We were swatted by low-hanging branches and accosted by mosquitos. An air of helplessness gradually faded to hopelessness in the impenetrable wilderness.

Then Catalina yipped with joy. "Anna, look, a dock and a cabin. Out here in the middle of nowhere. Praise Jesus, we're saved. Oh, a dock. Don't miss it."

I lacked confidence in steering for a delicate pass at the end of the dock. Should I miss, there would be no way to row back upstream with a single oar. Instead, I opted for a broadside strike on the upstream side of the dock. We hit the dock with a bone-jarring thud. There was no need to tie up the boat, as the current pinned it against the dock. Catalina crawled out first. I handed each girl to her, then pulled myself onto the dock, willing to sleep there the rest of the night if nothing better presented itself.

A girl in both arms, Catalina rushed across the dock onto solid ground. "A cabin and a driveway and a road. We're saved." I tied the boat to the dock in case we needed it again, but I was truly hoping my boating days were over.

Catalina knocked boldly on the cabin door. She knocked again and called out, "Help us! Please help us." Again, no response. Catalina tried the front door. "The door is locked. Help me find a way in. The mosquitos are eating us alive."

My curiosity engaged by the thought of a warm shower, a bite to eat, and a cozy bed, I circled the cabin, pushing on each window. One gave way. "Found an open window. I'll crawl through it and open the door."

I closed the window behind me to keep out the mosquitos. The cabin was small but tidy. I made my way to the front door where I turned on a light. I opened the door for Catalina, then locked it after the girls were in. "They have electricity here. We can't be as far from civilization as we seem."

Catalina ran a warm bath for the girls, who were shivering uncontrollably. I'm not sure they could have survived the wet and cold much longer. She sang to them as they splashed in warm water. I was impressed by their resilience. They took all we had gone through in stride and seemed no worse for it. Perhaps they didn't know how close we had come to being alligator food. Catalina was also a trooper. There was nary a whimper from her. She bore the hardships with composure if not grace. I found cans of chicken noodle soup in the cupboards and heated them on the stove. Then I looked for a phone without luck.

I rummaged through the clothes drawers and found a sweat suit that was about two sizes too big for me. I stripped and slid into my new outfit. I didn't find anything that would fit the girls, so we wrapped them in blankets. Catalina was more petite than me. She found a pair of jeans that fit pretty well, probably from a teenage girl, and a T-shirt that was very tight. I gathered up everyone's dirty clothes and started a load in the washer. After we ate, I moved the wash into the dryer and crawled into bed. I gave Catalina and the girls the queen-size bed while I chose the lower of the bunk beds. Despite the musty blankets, I fell asleep instantly.

CHAPTER 28

THE BAYOU

E mile expected a thud as the bullet hit. The shot missed him. He held his breath, expecting another shot, then exhaled sharply when Louie lowered his gun.

He exploded. "Louie, you're a crazy son of a bitch. You want me to shut up, ask."

"I've wanted to do that all my life," Louie said smugly. "I can take that off my bucket list."

"What? Give your partner a heart attack?"

"No," said Louie, nodding his head to have Emile look behind him. "Shoot a giant gator. Back her up a bit."

Emile put the boat in neutral while he pulled a flashlight out of the dry box. He shined it behind the boat where the water was churning. Then he put the motor in reverse and backed up. A monstrous gator floated there, blood gushing from a wound in the head. His tail was still thrashing.

Emile marveled at the size. "Geez, he's as long as two people."

"Hit him right between the eyes. Not bad, considering the boat was rocking, huh?" said a smug Louie.

Emile backed up beside the dead beast, careful to avoid being battered by the tail. "Excellent shot. Didn't even know he was there."

"He's been stalking us for a while. Started cleaning my gun as soon as I saw him. I don't do much right, but I had your back on this one."

"I have no doubt," said Emile, happy things were resolved. "Now we need to decide how much longer we're going to keep going downstream."

Louie answered with confidence. "Second dock, only because they might miss the first one. If they're not there, we can turn around."

Emile checked the gas can. It was over half full. He put the engine in forward and began moving downstream. "Sounds like a plan."

Louie changed the subject. "You have what every man wants, a charming wife and two beautiful kids. I don't want to see anything happen to them. Your daughter is not much younger than Catalina. You got to protect her. I'd hate to see her working for Boss."

"Thanks." He was ashamed that he had thought Louie might shoot him.

"I'm really tired of this line of work. What we're doing with these girls isn't right. They don't want to be hookers. They want the American dream same as you and me. Many of Boss's girls want to be hookers. Pays well. They earn in a week what I earn in a month."

Emile cocked his head in Louie's direction. "So get to the point. We can't back out now. Boss would be truly angry."

"I know," Louie answered meekly. "We got no choice. But it's nagging at me. I think I made a bad choice working for Boss. I used to work for my uncle as an auto mechanic. I liked him. I liked the job. I was good at it. Rarely screwed up. I left because I wanted something bigger. Didn't know what I wanted, I just knew it was time to leave. Now I miss it. An auto mechanic has a good, clean life, a chance to be proud of his work, to do something constructive. These girls don't want to be whores. I feel so guilty. And what will happen with the little ones?"

Emile nodded. "I feel guilty too. But that doesn't change the fact that we're committed to finishing this job. We got no choice. Agreed?"

"No choice," Louie agreed with obvious reluctance. "None at all. But I don't like it."

They motored in silence for a bit, the steady putt of the outboard motor augmenting the feral night sounds. Louie changed the subject. "How did you meet your wife?"

"We met in high school and liked each other well enough. But we didn't start dating until a few years later when I had a steady job—this job. It wasn't exactly love at first sight, but we were on the same page.

Better than many classmates who are divorced now. That's important, finding someone with similar values."

"Does your wife know what you do for a living?"

"Kind of, but not really. She knows I work for Boss. She doesn't like him personally. She has no idea that he deals in girls, drugs, and gambling—or maybe she does and knows to never mention it. I make good money, and that sweeps a lot of things under the carpet."

"Does she know what you're doing now?"

Emile paused, clearly uncomfortable. "Not really. She thinks I took a business trip to El Paso. That's what I told her. She doesn't know the details. She wouldn't like it if I told her the truth, so I shield her. If she asks too many questions, I tell her it's a company secret. And it is. Boss would be furious if I started blabbing about the day-to-day details of his business."

Louie puzzled this out as if it were a new revelation. "It must be hard living one life and pretending about another to your wife."

Emile responded with perfect frankness. "It was hard at first, but we've fallen into a pattern. She knows not to ask questions, and I know not to give her reason to. It won't be that way forever. The kids are nearly grown, and eventually I'll retire."

"If Boss lets you," countered Louie, who hadn't noticed people retiring from Boss's enterprise. "From what I've seen, disappearing like Vinny is more frequent."

Emile became defensive. "Doesn't have to be that way."

"I think it does. As long as you're on the payroll, you got no reason to talk to the police. Once you retire, you might be inclined to sell certain information."

"To whom?" snorted Emile. "You know that Boss controls the cops. Many are on his payroll, and those that aren't want to be. He's created a comfortable place for himself. So who exactly would pay me for information?"

"I don't know. It was just a line of thought."

"You don't have any plans to sell information, do you? That could be a lethal mistake."

"No, no, no," countered Louie. "I don't know why I even mentioned it. You know, I've only been in this line of work for a year. I really don't care for it. Hate to see the little guys get screwed. Hate to see one guy end up with all the marbles. Doesn't seem fair."

"You do seem unsettled. It's not good to be so restless. Find a girl. Settle down. You seem to enjoy Maribel and Guadalupe. You spoil them rotten, and they really like you. Have some kids of your own."

Louie's tone darkened. "I got nothing like that going for me. Chicks don't dig me. Got no curb appeal, I guess. I don't know how to talk to them. Never did."

Emile winced. Louie was a handsome man by Creole standards with dark hair and broad shoulders. "Hey, I'm old enough to be your father, so let me give you some fatherly advice. You're young. Give it time. The ladies will come around. Anyone in New Orleans catch your eye?"

"Nope. I can honestly say I've never gotten to know a chick I really liked. You know, more than just physical attraction. Of course, I dream about marrying Miss Universe and what I'd like to do with her every night, but all boys go through that." Louie suddenly brightened. "You may think I'm crazy, but I find this Anna chick fascinating. Her friend Catalina looks like Miss Universe, but there's nothing there. No personality. She just kind of sits there, staring like a frog on a lily pad. Hard to know what she's thinking. Maybe nothing but the next fly. I like her little girls. I like the way they giggled when I gave them ice cream. I could enjoy being a father, I think. But not married to her. She's like too many girls in high school who had no spunk. At least that's the way she comes off. Anna's not a ravishing beauty, but she's attractive in her own way. What I find fascinating is that while we hold all the cards, she's doing her best to beat us at our own game. She tried to broker a deal with a wealthy cousin who was willing to pay big bucks to get her back. I still think we screwed up there. She used lipstick to write an escape note in the bathroom, and she did finally escape in this mosquito-ridden place. She's put together in a way that appeals to me."

Emile interrupted. "But there are also problems. Number one, she's too damn smart for you. Hard to hide anything from her. Number two, she has her own agenda, and she might let you play, but only if you wanted to tag along. I never liked that sort, probably because I prefer to have my own agenda."

"It was just a thought," Louie answered despondently. "I guess you're right, but that doesn't stop me thinking about it. I have the hots for her."

Emile nodded appreciatively. "Look, this doesn't have to end badly for her, assuming we get her back. When we get to New Orleans, you and Anna could disappear. I don't want to know anything about it. Just vanish. I don't think Boss would hold it against me. But take my advice. Move to Alaska. Change your name. Get a real job. If it works out, maybe her wealthy cousin will lay a few grand on you."

Louie's voice trailed off. "I guess it doesn't hurt to dream . . . I know she hates my guts, and I don't blame her. Truthfully, I hope we find her before the gators do. It's not about the money. Like I said, I like her spunk."

Emile wanted to be reassuring, but he wasn't certain they'd ever see the girls again. There were many river channels and countless dangers. He tried to put a positive spin on it. "I know what you mean. I don't want them to die here. Not about the money."

Suddenly, gators bellowed up ahead. Emile said, "How many rounds you got left?"

CHAPTER 29

HACKBERRY, LOUISIANA

A s I rolled over in my bed, I thought I smelled coffee brewing. Just a dream, I surmised as I snuggled with the pillow. The rattle of cups in the kitchen drew me to full alert. I looked over at the Catalina's bed. Moonlight streamed in through the window, illuminating one large and two tiny sleeping figures. More rattling in the kitchen, then a hulking figure walked through the doorway. "Would you like your coffee with cream and sugar, Anna?"

Reflexively, I covered my body with blankets, though there was nothing to hide since I was dressed in a sweat suit many sizes too large. That's when I winced at the pain in my hands. They had been oozing blood and other fluids where the blisters had broken and were raw in other places. My wrist and hand joints ached from the pounding I gave the gator. My shoulders were so stiff I could barely move them. Sleep-deprived as I was, I recognized Louie's voice. On another day, I might have bolted out the window. Today, I was too exhausted to move.

Anxiety gripped me. They must have come down the river looking for the rowboat. How else could they have found us? I should have set the rowboat adrift downstream. I had been reluctant to abandon it, because we might need it if there was no other way out of the wilderness. Another costly mistake. "I'll take mine black."

Louie turned and left. I rolled out of bed and shook Catalina awake. "They're here. We're trapped."

Catalina sat up and pulled her girls toward her. "Outside?"

"No, in here. I know I locked the door. I don't know how they got in."

Louie returned with a steaming mug of coffee. He flicked the light on and handed it to me. He winced at my hands. There was kindness in his eyes for a change.

"And how would you like your coffee, Catalina?"

She raised her head proudly and glared at him. "I don't want anything from you except our freedom."

Louie gave her a manufactured pout. "Can't do that. We've got to leave soon. Have to get to the dock before they find out we borrowed their boat. Your hands, that's more than just damage from rowing."

Catalina spoke with admiration. "She fought off an alligator that tried to eat us. She's the bravest person I know. It's my fault that she's here, and I'm sorry. Can you see it in your heart to let her go?"

Louie shuffled his feet uncomfortably. "I don't want to hurt anyone. Deep down I'm a nice person. Perhaps I've lost my way. I have to take you to New Orleans. It's my job. I may be killed if I don't deliver you to Boss. We all have our problems, and there is no easy way out. Emile's cooking breakfast. We're gonna leave soon. Get dressed and come on out." He looked at a dark window, then pleaded, "There's nowhere to go. It's the middle of the night. Snakes and gators are on the hunt. It could end poorly for you this time. I have the key to my boat in my pocket. I'll give you three minutes to get dressed, then I want to see you in the kitchen."

"Our clothes are in the dryer," I blurted out.

"I'll get them," he answered, like a perfect gentleman. He returned with our clothes in less than a minute and tossed them on my bed. They were still warm, which meant that I couldn't have slept for more than an hour.

Louie continued, "I'm going to close the door to give you some privacy, but only for a moment. So hurry up and get dressed. Do not touch the window."

I heard Emile chuckle to Louie. "That was charming. You clearly have a way with the ladies when you want. You've given Anna the chance to see your kinder side. No doubt she'll come to breakfast with a big smile on her face."

Louie responded as he closed the door. "There's a thin line between respect and submission. They got to know who the boss is. I don't think there will be smiles, but they'll be out in a minute."

I emerged from the bedroom first to look for bandages for my hands. I rummaged through the closet and found a roll of gauze and some tape. I couldn't find antibiotic cream. Breakfast was nicely done. I could tell Emile was a good cook because he didn't have much to work with. He handed me a plate and gave me a miserable look. "It's been a long night for all of us. I'm tired and ornery. I could have had a good night's sleep except for you. You might want to go easy on me, lest I become irrational."

I couldn't help myself. I moved closer. "You ought to be ashamed of yourself for kidnapping us and terrorizing these poor girls. Real men don't behave this way. Your mamas would be ashamed."

I expected an angry arm to strike me. Surprisingly, Emile addressed me in a fatherly tone. "I'm doing my job. My family lives in New Orleans, and Boss may take revenge on them if I show up empty-handed. You're a wildling, and I know you're doing what comes natural to you in trying to escape. I respect that. I'm also tired of your antics."

I exploded. "Louie gave me the same old crap. I'm sorry your job sucks. So get a new one. I'm sorry your boss is a bastard. It's your choice to work for him. These are not valid excuses for kidnapping and torture. I hope you get busted and spend the rest of your miserable lives in jail."

Louie stood behind me, snickering. I turned and reared back to slap him, but he ducked out of range. Big, black, soulful eyes returned my stare. "Anna, don't push your luck. We're all running a sleep deficit."

I handed him my plate and sulked into the bathroom to bandage my hands. Out of the corner of my eye, Maribel and Guadalupe emerged from the bedroom, followed by Catalina. Louie picked Maribel up. "I have some hot chocolate for you and your sister. It'll warm you up for the long boat ride back to the car. Show me what you want to eat, and I'll put it on your plate." She did, and he repeated the process with Guadalupe.

Maribel nudged Guadalupe. "Señor Louie is trying to be a good guy."

Guadalupe shook her head. "He has a gun."

Her words left a sad impression with Louie. He squeezed Guadalupe. "I'm not gonna let any bad guy get you."

Catalina's voice was cautious. "You're just as bad as Francisco. Only you try to hide it from the girls."

When my hands were decently bandaged, I returned to stand beside Catalina. She gave me a sad smile. "We nearly made it. It was a good try. Thanks for beating the alligator off last night. I was so scared."

Emile studied my hands. "Alligator?"

Catalina found her voice. "She's the bravest woman I know. It tried to tip our boat over and eat us. She pounded him over and over with the paddle until he left."

Louie followed me with something that seemed like admiration in his eyes. I held his gaze, and hoped he didn't notice the folding knife I stuffed in my pants pocket.

Emile chuckled. "Louie, she put a knife in her pocket just now. She never gives up. Reminds me of a she-wolf."

Louie's face reddened from embarrassment. He held out his hand, and I handed him the knife. I still had the smaller one I used to pry open the window at the first cottage. But it was so small it was almost useless.

Emile caught Louie's eye. They seemed to exchange some private joke about me. "She's a tough one, Louie. Don't blame yourself. She might never adjust to life in New Orleans; she's so headstrong. I wonder if the knife was meant for us or for her. At this point, even she might not know. Last chance for food."

I shook my head and waited by the door for the forced march to the boat. The place was a mess. Maybe the owners would come back soon and call the cops.

Louie called to me in jest. "No notes on the mirror. I'm going to do a walk-through."

I turned and trudged out the front door, head high, Maribel in my arms. Emile indicated with a sweeping arm gesture for Catalina to follow, which she did. Louie brought up the rear, no doubt looking for messages. If he found mine written on a scrap of paper and hidden under my pillow, he never mentioned it.

At the dock, Emile tied the rowboat behind the larger motorboat. As the engine started, tears welled up in my eyes. I couldn't help feeling defeated. It was a good try, and I would do it again. I never thought my life would take this course. I wanted to go a different way, have a successful career, and be happily married with two kids. I had made a series of hasty decisions that proved to be disastrous. I choked up, realizing I would never see my family again. I would become a modern-day slave.

CHAPTER 30

LAKE CHARLES

S cott drove to the boat rental place, the last known location of the SUV. The parking lot was empty. Next, he drove to the house just downstream from the site where the SUV had been parked earlier. Scott knocked on the door. No one answered, but since the front door was open, he and Alvarez entered. There was an opened beer with condensation still on the outside of the can. The lights in the kitchen and bedroom were on. The TV was on. The remains of a shrimp boil were on the stove and heaped on several dishes. Much of the food had not been eaten.

Scott studied the kitchen. "Clearly left in a hurry. Hungry?"

Alvarez shook his head. Then Scott went in the bedroom. "Look at this. The window is open and the paint around the edges is newly chipped. I'll bet the girls used a knife to pry the window open and escape. They probably went to the dock." Through the window he saw Linda studying the boat.

They met Linda at the dock where she described her conclusions. "One of the rowboat oars was recently broken, as there is no weathering on the broken part. I assume that the women made a getaway but broke an oar and were subsequently captured. The muddy water inside the boat points to recent use. Rain would have left clearer water. This hypothesis is also consistent with the Creole man's story." She placed her hand on Alvarez's shoulder. "I think Anna was recaptured. The men may have borrowed a boat to track them down. A motorboat could have quickly overtaken a rowboat, especially one with a broken oar."

<hr />

When the stores opened a few hours later, Linda drove to a phone store in Lake Charles. She was waited on by a middle-aged man with a dark complexion and a Creole face. She gave him a sheepish smile while handing over the mason jar containing the phone. "This is my cousin's phone. I had a little accident with it yesterday. We were out on the lake, and I dropped it overboard. Retrieved it with a fishing net before it hit bottom, if you can believe that. I'd like to replace it with a comparable phone." Then she cast him a conspiratorial look. "He told me accidents happen and not to worry about it, but I'd like to do the responsible thing."

The man nodded as he unscrewed the lid and pulled the phone out of the jar. Something about the situation caught his fancy, and he started to chuckle. "Ah, the smell of Lake Charles. Can't tell you how many times a phone in a rice jar makes its way through my door. Sounds like you're both nice people, perhaps too nice to each other. My cousin would have dragged me to the phone store immediately, and insisted on a new and better phone. Now, how long was it submerged?"

Linda gave him her most sincere look while making up a story. "A minute, maybe even less."

"In that case, the SIM card is probably fine. Let's take a look."

He pulled out the SIM card and placed it in a SIM card reader. "I see here that your cousin's name is Johnny Depp. That correct?"

Although he kept a straight face, something about this name seemed wrong. "Excuse me?" said Linda, her face turning red.

The man chuckled at her embarrassment. "Just kidding. We all wish we had a rich and famous cousin. Mine is fat, ugly, and on welfare. I'd normally like to have the cousin here with you, you know, for privacy issues. But, since you have a sad story and are doing the right thing, we'll dispense with all of that. Your cousin has a nice French name. Louie Beaudette has a nice ring to it, don't you think? Kind of regal."

Linda suspected this was a trap and began evasive tactics. "I love the sound of French names. Mine is pretty plain, Linda Williams. You don't get much plainer than that. Of course, I married into the family. How about you? You look Creole. You have a French name?"

The man glanced at her hand and was visibly disappointed to find a wedding ring. "Just about everyone does in these parts. Mine is Jacques Giroux."

"Beautiful name," Linda added, hoping she passed the test.

"I see he has a New Orleans area code. Bet he's excited about the Super Bowl."

"It's all he talked about, though I don't think he can afford tickets."

"I know the feeling," said Jacques. "The SIM card looks fine. The address book is there, along with a log of calls. Turns out I have a similar phone in stock. Run you three hundred, including tax."

Linda smiled as she opened her purse and fished three Franklins out of her wallet. "You've been really sweet. I'll mention you to my cousin, Jacques."

In five minutes, she was back in the driver's seat, tickled pink. "Some days, I'm unstoppable."

Scott scrolled down the log of calls. "Let's see, his partner would get the most calls. His name seems to be Emile Marceau. New Orleans area code. The address book has an entry named Boss, also New Orleans. Think he's the boss? He gets regular calls."

Linda shrugged. "How would we know? Okay guys, where to?"

Scott answered quickly and confidently. "Let you know in just a sec."

Scott placed his forefinger over his lips to indicate quiet as he dialed Emile and placed the phone on speaker. Emile answered on the second ring. If he knew the call came from Louie's SIM card–activated phone, he didn't let on.

Scott deepened his voice and softened it to a whisper. "Boss wants to know how many broads you have and when you'll be back."

Emile answered, "Only two, but one is hot, hot, hot. We just left Lake Charles and should be back in three hours."

Scott clicked off and gave Linda a big grin. "It's three hours from here to New Orleans. Let's hit the road."

"Any chance he was lying?" inquired Alvarez, who was not good at reading English intonations.

"Not a chance," said Linda. "You don't promise your boss a delivery time if the goods are missing. You'd stall for more time."

"What if," Alvarez continued with a suspicious frown on his face, "he knew the call was bogus? His phone might indicate that the call was from Louie if Louie was in his address book."

Scott rocked back and forth, contemplating Alvarez's statement. "What you say is true for many phones. He sounded sincere. He could have been a good liar, but don't you think he would have said the opposite to throw us off? He wouldn't want us to follow him, or precede him to New Orleans. He'd send us on a wild goose chase in a different direction."

"Maybe he just did," countered Alvarez.

"Doubt it," said Linda. "New Orleans is the most likely destination for trafficked girls. And with the Super Bowl just around the corner, prices are sure to rise."

Alvarez nodded, but seemed unconvinced. "Well, let's go. Maybe we'll get another clue on the way."

Linda shook her head. "We can't count on another clue. Time to plan our attack. Alvarez, I want you to find Boss's address from his phone number."

"Already did. The Great River Road. Has an interesting name. Ring a bell?"

Scott got excited. "Oh, that's the pricy real estate. Antebellum plantation houses along the Mississippi. We may get a taste of the wealthy cut of old New Orleans. Many of the city's most prominent citizens came from landed gentry that made their wealth on these plantations. Could be fun."

"What are we going to do there?" came a cautious reply from Alvarez.

Linda jumped in. "We're going to approach Boss with a business proposition."

Scott pouted. "Hey, let me plan the attack."

Linda shook her head. "Not a chance. To use one of your favorite expressions, stay in your lane. This was my specialty at the FBI, and I know exactly how I want to play it. We'll need a professional wardrobe, of course, and we'll need to pick up a Bentley at a rental agency. Alvarez, you'll be my chauffeur. Scott, you'll be my secretary. I'll be director of a concierge service arranging wine, women, and song for wealthy clients from New York during the Super Bowl. Scott, call Boss to arrange a meeting tomorrow. Don't take no for an answer. Alvarez, I need you to make a web page for our business, complete with pictures and testimonials. We'll need business cards. We'll call the business 'WanderLust.' One word, capital *L*."

CHAPTER 31

NEW ORLEANS

W e stopped at a stately old house near Jackson Square. Emile said there was a good chance we would live in this house if Boss liked us. My room had a window with a lovely view of the yard, including a live oak dripping with Spanish moss. It was far nicer than my house in Juarez. We took showers and were given makeup and clothes for our interview. The makeup was too bright for my tastes, but I put it on heavy to hide the bags under my eyes and my sickly pallor. I thought the miniskirt was a headband at first, but it stretched as I slithered into it. I managed to get it halfway down my thighs. The top was tight and low-cut, but since I don't have big breasts, I was modest enough.

Then we headed to Boss's house. I was in awe of the stately homes we passed on the Great River Road. They were enormous white houses fronted with many tall white columns. It was hard to believe that only a single family occupied each house. My family's home in Juarez would have fit inside one of these mansions dozens of times over. What did they use all the space for? I guessed we were about to find out.

Louie had been quiet all day. He stole glances at me but turned away when I met his stare. Could have been the contempt in my eyes. There was something odd in his eyes that I didn't quite understand. I drew some strength in recognizing that it was not anger. It seemed more along the lines of shyness or curiosity.

Emile pulled through a magnificent metal gate and up to a guard shack. The guard was dressed in a uniform and carried an air of self-importance. The guard stooped and surveyed all the people in the car. I sat in the back seat with Guadalupe on my lap while Catalina held Maribel. Emile caught my eye in the rearview mirror and announced sarcastically, "This is Austin. He'll shoot you if you try to escape."

Austin rolled his eyes at the quip but gave Catalina a lengthy second glance. He motioned us forward with a sharp jerk of his forearm. The road to the house was landscaped in southern elegance. Had I been here for any other reason, I would have probably enjoyed myself. Now, my stomach was in knots. I was about to meet Boss, a modern-day slaver. I grabbed Catalina's hand and squeezed it for reassurance. Her hand was cold and clammy despite the warm temperatures. I could tell she was nervous too. The girls were remarkably quiet and had been for a while as they stared at unfamiliar scenery. They were exhausted and should have been sleeping, but everyone was wired.

The car stopped in a parking lot adjacent to a large white mansion, similar in size and shape to those along the Great River Road. The house was perched atop a small hill that receded in the other direction to the river valley. Across the river, other houses of this ilk lined the river. Further away, a factory spewed dark smoke. It seemed odd that city planners would allow a factory to take up space next to these stately residences.

Emile opened the car door for me. "Anna, please understand that Boss does not like girls who speak out of turn. Address him with 'Yes, sir' or 'No, sir' and keep your responses to the point. Simple works best with him. It's probably best if you don't describe the trouble you caused along the way. He deals harshly with troublemakers. You may have heard me talking to Louie about my cousin Vinny. Vinny passed away years ago under mysterious circumstances. You don't want to get on Boss's bad side. He carries a grudge forever."

Another reason to make me nervous. I was marched up a set of winding steps as if to the gallows. I wobbled on heels that were higher than anything I had ever worn before. I carried Guadalupe in one arm and hung on to the banister with the other. Louie held the enormous front door open for me but did not meet my eyes. I gave him a contemptuous stare anyway. This was all his fault. I hated him for what he was doing to us, and the worst was yet to come. The entry room was enormous with a marble floor. A chandelier that was larger than me hung over us. The only other person in the room was a sullen guard dressed like Austin. He was flanked on either side by two enormous dogs. To the back, a graceful stairway led to an upper floor.

Boss descended the steps slowly, with a regal bearing. His attention was focused entirely on us. He was about fifty with fair skin and light hair. No trace of Creole in him. He was wearing a tan suit that fit his lean frame. In his hand was a small black stick. His face lacked expression. His brown eyes were cold.

"Pickin's were slim, Boss," said Emile with a sly smile. "We thought there were four, but two of them turned out to be munchkins."

Boss surveyed me first. He began circling while scanning me head to foot. His eyes bored into me as a potential buyer might look over a horse. He ran his stick underneath my chin and forced it up to meet his gaze. "You have pretty eyes. What's your name?"

"Anna," I answered meekly as I pulled my eyes away. I was immediately ashamed by how weakly the word came out.

"Anna, you have a few good years left. You ever been an escort?"

I shook my head.

"What did you do for a living?"

I cleared my throat and announced proudly, "I do genetic testing."

He gave a faint smile of surprise. "Genetic testing? That's a first among my girls. So you can pick out the bastards and the perverts. You must be smart. Any new genetic tests coming out?"

"There's one for a gene that causes people to become heartless bastards."

He tapped his stick against my cheek firmly, but not hard enough to leave a welt. "You're a wildling. Bad sign. My girls learn how to hold their tongue. You'll soon learn the difference between master and slave."

He studied the gauze around my hands. "What's wrong with your hands? Unwrap one."

I unwrapped the worse of the two and held it up. The broken blisters were still oozing blood.

Boss winced. "What did you do to your hands?"

"I got blisters rowing a boat."

He tapped my wrist with his stick. "Was it a race?"

I nodded.

"You're a competitive woman. I like that in a person. Most people would quit before it got this bad. You have fortitude, but apparently no common sense. Did you win the race?"

"The race hasn't ended yet," I said proudly. I kicked off my uncomfortable shoes to try to avoid further questions. Boss brushed his stick on my thigh. "You have nice legs. You a runner?"

"Soccer," I said.

"Not much soccer here. Some of my clients prefer the thin, athletic types. It's become more popular. Reminds the old men of their fraternity days, I guess. Stay in shape."

His gaze drifted to Maribel and Guadalupe. "These your girls?"

I shook my head. He stepped over to look at Catalina, then addressed Emile. "They have quite a few marks on their skin. What are those?"

"Mosquito bites." Emile cleared his throat. "The coyote was a little careless when they crossed the Rio Grande. I don't think it's anything to worry about. They'll heal in a few days."

Boss nodded. "Didn't know Mexico had mosquitos. Thought it was too dry. Those damn things are everywhere. Have the doc check out the blisters on Anna's hands and the bites."

He walked around Catalina and studied her as one might study a Rodin sculpture.

"You have a beautiful face. Where are you from?"

"Guatemala," she replied with lips trembling.

"And what is your name?" he asked with a stern face and expressionless eyes.

"Catalina."

"Catalina," he said with a sigh. "What a pretty name. How did you make your way from Guatemala to Juarez?"

"I ran away from home."

"Going anywhere in particular?"

"Hollywood," Catalina answered, full of pride.

"You know, many famous Hollywood people visit New Orleans. I'll make a point of introducing you when the time comes. Hell, you're so pretty, they'll fall in love with you. Maybe you'll even get a part in a film. Did you know that over two hundred movies have been filmed here? And several TV series. You don't need to go to Hollywood. Hollywood comes to us. There are four movies being filmed here right now. Hey, did you ever see *The Big Easy* with Dennis Quaid and Ellen Barkin? It was filmed right here. Now that's a quality film."

Catalina shook her head.

"How about *Easy Rider* with Peter Fonda and Dennis Hopper? It's a classic. Or there's *King Creole* with Elvis Presley."

Catalina's face perked up. Boss pulled the right strings talking about Hollywood. Then Boss turned his attention to the girls. They were fearful. They had their arms wrapped around our legs and were hiding from him.

"They look like twins. Cute," he said. "I'll let you keep them, but only as long as you remain on your best behavior. Both of you."

Catalina's eyes grew wide at the thought that he might actually take her girls. She pulled them both toward her as if an evil presence had suddenly invaded the room.

Boss gave a snide smile and cast a malicious eye toward us. His eyes moved between Catalina and me in quick succession. "Let me be clear. I'll take care of the girls if you take care of my clients. Otherwise . . ." His voice trailed off with a shrug that indicated deleterious consequences. "I don't kill the women who won't cooperate. I just make sure their lives aren't worth living. There's nowhere to run and nowhere to hide. Emile may have told you this already, but I own the police and most of New Orleans. Play it my way, and your girls will grow up healthy and well educated. Fight me and bear the consequences. Most of my girls are very happy working here. It takes some time to adjust, but you'll settle in. I pay well. You'll earn more than you can in most other lines of work, even"—he cleared his throat for emphasis—"genetic testing."

His voice was firm, his tone flat, as if he'd been through it a hundred times and was tired with it. He scanned us for signs of resistance. I'm embarrassed to say I offered none. "Emile, take them to the doctor for physicals. Don't want any of my clients getting STI's. Take the girls too. They'll probably need some vaccinations."

I finally found my voice. "Excuse me," I said indignantly. "It's the other way around. You need to protect us from your clients."

Boss raised one eye at me and spoke with such enmity that I lowered my eyes and quivered at the knees. "You speak only when I ask you a question. You know what a condom is? Make sure you use one."

"Emile, get them measured for work clothes. We can do better than these. You know the drill."

"Yes, Boss," answered Emile submissively, probably embarrassed at my outburst.

"Get right on it. I'll work them into the client register soon."

My heart sank. I was about to become a prostitute, and there seemed to be little I could do about it.

CHAPTER 32

GREAT RIVER ROAD

"Slow down, Alvarez, so I can see the gate," Scott cautioned as they approached the entrance to the manor. The open gate was elegantly designed with a curved pattern in shiny metal that spoke of country gentry. It was also secure. "It's made of reinforced steel. You'd need a tank to bore through it when it's closed. Might be better to bring a boat around the Mississippi side."

Many plantation houses faced the Mississippi River, which had been the plantation entrance when the houses were first built. Roads came later. Over a couple of centuries, the Mississippi was altered to make the river an unfeasible entrance. In the early twentieth century, a levee was constructed to keep the river on course. Then, the Bonnet Carré Spillway was added to protect New Orleans by absorbing overflow water during flood years.

Alvarez pulled up to the guard gate. "We have an appointment with Boss."

The guard studied his clipboard. "What's the name?"

"Stephanie Orie, owner of WanderLust."

Alvarez flashed the guard a business card. The guard squinted to see Stephanie in the back seat next to Scott. "Just the three of you?"

"Yes, sir," responded Alvarez.

The guard handed the card back. "Follow the road to the manor and park in a visitor parking spot." He pointed at Alvarez and spoke firmly. "Stay with the car. There are dogs, guards, and security alarms on the grounds. You are not permitted to walk around."

"Yes, sir," said Alvarez meekly as he tucked the card in his shirt pocket and put the car in gear.

"What an inviting place," said Scott sarcastically. "Clearly they have something to hide."

Alvarez parked in a visitor parking spot adjacent to the manor. Scott and Linda made their way up the elegantly curved steps to an entrance that was far above ground level. Alvarez waited until Linda and Scott were inside the manor and opened the trunk. He understood that they would be the major focus for a short period of time, so this was his window of opportunity. Inside the trunk were the drones he bought in Houston and hastily outfitted with cameras. He pulled the first one out and launched it with the remote. The electric engine whined as the propellers bore the craft straight up. Alvarez sent it toward the top of the house. He succeeded in turning the craft and landing it on the edge of the roof. He activated the camera and looked at real-time images. The screen showed the entire parking lot and a swath of landscape to either side. He had planned to use the other drone to monitor the guard gate, but Linda convinced him to place it on the back side of the house facing the Mississippi River. The idea made sense. If there were two ways in and out of the plantation house, they should both be monitored. He didn't expect the Mississippi side to be used since the levee reduced the navigability of the river. But small crafts could move across the river without difficulty.

Landing this drone would be more difficult since he couldn't actually see the back side of the house. The key point was to keep the drone away from the edge of the roof where a storm might blow it off. He turned the camera on for drone number two and let it be his eyes. He hugged the roofline until he had a view of the river. Then he gently landed it on the rooftop and turned the motor off.

Just as he finished closing his computer, dogs began barking. Two large Danes bounded around the side of the house toward him. He thought the whining of the electric motors might have agitated them. Alvarez had suspected there might be dogs, so he had brought along two balls. He pulled them out and closed the trunk. As the dogs neared the car, they pulled up and began snarling. Alvarez retreated toward the driver's door, a ball in each hand. One dog circled the car menacingly. The other dog stood back about ten feet, barking. Alvarez pitched a ball to the farthest dog as he scrambled inside the car. The nearer dog became intrigued and lunged for the ball. Seeing this, the other dog tried to take it back. A battle ensued over the ball as they lost interest in Alvarez. Alvarez pitched the second ball out the window and they each chewed intently. Alvarez had coated the balls with acepromazine, a drug frequently used to treat dogs that are anxious, uncooperative, or hostile. As they chewed, they mellowed. He hadn't realized the dogs would be Great Danes, or he would have used a larger dose.

About this time, a car pulled around and parked on the other side of him. Two men got out and studied the dogs.

"Would you look at that, Louie? I haven't seen these dogs so well-mannered in a long time." Emile sauntered up to Alvarez, who stiffened. "You give them those balls?"

Alvarez nodded but said nothing, lest his accent betray him.

"I knew it was you," Louie continued. "Boss doesn't give them those kinds of balls to play with. He prefers they chew the balls of trespassers." Louie snickered, but Alvarez said nothing. "Just a joke, man. Lighten up. You may wish to stay in your car. Where you from?"

"New York," answered Alvarez.

"Ain't that a fact," said Louie. "Where'bouts? Emile, don't you have an uncle who lives there?"

Alvarez didn't know much about New York but said the first thing that popped into his mind. "Manhattan."

"I've never been there, but I hear it's pricey real estate. My uncle lives on Long Island. You like New York?"

"It's okay. Like you said, expensive."

Emile shook his head in disagreement. "You don't sound like you're from New York. You sound like you're from the Southwest."

Clearly uncomfortable, Alvarez muttered, "Just moved to New York from Arizona."

Emile challenged him. "Your name Carlos Alvarez by any chance?"

Alvarez swallowed hard. "Carlos? No. I'm Juan Perez." His voice was strong, as this was the name he rehearsed, but his face looked guilty.

Louie nodded suspiciously. "Reason we ask is that one of the babes mentioned a Carlos Alvarez. Said he might ransom her. I know where she is. I could cut a deal, strictly under the table."

Alvarez shook his head. It wasn't time to go rogue. Then Emile and Louie walked a meandering path around the mansion. The dogs followed with their balls. Alvarez noted the faint trail they took, using various trees and bushes as landmarks. He suspected that it avoided buried alarms and could be used in an escape.

CHAPTER 33

GREAT RIVER ROAD

Entering the front door was like stepping back in time. The marbled foyer was lit by a crystal chandelier. Directly across the foyer, a staircase curved upward. The only thing out of place from a bygone era was the armed guard who sidled toward them.

"I'm Stephanie Orie. This is my secretary, Shaun Finnerty. We have an appointment to see Boss."

"Any weapons? I always ask politely before the search to avoid embarrassment. Sometimes male secretaries come packin'."

Linda and Scott shook their heads.

"Okay, raise your arms. This will only take a moment."

The guard frisked them thoroughly. His hands lingered on Linda longer than they should have. Then a voice called from the top of the staircase.

"Welcome to my humble home, Stephanie." The man, dressed in an expensive Italian suit, descended the stairs with practiced grace, his eyes fixed on Linda. "This home has been in my family for five generations. There is a rumor that my great-great-grandfather won it in a poker game. I know it isn't true, as I have the original receipt. People can be so unkind. Poker may have influenced the price in the end, but this lovely plantation wasn't a gift from the poker gods."

His eyes remained on Linda as he ambled across the room. When he reached her, he extended a hand. "Now, how can I help you?"

Linda got straight to business, as New Yorkers do. She had practiced a bit of an accent and hoped it would carry the day. "I represent some wealthy clients who are planning to attend the Super Bowl. Perhaps we can discuss this matter someplace more private."

"Of course. My office is this way." Boss led them toward a room facing the parking area. Scott suspected that Alvarez might be flying his drones and be visible from a window. He stalled.

"Excuse me." Boss turned, an annoyed look on his face. He turned to Linda for clarification, since secretaries were to be seen and not heard. Before she could say anything, Scott continued, "I was wondering whether your family used bousillage for insulation."

Linda said, "I'm sorry for the interruption, Boss. Shaun has had a longstanding interest in French art and architecture. He gets carried away." This was perfectly true. She cast Scott an angry look, but it was all an act, and she understood the reason for it. "Shaun, I have no idea what bousillage is."

Boss fixed his attention on Linda again, ignoring Scott. "Bousillage is a mixture of horsehair, Spanish moss, and mud. The older planta-tions like Destrehan still use it for insulation. This plantation has been extensively remodeled over the years. I'm not aware that bousillage was ever used in this house, and if it was, it was completely removed. We have all the amenities of a modern house in antebellum splendor. Now, can we proceed?"

"Certainly," said Linda. "No more interruptions, Shaun."

Boss turned and led them into an ornate office furnished in period antiques. Scott cast a surreptitious glance out the window and saw Alvarez behind his open trunk. He had to keep Boss from looking out the window. Boss led them to chairs opposite his desk. "May I offer you a drink? First-time visitors seem to like mint juleps. Never cared for them myself."

"Nothing for us," Linda said. Boss made his way around the desk, never casting a glance out the window. Linda continued, "As I was saying, I represent a wealthy group of travelers. You could think of WanderLust as a high-end travel company. Our clients are mostly male and mostly interested in sporting events—Super Bowl, World Cup, Summer and Winter Olympics. They are older men in midlife crises who want to relive their fraternity days. I provide the venues, and I look for a local business to provide the sorority girls, if you get my drift. We'll be here the week of the Super Bowl. I hear you have discreet girls who might make the occasion memorable to my clients."

"I have the cleanest girls in New Orleans. They have all their vaccinations. They get physicals and blood tests every month. No drugs, no venereal diseases. I have girls to suit a variety of tastes—black, white, Asian, Creole, Latino. Even have a beauty queen from Guatemala."

"I need girls who are smart. My clients are self-made men, college educated, and they want an escort who can show them around town, converse with them, make them believe they are special. Some want to take in the music scene. Some want the restaurant scene. All want a lovely and interesting lady on their arms who will turn heads."

Boss nodded appreciatively. "They've earned that right with their storied careers. I have the girls for them, but you're talking about the cream of the crop, so they won't be cheap. Here, I have some pictures."

He pulled a photo album out of his desk drawer. "I don't have pictures of all of them, Stephanie. But this will give you an idea of the quality and variety."

He handed the album to Linda. The shots were professionally done. Each girl had an entry in casual attire, evening wear, and a swimsuit. Scott pulled his chair closer to get a better look. The girls were stunning. Linda leafed through them quickly, looking for one that resembled the Facebook photo of Anna that Alvarez showed them. She wasn't there.

Linda said, "They are lovely. And there are more?"

Boss beamed. "More girls have joined the group recently, and I haven't updated this book. If you had given me more notice of your visit, I could have prepared a more complete display."

"Sorry for the last-minute rush. We only recently became aware of your services. You come highly recommended."

"Good. Well, let's talk price. I charge fifteen hundred per hour per girl with a ten-thousand-dollar per-night max."

"I was thinking more along the lines of one thousand per hour and four thousand per night."

Boss placed his fingers together and studied Linda. "Quite reasonable for almost any week of the year, except for Super Bowl week. I get top dollar that week. You want to schedule a different week, we'll go with your number."

Linda handled it in stride. "I'm thinking twelve girls, five days each. You wouldn't charge them for taking the girls to the Super Bowl, would you?"

Boss shook his head. "I'd throw the Super Bowl in for free. The girls would get a kick out of it. I'd even be willing to host a private Super Bowl party here."

Scott nodded and pulled a calculator out of his pocket. "So let's see . . ."

Boss saved him the trouble. "That's six hundred thousand for five days."

Linda nodded. "Agreed. Now, I'd like to match the girls with my clients." She flipped the photo album pages to the spread of an African American girl. She held it up for Boss to see. "For example, she's a real beauty. My client, Robert, is black and has always preferred dark-skinned women. He's a surgeon who likes to talk about himself, and I would prefer a girl who can talk medicine with him, or at least listen in an educated way."

Boss placed his hands together and held them on his lips in thought. "Well, I don't have any MDs in my group," he chuckled. It was the first bit of humor he showed. "I do have some pretty smart girls. Some. One does genetic testing. Were you thinking of personal interviews?"

"I'd prefer a spread like this for each girl and a short bio. Who they are, what they enjoy, where they come from. Something to share with the clients so they know what to expect. A few don't like surprises. Then we'll talk about interviews if necessary."

"If necessary," Boss mimicked. Just then his dogs began growling out front. He swiveled his chair to take a look. "That's odd. They usually don't approach strangers in the parking lot unless something is amiss. They seem to be growling at your chauffeur. No, they're fighting over a ball."

Linda and Scott rose and looked out the window. Alvarez was inside the car. He lowered a window and tossed another ball. Each dog chewed intently on their new toy and things quieted down.

"Clever chap to bring balls along for edgy dogs. I don't approve, but I'll let it ride this time. My personal driver is not that clever."

Boss swiveled his chair around to face them, and they sat back down. "So, Stephanie, we seem to be agreed on the price. I'll allow you to match them with your clients based on pictures and bio."

"And an interview, if necessary," Linda added quickly.

"I hope it doesn't come to that," added Boss. "These girls have street smarts and worldly ways, but they're not college grads. At their age, your clients want girls who will make them feel young again. These girls know how to do that. Now, how do you propose paying for it?"

"One hundred thousand down and the rest at the end of the Super Bowl."

Boss shook his head. "Three hundred thousand down and the rest at the end of the Super Bowl."

Linda gave him a coy look. "I don't have that kind of cash in my purse." She held up her small purse for emphasis.

"When do you propose to get the money to me?"

Linda's eyes hardened. "When do you propose to draw up the contract?"

"Contract?"

Linda stiffened. "For half a million dollars, I need a contract and a receipt. I run a legitimate business. Look at it from my perspective. If I show up with my clients and there are no girls, WanderLust goes down the tube."

"That's not gonna happen, trust me. Okay, I'll have my lawyers draw up a contract. It will be written in a way that doesn't appear to break the law. We use the term *escort service*."

Linda's face relaxed. "May I stop by and pick it up tomorrow? I'd like to head back to New York in the next day or two."

Boss frowned. "How about late tomorrow? That should give the lawyers enough time. We'll sign the contract. I'll give you a week to deliver the money. By then, I'll have the new spreads and the bios."

Linda stood and extended her hand. "Agreed."

Boss stood and shook her hand. "I'll walk you to the door."

As they neared the door, Scott said, "I have a favor to ask. Would you show us the view from the Mississippi side of the house? That used to be the front when the house was built. Samuel Clemens was in awe of the plantation houses lining the Mississippi from the perspective of the steamboat."

Boss shuffled his feet in irritation, but Linda added, "That would be interesting. I'm sure you have a lovely view."

"This way," Boss sighed in a grumpy tone. He led them to a porch with a grand view of Ol' Man River.

"Magnificent view," said Linda. "I see a dock down there and a boat. But I also see a levee, so there's not really anywhere to go with the boat. It's like a big lake."

"That's right. We can visit the neighbors across the way. It's quicker than driving. But I don't do that very often. We mostly use the boat for taking clients fishing. We don't eat the fish, of course. Lord knows what they're contaminated with. Stuff that'll rot your brain, no doubt."

"What's that grassy plant?" Linda asked.

"Sugarcane. That's how the plantation owners became wealthy. We don't harvest it anymore. It's just there for visual effect."

Linda sat in a rocking chair and crossed her long thin legs. She smiled up at Boss. "I can see why your great-great-grandpa liked the place. What a nice place to sit on a sunny day."

Boss cast his eyes downward at her legs, seeming to realize for the first time what an attractive woman she was. She wore a blouse that accentuated her bust and a skirt that revealed shapely calves. His tone became more accommodating. "On a sunny day, yes. Not a nice place to be when a hurricane comes through, perched as it is on a hill. Suffered a lot of damage with Katrina. But that's how life is. You take the good with the bad."

Linda stood. "Thanks for the tour. We'll be back tomorrow for the contract."

CHAPTER 34

GREAT RIVER ROAD

"Everything go well?" Scott inquired as Alvarez drove off.

"I don't think so. Two men came by named Emile and Louie. They asked me point-blank whether my name was Carlos Alvarez. How could they have guessed who I was? Caught me completely by surprise. They told me they knew where Anna was and were willing to cut a deal. I wanted to say yes but was worried it was a trap. I denied it. Told them I was Juan Perez like we practiced. I don't think they believed me."

Linda and Scott sat in stunned silence as they mulled over possibilities. Linda offered a hypothesis. "Well, you look Latino, and you don't have a New York accent. If they were the kidnappers, they know that someone with that name offered to ransom Anna and might be in pursuit."

"Sure, but why a chauffeur?" Alvarez nodded to the guard and passed through the gate.

"Anything else happen?" asked Scott.

Alvarez smiled broadly. "I managed to land both drones on the roof. The bad news is that the roof is much farther off the ground than I anticipated. I should have used a telephoto lens instead of a wide-angle lens. I can see people, but I'm not sure how well I can recognize faces. Anyway, I should have pictures of these two men to show you when we get back."

"We saw you throw a ball to the dogs when we were in Boss's office. How did the sedative work?"

"The dogs were huge. The acepromazine calmed them down, but I'll need a higher dose to knock them out."

"You did well," said Scott. "As I see it, we have two options: cut a deal with Emile and Louie, or stick with the original plan of rescuing them in one fell swoop."

Alvarez was tentative. "I can't believe they mentioned a deal in the shadow of Boss's house. I think it must be a trap. I think if we admitted who we were, that would identify us as the enemy and make it easier to eliminate us. What's another option?"

Linda shook her head sadly. "We don't know where Anna is being kept, and can't do anything about rescuing her until she surfaces. We have a second visit with Boss planned for tomorrow. We have to find her by then."

A despondent silence set in. Even the best-laid plan rarely survived the first encounter with the enemy, and this one was already developing large cracks. It had to be wrapped up soon, or it was going bust.

CHAPTER 35

NEW ORLEANS

Emile and Louie swept through Boss's plantation, looking for unwanted visitors and anything amiss with the electric fence. Occasionally, they found a vagrant looking for a secluded place to crash, but nothing today. They returned to the parking lot, disappointed the car was gone. Louie said, "I really think this guy is Carlos Alvarez. Did you see the guilty look on his face?"

Emile didn't see it that way. "That guy didn't win no Presidential Medal. He was a big fat wimp. He was scared of us. And why would he be disguised as a chauffeur? I think you just got him flustered. I don't see any way Carlos Alvarez could have followed us to New Orleans, let alone Boss's place. And, how could he have arranged a visit with Boss on such short notice? It's a little hard to believe."

Louie was adamant. "Scared of us? I don't think so. He was hiding something. Look, you and I both know he was lying about something."

"I agree he behaved suspiciously, but I don't know about what. Maybe there's something else going on."

"Like what? Hey," said Louie, pointing to the roof. "What's that?"

Emile cocked his head. "What are you looking at?"

"There's something big sitting on the roof. Here, let me get my binoculars out of the glove compartment." Louie returned with binoculars and focused them on the roof. "It's one of those flying saucer things. It has legs and wings and something that looks like a camera. It's pointed right at us."

Louie handed the binoculars to Emile, who studied the object. "You're right. It's a drone. You think Boss put it there to check on us?"

Louie shook his head. "Why would Boss do that? He could build cameras into the house and make them invisible. This drone is actually in a dangerous place. A strong wind could blow it off the roof. I'll bet the chauffeur did it."

Emile disagreed. "The chauffeur? Today? It could have been here for weeks. When was the last time you looked?"

Louie became defensive. "I wasn't looking there today. It just kind of caught my eye as something unusual. I'd like to think it would have caught my eye another day if it was there. I doubt it was there when we left for Texas. Maybe we should tell Boss."

Emile drew back, clearly worried. "I don't think that's a good idea. Boss would certainly blame it on us, especially if the chauffeur is Carlos Alvarez. Damn, we could have drawn the FBI here. This is bad. You can leave anytime, just disappear. He won't care enough to track you down. I have a wife and kids. We live here. Boss's wrath will follow me forever. Hell, I have visions of Vinny floating in the bayou."

Louie rolled his eyes. "Don't start with the Vinny shit again. You're not Vinny. I'm not Vinny. You're too paranoid."

Emile shook his head despondently. "I'm not so sure. This has never happened to me before. For years I did what Boss asked without question. He paid me well and he owns the law around here. Maybe my luck has run out. If it's the FBI or some federal bullshit and Boss goes down, we go down with him. We kidnapped girls. We brought them across state lines. We help run a brothel. Hell, we're looking at years in the slammer. So what are we gonna do?"

Louie shot the camera the bird. "I have no idea. A one-way ticket to Alaska is looking pretty good right now. Maybe you want to pack up the wife and kids and join me?"

CHAPTER 36

NEW ORLEANS

lvarez programmed the cameras on the drones to take a picture every five seconds and send them to a secure cloud. He collated the time series and was studying the photos in chronological order. "Look at that view," he exclaimed as he began reviewing the dockside pictures from drone number two. "The Mississippi River cuts a broad valley, and the edges are lined with cane of some sort."

"Sugarcane," Scott offered. Across the river were more antebellum plantation homes. "The area is little changed. At the time of the Civil War, the plantation owners harvested sugarcane off the backs of black slaves. Some plantations had over one hundred and fifty slaves. Today, Boss's plantation has modern slaves who offer tourists 'sugar' of a different sort."

"Nice historical note," Linda offered wryly at his play on words. "It's vast but manicured. Many places to be intercepted. I hope we don't need to escape in that direction."

The dockside series was not interesting. There were no people and the boat didn't move. The series overlooking the parking lot was more engaging. They watched Alvarez open the car door for Linda, close it behind her, then drive off. It wasn't long before he let out a long breath.

"The drone's already been discovered by Emile and Louie. There's Louie saluting the drone with his middle finger."

Linda and Scott huddled around the computer screen as Alvarez replayed this part of the series several times.

Linda sighed. "Didn't take long for them to find a drone. Do you think they know you planted it? If our cover is already blown, we'll have to act quickly. Let's see what else you have."

The evening pictures showed the security guard driving off in one car and Emile and Louie driving off in the remaining car. Nothing happened during the night. In the early morning, a man in a security outfit arrived. He was carrying a box that could have contained food. In the late morning, Emile and Louie drove back, this time with passengers. The first woman out was followed by a small girl. Out the other side popped another woman and another small girl.

"It's Anna," Alvarez exclaimed with obvious joy. Then his voice became more pensive. "She seems to be staggering. Looks like they drugged her."

Anna held on to the railing as she slowly made her way up the steps. Then, she was out of view. Linda went backward and forward several times. "I don't think she's drugged. I think she's wearing stiletto heels and having trouble keeping her balance. The other woman is doing much better."

Alvarez stared hard. "I can't see heels."

"I'm not saying I see heels. The camera is too far away. I'm speaking in first principles. Hookers wear heels. That's what they're training her for."

Alvarez nodded. "Makes sense. She never liked heels of any sort. She was always practical about footwear. So the other woman might be Catalina, given the two girls with them."

Scott became agitated. "I think we make our move now. We know of four guards. There may be more if they sleep there, but probably not. No evidence of another car. Those are better odds than we bargained for. There doesn't seem to be a cooking or cleaning staff, perhaps because this is Sunday. The girls are all contained in one place. It's snatch-and-go time. We can bring them back here while we ditch the Bentley."

CHAPTER 37

GREAT RIVER ROAD

Austin greeted them at the guard gate, clipboard in hand. Gruffly, he asked, "Name?"

Alvarez answered politely. "Stephanie Orie and Shaun Finnerty. We were here yesterday."

Austin was sharp. "Of course you were. I'm not an idiot. But your name isn't on the list for today. So back up, turn around, and leave. Don't come back until your name is on the list."

Linda rolled her window down. "Please, let me explain. We don't have an appointment with Boss. We just need to pick up a contract his lawyers drew up. It'll only take five minutes."

Austin looked at her, then Scott, then back to Linda. "Let me call the house. Wait right here."

He pulled his phone from his pocket and spoke into it as he walked away from the car into the guardhouse. Scott glanced up the hill toward the mansion where he noticed a car approaching. Remembering Alvarez's video feed, he recognized Emile's car that had carried the ladies to the mansion earlier in the day. He whispered to Linda, "There's some good news and some bad news rolling down the hill."

Linda leaned forward and peered through the windshield. "The good news is that there will be fewer guards. The bad news is that the girls may have been split up. Try to see who's in the back seat. If it's Anna, we can leave right now and follow that car."

Austin motioned Emile forward with little more than a sideward glance. Emile slid through the open gate without slowing down.

"I saw two guards in the front. Didn't get a clear view of the back seat," said Linda. "The guard booth was in the way."

"Nor I," said Alvarez. "The car didn't even slow down."

Scott whispered, "I saw only one lady in the car. I couldn't tell which one. And I don't know about the girls, since they are so short. Fifty-fifty chance Anna is still in the house. Decision time. In my opinion, we have no choice but to beg our way into the house now, in case Anna is there. This may be our last chance."

Linda said, "Scott's right. If we turn around and follow the car and it's not Anna, then we may never get another chance to enter the house."

Alvarez nodded in agreement as Austin came back to the car somewhat apologetic. "Apparently a contract is awaiting you. You can pick it up from the security guard just inside the house. He wanted me to let you know that Boss has a full schedule today and can't meet with you."

Scott leaned over and spoke through the open window. "Hey, where was Emile going? We wanted to speak with him."

Austin backstepped to the guardhouse. "That's none of your business. Proceed."

Alvarez drove up the hill where he parked the car in full view of his drone. "They let it live," he said in a mocking tone. "At least for now."

He got out of the car and opened the door for Linda. Scott hopped out the other side. He adjusted his sport coat and the things beneath it. "Good luck, babe. I got your back."

As they sauntered up the steps to the front door, Linda said, "I'll take the bottom floor, you take the top. I'm not very good on steps in heels."

Scott looked down at her feet. "You look good in heels. But I say kick 'em off when you're clearing rooms."

Scott opened the front door for Linda, then stepped in behind her. A lanky guard was waiting for them with a package in his hand. They approached the guard at ninety-degree angles to each other so he couldn't watch them both at the same time. Both Linda and Scott stuck out their hands to receive the package. The confused guard vacillated between one and the other.

Linda chuckled.

"Give it to her," Scott said politely. "She's my boss."

As the guard turned to hand the package to Linda, Scott palmed a Taser and zapped the guard in the neck. The guard collapsed immediately. Linda scanned the second floor to see if anyone was watching. She kicked off her heels. Scott sealed the man's mouth with duct tape and immobilized his hands behind his back with flex cuffs, then did the same with his feet. He stuffed the guard behind the nearest interior door, which turned out to be a coat closet.

Just then, two snarling Danes emerged from the back room. Linda backed up a step. Scott slid forward and bounced a ball laced with acepromazine to them. They both lunged at the ball. One dog was victorious and chose to retreat to a different room with the ball in his mouth. The other dog snarled at Scott, who tossed a second ball. This appeased the snarling dog, who retrieved it and left to be with his companion.

"Alvarez told me they'll be out cold in about twenty minutes. Close the door if you see them in a room to contain them."

Linda pulled a gun and latex gloves from her purse, and left her purse by her shoes. She started on the right-hand side, opening doors while pointing her gun inside. "Clear," she said, mostly to herself as she moved to the next room.

Scott knew he should follow her as backup, yet the pictures from the drone seemed to suggest that the only other people in the house were Boss and one of the girls. He suspected Boss would be giving the young lady a lesson in the art of womanly behavior. Where would that lesson take place? The master bedroom, of course. Confident in Linda's ability to secure what he believed to be an empty downstairs, he took the steps two at a time to the upper floor. He donned gloves and started on the right as well, methodically checking each room. When he came to the master bedroom, he took a deep breath. He thought he heard voices inside. Or was it music? He should wait for Linda, but time was of the essence.

Gun in his right hand, he turned the doorknob slowly with his left hand. He took a deep breath, then burst in. He scanned the room quickly. He panned past the standing girl, then pointed his gun at the reclining figure on the bed.

"Hands where I can see them."

Boss was startled, but raised his hands slowly in a surrender that somehow seemed to mock him. Scott fought back the insult. "Roll over on your stomach. Place your hands behind your back. I'd love to shoot you, so make my day."

Boss had a horrified look on his face at this unexpected turn of events. He recovered quickly, speaking in a mocking tone that seemed to suggest this was but a temporary setback. "You lack creativity, son. Think of something original. Something worth memorializing when you die."

Scott stepped forward and dug his knee into Boss's back. He cuffed the man's hands behind his back with flex cuffs. Then he pulled the covers away. No gun, no knife. Just a naked man, older and more fragile in his nakedness than he appeared yesterday.

Scott glanced at the woman briefly. "You Catalina?"

The woman nodded, her delicate hands cupped over naked breasts that were too large to conceal. "Grab your clothes. Move it. We're here to rescue you. Where's Anna?"

"I don't know."

"Go downstairs. Call for Linda. She'll take care of you. There's a car with a chauffeur waiting for you in the parking lot."

When Catalina was out the door, Scott spoke to Boss. "I want two things from you."

"Speak," said Boss defiantly.

"I want to know where Anna is, and I want safe passage for all of us out of New Orleans."

Despite his compromised position, Boss spoke indifferently. "You're asking a lot. The first request is easy. She's in a house near Jackson Square."

Scott growled at him. "You got an address?"

"Don't know it offhand. The second request is more difficult. I can't control your destiny, your karma controls that."

Scott growled at him. "I'll need some insurance that you have my best interests at heart. I'm going to raise my knee. I have my gun trained on the back of your head. Any unexpected move, and you get a bullet in the brain. Midbrain, you're gone. But I'm gonna aim a bit lower, and you'll be a quadriplegic unless you do as I say. You're going to walk into your office. You're gonna open your safe. You hit an alarm of any sort, and you'll never have another woman again."

Boss was defiant. "Your karma will be fine if you leave right now. I'll let you go. Pick up the girls and beat it out of town. No problem."

Scott said, "I'd rather see what's behind door number two. Up."

Boss stood, and Scott muscled him toward the door. "To your safe."

Boss led Scott down the hall to a study. The door was closed.

Linda made her way up the steps, breathless.

Scott said, "You're just in time. Boss is about to gift us the contents of his safe. Could you get the door, please?"

Scott pulled back on Boss's flex cuffs with his left hand. The pressure made Boss's shoulders arch up, and he gave a yelp of pain. The gun in Scott's right hand never strayed from Boss's head. Linda stepped aside while Scott pushed Boss through the doorway. "Where's the safe?"

Boss nodded toward a painting of a boat silhouetted in the sunset. Linda removed the painting from the wall. "Combination?" she said anxiously.

As Boss recited the numbers, she spun the dial and pulled the door open. In it were stacks of hundred-dollar bills lying on top of an old ledger and some manila folders. Linda pulled out the ledger and folders, but left the money behind. She opened the ledger and studied it briefly. Then she opened one of the folders. She nodded to Scott.

Scott said, "This is my karma for the next few days. I'm giving this to my lawyer with explicit instructions. You let us go, and she returns this to you. You harm or kill us, and the folders go straight to the FBI. You could spend the rest of your life in jail. Don't make an impulsive decision you'll regret a few hours later. Understand?"

Boss nodded with a grumpy look, seeming to understand for the first time he wasn't dealing with amateurs. Scott sealed his mouth with duct tape. He shoved him in a closet and closed the door. "Where's Catalina?"

"In the car. Let's beat it."

CHAPTER 38

NEW ORLEANS

S cott drove, since he was more experienced at high-speed chases than Alvarez. He came down the hill fast, expecting to be able to pass right through the gate. He hit the brakes hard and squealed to a stop at the closed gate. He nodded to Austin. "We're leaving now."

The guard shook his head dismissively. "No one's going anywhere. We're on lockdown."

Scott scowled at him. "Detaining people against their will is kidnapping. Kidnapping is a felony."

"I'm not detaining anyone, wiseass," he said with a smirk on his face. "The gate is locked with the master switch in the house."

Scott spoke calmly but with a sharp edge. "And you don't have an override switch in your cubicle?"

The reply seemed almost too quick. "No, sir."

"Any idea why we're on lockdown?"

"No, sir. Could be that Boss opened the safe. Gate always locks when the safe is opened."

Scott figured the guard was barely out of his teens. He nodded thoughtfully, then gave the guard a kindly smile. "Well, we can sit here a piece until Boss closes the safe. What's your name again, son?"

The guard seemed relieved. "Austin, sir."

"Austin, mind if I stretch my legs?"

"No, sir."

Scott opened his door and got out of the Bentley. He stretched a little, then sidled over to the cubicle where he pulled his gun in a fast, fluid motion. "Austin, I want your gun, slow and easy. No one has to get hurt here. Move slowly and keep your hands where I can see them."

Austin shook his head ruefully but did as he was told. Scott pocketed the weapon. "That your truck over there?"

"Yes, sir," Austin answered halfheartedly.

Still pointing his gun at Austin, Scott continued with a smile. "She's a beauty. Late model?"

Austin didn't return the smile. "Brand new. Just got her."

"She's built like a Sherman tank. How about handing me the keys? I'd like to take her for a spin."

"What? Where? There isn't anywhere to go."

"Hand me the keys," Scott insisted as he pushed the muzzle of the gun in Austin's direction.

"Okay, okay. Where you gonna take her?" he inquired as he handed the keys over.

"I'm gonna back her up about fifty yards, then floor it. I hope to ram the gate going full speed. Think the gate will budge?"

Austin winced. "Please don't. I spent every cent I had on her."

"I'm afraid it was a poor investment, unless of course there's an override switch in the cubicle that will open the gate."

Scott didn't wait to find out as he climbed into the truck and fired the engine. "Nice sound. I like the way the engine just roared to life. Be a shame if anything happened to it."

Austin grimaced. Clearly, there was no override switch.

Scott backed the truck up and pointed the front end at the gate. Austin winced as he yelled, "I'm telling you, man. I can't open the gate. It's locked from the house."

"I believe you," Scott yelled back. "That's why I'm in your truck instead of my car. But don't worry. I'll have this troublesome gate open in no time at all."

Scott floored the pedal, and the tires squealed as the truck lunged forward. While the hinges held, the truck blew a hole in the gate large enough for the Bentley. Scott pulled a u-ey so that the front end faced Austin and hopped out. "Great pick-up-and-go. I've got to get one of these for my ranch. Sorry about the front end. The check engine light just came on. You might want to have that checked out while it's still under warranty." Scott shrugged in consolation.

Austin looked devastated as he surveyed the damage to the front end from the safety of his cubicle. Linda pulled the Bentley through the gap and stopped long enough for Scott to jump in. "Hit it, babe."

Scott rummaged through the stack of papers. He handed half to Alvarez. "Photograph anything important looking. Boss is going to come calling. I want as many images as possible in case we lose the papers." Then he glanced at Linda. "Would you look at this? I found his black book of client names." Scott was silent for a while as he studied the names. "You'll never guess who's on this list. It reads like a *Who's Who*. Small wonder he wants it back."

CHAPTER 39

E mile and Louie dropped us off at our new home, a stately antebellum house near Jackson Square. As I explored the house with the twins in tow, I discovered a small room that contained some children's toys. There was a dark-skinned woman there with a mixed-race boy just slightly older than the twins. The boy was playing with a model of a red pickup truck. The woman was crying. Guadalupe and Maribel found a doll and began to fight over it, pulling it back and forth. I plucked the doll from their hands and approached the woman. I tried to be bold. "Hey sister, what's wrong?"

She was surprised to see me. "You new here?"

"Got here moments ago. Hate it already."

The woman used a Kleenex to dry her eyes. "It's not so bad. It grows on you. Got here when I was fifteen. Boss may be an asshole, but he takes good care of you as long as you stay clean."

"Clean?"

"Blood tests," she answered matter-of-factly. "No drugs. No germs." Then she burst into tears again.

I pointed at the gauze taped to the crook of my arm where the doctor had drawn blood earlier. "This a regular occurrence?"

"Random, but about once a month, hon. And they better come back clean, or you're out on the street."

I tried to puzzle out the meaning of her words in the context of her crying, but my silence hung heavy in the air. Then Guadalupe began whining.

"Give me back my doll. I'm gonna tell Mama on you."

I was too distracted to argue and handed her the doll. Maribel immediately lunged for it, and the two resumed their tug-of-war. I ignored them and took another step toward the woman so I could hear her over the din. "So was it drugs or germs?"

"Germs," she answered meekly. She waved a paper at me. "Says I'm HIV positive. I try to be careful, but some johns don't want to use condoms. Now Boss will kick me out of here. I don't know what I'll do. You know what it's like on the streets? I won't last long as a street-walker. When I get AIDS, Charles won't have a mother. Look at him. He's four. Without health care, I could be dead by the time he's ten. This really sucks for both of us."

I was horrified to hear that her job was about to take a turn for the worse. I didn't realize that there were things worse than Boss's seedy enterprise. "What's so special about this place?"

The woman stared wide-eyed at me as if I was a real bimbo. "A high-end escort service is the best place to be in this line of business. Boss has very wealthy clients who are well-behaved. They like us because they know Boss has clean girls. They're not the usual drug-addled pervs you see on the street. They want to be seen with pretty girls in public as much as screw them at the end of the night. You'll go to fancy restaurants and interesting events, mostly casinos and sporting events, but some like the music scene. It's a male ego thing. Like 'my girl has bigger tits than your girl.' If you act interested and can hold a conversation, you can expect a nice tip. This is the only thing I've ever done, and now it's gone."

She lowered her head and began sobbing. A life of one-night stands with old men didn't appeal to me, but I was curious about the alternative. "So what's it like on the streets?"

"It's brutal. You need a pimp to work almost any corner. The closer you get to the French Quarter, the more money the pimps want. The pimps expect streetwalkers to pull the clients in by shaking their ass in short skirts and high heels. The pimps will beat you if you have a bad night. The johns are rough too. Some try to skip out without paying. Some beat you. Not a good environment to raise Charles. Last girl who left here, oh, about a year ago, is dead now. Got shot by a pimp in a territorial dispute. The pimps control certain corners, and you better not trespass. Streetwalkers don't last long."

I could see her lips quivering. I wanted to wrap my arm around her and provide some comfort, but my feet seemed glued to the floor. "Maybe it's a bad test. A false positive."

Her face brightened a bit. "Maybe." She pointed to the crook of her arm. "This is test number two. I'll know in a week."

Then I had a sudden revelation. "Is there any way we can switch blood test results? I just had my blood drawn by the doc." I pointed to the gauze around the crook in my arm. "I wouldn't mind getting kicked out. I'm getting cold feet."

She shook her head sadly. "The doc keeps the records. This is just a copy. See? It says 'copy'," she said, pointing the paper at me. "You only get a copy when the news is bad. First bad one in five years, but that's all it takes."

CHAPTER 40

NEW ORLEANS

I found a full-length mirror in the hallway. I put on my heels and studied myself from several different angles. The new clothes were bright, tight, and light. The top was skimpy and the hemline short. But the colors worked for me, and the fabric was soft on my skin. The earrings seemed to be made of real jewels and gold, or were at least good imitations. I twirled slowly in front of the mirror. I didn't have Catalina's voluptuous figure or beautiful face, but I wasn't bad. I had nice ankles, shapely calves, and thin thighs. My legs were probably my best feature, and the shoes made them look hot. I had small hips and a petite waist. I didn't have much up top, but what I did have was hanging out for all the world to see. I thought I had style. But did I have sex appeal? I hadn't been on a date in nearly two months. I hadn't had a good date in nearly a year. Would someone actually pay a thousand dollars an hour for the pleasure of my company? Boss seemed confident it would happen. I had my doubts.

Then the method of seduction became crystal clear. This was exactly why the mirror was placed here. They buy you expensive clothes. They dress you up. They provide you with a measure of confidence that you can hang with the other girls in the house. Many girls probably wanted to go the next step just to see if they could bring in a grand an hour. It took me over two weeks to earn that much at GenWiz. Hot clothes, expensive jewelry, and a full-length mirror might persuade just about any girl to go for a test drive.

I shuddered to think about what I might have to do in return. The padres had definitely left their mark on me. I had to find a way to leave. I shuddered to think of what Catalina must be going through this very moment with Boss. Poor thing.

I walked the girls back to my room and kicked off my heels. The girls settled in on the floor, coloring. They were remarkably adaptable and good-natured. They found solace in each other and rarely complained to me. Part of this I could see in Catalina's personality. She was more malleable than me. She went with the flow, while I tried to bend the world to my tastes. She was a quiet stoic. I was a drama queen. She had not been one to plot escape but had acquiesced and even encouraged my plans. What would become of her and her girls in the long run? Would they settle into this career like their mother? Would they find themselves out on the street, motherless and home-less, victims of HIV?

I could leave now, but with no friends and no money, I wouldn't get far. I could steal away to the police. They might ship me back to Francisco's waiting arms. Or, if they were a corrupt bunch like the Juarez police, they could notify Boss, and I would place us all in jeopardy.

There was a knock on my door, and before I could get up, Louie stuck his head in. When he saw me, he stepped in quickly and closed the door behind him. Maribel giggled and walked over to him.

"Are you a good guy or a bad guy?"

He bent down and handed her two lollipops. "Definitely a good guy. Give one to your sister."

Maribel toddled off. Quite surprisingly, she shared the bounty with her sister. I admired and hated this about Louie. He loved the girls and they him. Yet they never noticed that he was the source of our misery.

Maribel called out, "See me pretty?" She had on my heels and a necklace wrapped around an arm like a bracelet. She couldn't walk in the shoes, but she slid them forward a little at a time and wobbled over to Louie with a cute smile. "I'm gonna be like Mama."

His smile faded immediately. "Wouldn't you rather be a doctor or a lawyer?"

She shook her head defiantly. "No, just like Mama."

He patted her on the head and spoke absently. "I hope for your sake you do better."

I stood to face him. All my anger began working to the forefront. Louie studied me top to bottom and I became uncomfortable. Before I could open my mouth, he began a nervous sentence.

"I . . . uh. Now that you are settled here, uh . . . I was wondering if I could be your first client?"

I reared back and slapped his face as hard as I could. I was surprised by my force and fury. "I'd rather die."

A solid mass of muscle, Louie barely flinched from the blow. I broke down crying. I tried to hide the tears from the girls, but they noticed my distress, and each one wrapped arms around a leg.

I bent down and hugged them. I needed it. "I'll be all right. Go back to coloring."

I lifted Maribel out of my shoes and gently guided the girls in the direction of their coloring. Then I stood toe-to-toe with Louie. I drew some satisfaction in watching a red mark appear on his face where I had slapped him. When he caught my eye, he apologized.

"I'm sorry about all of this. When I took the job, I didn't realize I could ruin so many lives. I'm especially sorry for them." He nodded toward the girls. "This is no place for them to grow up." His voice trailed off, a look of helplessness on his face.

I seized the moment. "If you're truly sorry, then why not stop?"

He countered quickly. "I intend to. I've been thinking about moving to California. I'm thinking of becoming an auto mechanic again. I can't right all the wrongs I've committed, but maybe I can help you out."

I didn't hesitate. "Can you drop us off in El Paso? The four of us?"

He shrugged with a hopeful look in his eyes, as if it were a possibility. "You have to understand that this is a dangerous move. This job is like the 'Hotel California.' You can check out, but you can never leave. Boss is worried about losing control of company secrets. He plants a bullet in the back of your head if he suspects you intend to run."

"All the more reason to do it now before he suspects anything. We can leave as soon as Catalina returns."

He grew wary. "Don't you have friends in town? There is a man, a woman, and a chauffeur. Odd things have been happening since they arrived."

This was the first I'd learned of it. My heart surged with hope. I tried to keep my eyes from showing that hope. I shrugged. "I don't know. I have a cousin, Carlos Alvarez, who would have ransomed me. You didn't want to deal, though. Was one of the men Latino, about five-five, late twenties, and overweight?"

Louie nodded. "He didn't look like a millionaire with a jet, though. He was the chauffeur."

My hope soared, but I became more guarded. Was Louie just trying to suck information out of me? Would he rat me out to Boss? Was Carlos really here? If so, who were the people with him? I played it coy. "My cousin is not a good driver, so I doubt he was the chauffeur. That general description fits a lot of Hispanic men."

Louie must have sensed promise in my voice. "I hope for your sake it's true. It won't be easy for them. Boss's house is a fortress with a guard at the gate and a security guard inside. He also gets a lot of support from the police."

He stared long and hard at me. I met his eyes with resolve and what I hoped would appear like a measure of contempt. To my surprise, he couldn't hold my gaze. He looked away and stammered, "I . . . I'm not very good with ladies, especially classy ones I like. I'm sorry I got you in this mess. Maybe it's not your Carlos Alvarez. Maybe you need another exit strategy. Look, maybe I can get you out. I don't want to stay here any longer. I want to make a clean break myself."

Maribel came over and wrapped her arms around my leg. "Where's Mama?"

"Your mama will be here in a bit." As I picked her up, a beeping noise rumbled through the house. It sounded a bit like a weather alert, though the skies were clear. Fearful of the sound, Maribel buried her head in my shoulder. "What's that?"

Louie gave me a frustrated look. "That's the . . . alarm. This place is on lockdown. All the girls are supposed to go to their rooms and wait. Something must be wrong."

Guadalupe came running, and I scooped her up on the other hip. I began to panic. "What does this mean? What should we do?"

He shrugged. "Nothing, I guess. Usually someone goes around and checks to make sure all are accounted for. You want them to find you here in your room."

He turned, leaving more questions than answers.

I blurted out, "Louie, if you're serious about leaving New Orleans, pick us up on the way out. The four of us, that is."

Relief flashed across his face.

"What about your friends? What if they're looking for you?"

"Give me your phone," I demanded. I hadn't had access to a phone for days. I dialed Carlos, who didn't answer. I left a message. "This is Anna. I've been kidnapped to a brothel in New Orleans. It's near a statue of a guy on a horse."

"Jackson Square," muttered Louie helpfully.

"Jackson Square. Big church nearby. Please help. I'm desperate. I may try to run away today. Not my phone. I'll call again if I can."

He gave a brief nod as he took his phone back. "Get your things together. Be ready to leave quickly."

While I changed into clothes more suitable for travel, an elderly woman stuck her head in. "Welcome, dearie, I'm Deloris. I see you have two little ones. They're so darling. Sorry about the noise. I'll get that thing turned off in a minute."

Louie stuck his head in shortly after the alarm was turned off. He handed me his phone. "It's for you." Then he entered completely and closed the door.

"Carlos?"

"Yes. I'm in a car with Catalina and two friends. We're on our way to Jackson Square to pick you up."

I let out an enormous sigh of relief and began crying. "I'm so sorry for the mess I made. Where can we meet?"

Louie spoke loud enough to be heard over the phone. "There's a line of horse-drawn carriages right off the square. We'll be parked as close to there as possible."

I added, "I'll bring Catalina's girls and her new clothes."

Within minutes, we were in Louie's car and on our way. We were lucky enough to find a parking spot close to the carriages. Then we waited and waited and waited.

Louie was suddenly anxious. "This is taking too long. Something's wrong."

He pulled out of the parking spot and began to drive back to Boss's place. We were almost to Great River Road when he spotted the Bentley pulled over with flashing blue lights behind it.

"This could be bad," he whispered as if the cops might be able to hear him.

"Maybe it's just a traffic violation," I said hopefully.

"Doubt it," Louie said matter-of-factly. "Boss has long arms and a short temper."

CHAPTER 41

NEW ORLEANS

Louie circled around and pulled up behind the police car. The flashing blue lights were blinding. I peered around the police cruiser. The officer was speaking with a female driver who seemed to be handing him her driver's license. He turned and glanced at Louie, giving him a shake of the head and a decidedly unwanted stare. Louie killed the engine anyway. He rolled his window down as the officer strolled over.

The officer pulled off his sunglasses. "Louie, I found them first. The reward money is mine. Please leave now."

Louie stuck out his hand to shake. The policeman accepted it half-heartedly. "I'm not here for the reward, Freddie. It's yours, completely and totally, if you want it."

Freddie pulled back and acted suspicious. "Why would you say no to five grand?"

I could wait no longer. I jumped out of the car and ran up to the Bentley. I banged on the window. Carlos jumped out and gave me a hug. I said, "I love you, Carlos. Thanks for coming for me." Then I called in the open door to Catalina. "I have your girls."

This move apparently frustrated Freddie. "Just a minute, Louie. Ma'am, back in Louie's car. I may be making an arrest here. I suggest you cooperate unless you want to spend a night in lockup with your friend."

I had no choice but to comply. Catalina hopped out of the car and ran back to Louie's car. Freddie raised his hand to stop her, but she blew right by him, dressed in practically nothing. "These are my girls. Boss took them from me, then tried to rape me."

Freddie was having none of it. "Ma'am, back in your car until we sort this all out."

Catalina ignored him and crawled into the back seat with her girls. She slammed the door closed and locked it. She gave Freddie a mournful pout through the window. Guadalupe and Maribel lunged for her. She wrapped her arms around them and buried herself beneath them.

Freddie stared crossly at her and spoke through Louie's open window. "Ma'am, do as I say or there will be trouble."

Louie tried to defuse a situation escalating out of control. "Freddie, leave the girls alone for now. They've been through a lot. We can deal with the girls later. Do what you need to do with the ones in the Bentley. I want you to understand before you do anything illegal that they may be participants in a federal investigation."

Freddie squinted as he read the driver's license. "Hardly. She's Linda Williams from Sierra Blanca, Texas. That's out in the middle of nowhere. That county has more cows than people."

Freddie paused to call in the license number. When he finished, Louie continued, "Linda Williams? That's not the name she used with Boss. Austin told me her name was Stephanie Orie and that she owned a high-end travel agency out of New York called WanderLust. I'm just saying things are not what they seem. If she's the boss, why is she driving, and why is the guy in the chauffeur outfit in the back seat on a computer? Something isn't right."

A call came in for Freddie, and he answered it. When he disconnected, he said, "Driver's license is legit."

"Seems legit," Louie said. "She could have another one for Stephanie Orie in her wallet. Right now, I don't think either of us knows the truth. When these people showed up, we found a pair of drones on Boss's roof. This isn't the work of ranchers from Sierra Blanca."

Freddie scowled at Louie. "Look, the FBI gets warrants. They don't pillage a safe, roll the owner, and make off with his papers. That throws everything out of court."

Louie seemed to ponder the statement. "You have a point. I have no idea why they rolled Boss and stole his papers."

I couldn't help myself. I blurted out, "My cousin won the Presidential Medal of Freedom for saving the president's life."

"President of what?" was Freddie's cautious reply.

"President of this country."

"Your cousin is the fat guy wearing the chauffeur's outfit?"

"Yes," I said proudly.

"That's a stretch," said Freddie dismissively.

"Could actually be true," Louie countered. "His name is Carlos Alvarez. Look him up."

Freddie looked genuinely puzzled. "What are you thinking, Louie?"

"I'm thinking Boss is being investigated for something. Maybe it has to do with the papers. Maybe the papers are a ruse to hide the real motive and flush something else out. All I'm saying is that if you piss these people off and they bust Boss, you could go down too. I can't wrap my head around this. Way too complicated. Let's just say, if you have a legitimate bust, do it, but do it by the books. If you're doing this off the record for the reward money, you might find it costs you more than it's worth."

Freddie was not convinced. "Seems pretty simple. They stole papers from Boss and he wants them back."

"And you have a warrant to search their car?"

"Not exactly."

"Then you'd be sticking your neck out if you just took the papers, assuming they are in the car. Maybe you just ask for the papers back and if they comply, you get the reward and it's all off the record."

Freddie kicked the gravel on the ground. "Ain't this my lucky day. Thought I had a clear shot at five grand. Boss wants more than the papers. He wants their asses. You ever hear what he did to Vinny?"

Louie's face contorted in exasperation. "I'm tired of hearing about Vinny. I never heard of the guy until two days ago. Now he's who everyone wants to talk about. Look, turning the folks in the Bentley over to Boss would be going way too far. There's nothing legal about it. Unless you got a legitimate reason to bust them, let them go. I'm telling you there's something fishy going on, and you better think twice about how deeply you want to get involved. Boss may be going down. You make a wrong move; you could go down with him. For myself, I don't want any part of this, not the bust, not the reward money."

Freddie seemed to reflect on this as if he needed only a slight push to let us all go. I spoke up. "Boss kidnapped four of us and my cousin is here to rescue us. We just want to go home."

"Ma'am, I'm not speaking with you. Please be quiet." Then he turned and walked back to the Bentley.

CHAPTER 42

NEW ORLEANS

E ven though he was many years her junior, Freddie gave Linda a paternal frown that was supposed to mean serious trouble. "Ms. Williams, there was a report of a robbery."

Linda interrupted him. "Is this a formal police report or something off the record?"

"Off the record for now, ma'am, but that could change. According to the report, a man and a woman held a man at gunpoint, rifled a safe, and stole some documents. They also assaulted two men and damaged a truck and a security gate. The victim gave a description of the people and the car. You and your car fit the description, and you just happen to be traveling away from the house."

"Could all be coincidental," said Linda matter-of-factly. "You have names?"

"Stephanie Orie. Your name doesn't match, but you could have been using an alias."

Linda grew agitated. "You don't have much evidence, and like I said, it could all be coincidental."

"Doubtful, ma'am. We don't see many Bentleys in New Orleans. Furthermore, the four of you match the description down to the chauffeur's outfit and the scantily clad woman."

"I see you have a camera on your person. Is it running, Officer Shannon?"

Freddie became agitated. "No, ma'am. I thought it best to keep it off for now."

"If we're as dangerous as you imply, you had best turn it on."

Freddie glanced at the others in the car. They were still and quiet, but stared intently at him. "Don't think that's necessary."

"Because there's no official police report?"

"That's one reason, ma'am."

"I gather you don't have a warrant to search our car."

"No, ma'am, but I don't need a warrant to take you downtown. We can sort it all out down there."

"Does the victim want to make this a matter of public record? Or does he just want his papers back?"

"He wants his papers back, and he wants to meet with you."

"I don't have the papers, and I don't want to meet with him. What do you intend to do, Officer Shannon?"

"I think you're lying about the papers, ma'am. There was too little time for you to get rid of them."

Linda stared at him with such spite that he glanced elsewhere. She dressed him down. "Officer Shannon, I worked for the FBI for twenty years. I've seen my share of agents who turned to the dark side. I believe you've gone rogue. Evidence in point—your video camera is off, there is no police report or search warrant, and you don't seem to want to arrest us but would rather hand us over to Boss. All of these things lead me to believe you're on Boss's payroll and acting outside of your jurisdiction as a police officer. You can either let us go now, or you can hitch your wagon to Boss's pony and get what's coming to him. As I see it, we have a case against Boss involving racketeering, income tax evasion, money laundering, human trafficking, prostitution, and murder. You want your share of the penalty for that? Could be years in prison. What's it going to be, Officer Shannon?"

CHAPTER 43

SETTING SUN RANCH

The sky was bursting to life with early morning pink-and-orange hues when Mateo and Francisco parked the trailer on a plot of farmland about one hundred yards south of the Rio Grande. The spot was well concealed from the US side of the river by brush and small trees. They crossed the river on horseback because they were unfamiliar with the hangouts of the Border Patrol and wanted the flexibility to bushwhack around police cars if necessary. There was a single road through the Quitman Mountains that went most of the way to Setting Sun Ranch. Mateo estimated that the trip would be ten miles each way as the crow flies. This would be an easy trek for their young horses. The trick was to keep a low profile to avoid suspicion. They were dressed in traditional American cowboy gear—boots, jeans, chaps, and cowboy hats. This gear was distinctly different from the traditional Mexican cowboy dress that often included a colorful poncho and a sombrero. They grew a bit of stubble on their faces to present an unkempt appearance that might belie a cowboy on the road. In their saddlebags they had guns, ammo, and food in case they were waylaid, though they expected to be back before nightfall. They also had wire cutters to negotiate barbed wire fences.

Francisco selected a mustang, which was the most traditional American breed. He reasoned they would be common in the US and wouldn't seem suspicious. Mateo preferred a paint because his ancestors believed that they possessed magical abilities based on their colorings. After crossing the river, they entered the Rio Grande floodplain. The weather had been dry, and there was little in the way of standing water or muck. At the end of the floodplain, they negotiated a small berm that provided protection against periodic floods. Both horses moved with quiet confidence up the uneven ground. They found their way blocked by a locked gate leading to a dirt road. They skirted around the gate through a wooded area, then cut a hole in the barbed wire. They swung onto the dirt road going north. They passed a homestead, unnoticed, as the fiery ball of a rising sun emerged over the Quitman Mountains.

At the end of the dirt road, they crossed Esperanza Road, then took a right onto Quitman Pass Road. The horses labored through the pass, but from there it was a straight and easy shot to Setting Sun Ranch. When they reached Fivemile Point, a Border Patrol car passed, going the other direction. Francisco suspected the car would turn back to check them out. He moved off the road to a barbed wire fence. He and Mateo dismounted and pretended to be repairing the fence. The Border Patrol car returned shortly and pulled off the side of the road. The patrolmen watched them work from the comfort of their cruiser. Francisco flashed them a friendly smile and waved. The Border Patrol agents left the way they came.

"You see how easily we fooled them, Mateo? These Americans are stupid. They don't study you carefully. They don't ask questions. They just sit on their fat asses and pretend to work. If we had a car with American plates, we could go anywhere."

They arrived at Setting Sun Ranch about thirty minutes later. The two ranch hands, Pedro and Jose, were moving cattle on the far reaches of the ranch, so the homestead was deserted. Scott's truck with the trailer still attached was there. Mr. Ed was in the corral along with Linda's horse. Jake, the family dog, tore out of the barn, barking. Jake followed the intruders to the house, staying just out of reach and barking all the while. This made the horses edgy. They stomped their feet and neighed, which in turn made the Mexican horses nervous. The young men were alert for movement in the outbuildings but didn't clear them before proceeding to burgle the house. Jake was left to his own folly.

Francisco and Mateo tied their horses up on the hitching post just off the front porch. They ascended the steps to incessant barking and growling that was more of a nuisance than a threat. Francisco pulled out his handgun and concealed it beneath his vest. He knocked on the front door. No answer. Francisco knocked louder. Still no answer. Jake continued to bark and snarl. Francisco fired a round at him. The bullet missed, and Jake wisely retreated to safer ground.

"That shut him up," Mateo said. He had been sucking up to Francisco all trip, trying to get him off his back about the money he owed the cartel. A stony silence followed, broken only by the whinny of Mr. Ed in the distance. "Hey, let's leave them a message," Mateo said gleefully.

There was a can of paint and a brush on the front porch the color of the trim around the windows. Mateo painted a message on the front door.

"Nice," said Francisco absently as he peered in the windows. "I see a shotgun, but nothing else of interest. They certainly don't seem like wealthy people. Hell, I have nicer furniture."

Mateo didn't care to compare fortunes. "The money will be in the bedroom. That's all we really want."

"Mostly," said Francisco. "I want Anna, but she doesn't appear to be around."

They tried kicking the front door down, but the door was secured with dead bolts. They worked their way around the house, trying to pry the windows open, but they were bolted shut.

Mateo's imagination went to work on the possibilities. "I think there is something valuable in there. Out here in the middle of nowhere, there's no need to secure your house so tightly. They're protecting something. We got two choices. We can sit here and wait for them to show, or we can bust out a window and see what we can find. How about if we bust out the window?"

Francisco nodded. "Throw the paint can through it."

As the window gave way, a burglar alarm began a piercing cry. There was no sign that this menacing call was recruiting help. "Let's go in."

Mateo kicked out the rest of the glass and Francisco entered first.

"Find the bedroom. That's where the cash will be."

The first room Francisco found was the study. Prominently

displayed on the wall were special commendations from the Federal Bureau of Investigation, one to Scott and the other to Linda. Next to them were two Presidential Medals of Freedom they received the previous year for rescuing the kidnapped president. Next to each medal was a framed picture of them shaking hands with the president. An alarm went off in Francisco's head. If they were this famous, no doubt the house alarm was wired to the police station.

"Hey, Mateo. We better go."

His instincts were spot on. As they mounted their horses, a police car barreled toward the house with blue lights flashing. They rode about two hundred yards into the desert, dismounted, and hid the horses in a thicket of mesquite. Then they worked their way back toward the house with a pair of binoculars to see what the US police would do.

CHAPTER 44

NEW ORLEANS

Officer Shannon stepped out into the road to stop oncoming traffic. He waved Linda forward, visibly upset but unwilling to carry the charade to the next level.

When Freddie and his cruiser were out of view, Scott grinned from ear to ear. "You were fabulous, babe. I'm not sure Boss will let us leave town alive, but you made certain we passed the first test."

Linda looked in her mirror. "The car with Anna and Catalina is following. I'll lead them to the car rental place. Then we'll pick up our suitcases at the hotel. Any idea who's driving the other car? I never got a good look. Looks like a large man."

Alvarez was busy photographing documents again and answered causally. "That's Louie, one of the kidnappers. He stopped by while I was sitting in the car at Boss's house. He seems to be a security guard. He's the one who flipped the bird at our drone. He also knows exactly who I am. Called me by name. This makes me really nervous. Don't let them out of your sight. I know that Anna had to have some help escaping, but I'm astonished it was him. Why would the kidnapper turn on his boss?"

Scott mulled over the possibilities. "He was clearly upset to see the drone, so as of yesterday, he was still loyal to Boss. Going back in time further, he clearly treated the girls so poorly that they tried to escape. In Texas, he inquired about a ransom. I'm left with the notion that he still wants to ransom them. Maybe he wants to cut Boss out of the deal and leave town. The moment of truth has to happen very soon, because at the car rental place, they get into our car."

"They won't all fit into your car," Alvarez noted.

"They seem to be falling back," Linda observed.

"Don't brake. Slow down and see if they catch up," Scott suggested. "Don't look back, Alvarez. Linda, you need to be our eyes so that we don't seem overly suspicious. If it's kidnapping for ransom, Louie might ditch us and hole up somewhere while he makes his demand."

Linda took her foot off the gas and cruised for a bit. "Relax, here they come. I may have been speeding. I need to pay more attention to the speed limit."

"Right turn coming up," said Alvarez, navigating from the back seat.

Linda turned right, and the car followed.

"Left turn in one mile," said Alvarez. "The rental place is only about a mile and a half from here. They're going to have to make their move soon."

Scott became anxious and began barking orders. "When we get to the car rental place, stop somewhere with lots of other people. I don't want it to come to a shootout. Surely he can't expect us to have a hundred grand on us." Scott pulled out his Glock and checked the magazine.

Alvarez's phone rang. "Dammit," Scott muttered. "This is where he makes his move. How far behind are they?"

"Very close. Four or five car lengths," Linda estimated.

"Doesn't make sense. He's in a vulnerable position," Scott noted.

Alvarez's phone rang again.

"But he has four hostages. He has all the cards right now. My Glock is in my purse, so you're the only one on our side who is battle ready. What are we going to do?"

Scott took a deep breath. "Wing it. Get your gun as soon as you stop the car."

Alvarez's phone rang again. He put it on speaker and answered meekly. "Hello?"

"Carlos, this is Anna. Maribel has to go to the bathroom. Are we almost there?"

Alvarez let out a long and audible sigh.

Anna said, "Carlos, are you okay? You sound tense."

"No more than usual when you're being held hostage by a madman who is liable to slit your throat."

"You mean Louie? I think he had a change of heart. He's moved from adversary to liberator. I wouldn't be here without his help. It'll be okay."

When they returned the Bentley and picked up their car, Louie was parked next to them. Scott went directly to Louie. He did not extend a hand and spoke in a demanding tone. The others fell silent, watching the scene play out. "I'm Scott Williams. What do you want out of this?"

Louie gazed at Anna, then spoke in an apologetic voice. "I'm Louie Beaudette, the man who kidnapped them. I hope to help them escape. I was young and foolish when I took this job a year ago. I realize now that this is not the life I want for myself. Anna offered me a chance at redemption, and I took it."

Anna verified with a nod. Wide-eyed, Scott continued, "And why should we trust you? You could turn us all over to Boss, and then we'd have a fine mess."

"No reason," said Louie glumly. "I just want to point out that you will need two cars to carry all these people back to Texas. I'm willing to make mine one of them. I'm eventually going to go to California and start a new life."

"Doing what?"

"Auto mechanic," Louie said quickly, his face brightening.

Scott spoke sharply. "Hell, those people are bigger crooks than Boss."

Linda elbowed him. Scott's face reddened. "Sorry. I'm not sure I believe your story, and I certainly can't trust you. If you don't mind, Linda or I will ride with you at all times. We have guns, and we have extensive training in hand-to-hand combat. Believe it or not, Linda could whip just about every man at the FBI. I would expect you to relinquish your weapon."

Scott held out his hand. Louie reluctantly handed over his gun. An alarm began sounding on Linda's phone. She recognized the sound immediately, even though this had never happened before. "Scott, we're being burgled."

Scott shrugged it off. "The boys probably forgot the passcode."

Linda had security cameras trained on the front porch, back porch, and living room. When activated by movement, each camera shot pictures at five-second intervals. When she viewed the feed through her phone, she gasped. "It's that coyote, Mateo, and another guy on our front porch. One has a gun. They're painting something on our door."

Anna and Catalina gathered around the phone where they agreed that Mateo was one of the two men.

Linda continued, "They broke the front window. That set off the alarm. Mateo's crawling through the window. He just opened the front door for the other man. How did they find our place? What do they want?"

"Bet Mateo wants his money back. They'll be surprised when the police arrive. Perhaps you should let the sheriff know that the burglars are armed."

Linda scrolled through the feed to the end. "They left out the front door. Perhaps the alarm scared them off."

Linda reached the dispatcher. "Hey, Dusty. This is Linda Williams."

"Linda, we just got a message that your burglar alarm is going off. Is everything all right?"

"No, that's why I'm calling. We're in New Orleans. I'm reviewing the feed from the security cameras and there are two armed men in our house. They painted a message on the door. I think they've left the house, but they may still be on the premises. Please tell the deputies to be careful."

"Did you recognize any of the men?"

"Oddly enough, one seems to be a Mexican coyote named Mateo. We had a run-in with him by the Rio Grande a few days ago. We left him tied up by the side of the road for the Border Patrol, but I hear he escaped."

Dusty replied, "I'll run that by the Border Patrol. Heard about a dead Mexican, snakebite or something. Didn't hear anything about a coyote. I'm looking at a map. The straightest path back to Mexico from your place is Quitman Pass Road. I'll see if the sheriff wants to post a car there. When will you be back?"

"Probably tomorrow. It's a fourteen-hour drive. We'll drive straight through. Could you have the deputies check on Jose and Pedro? I'll try to call them now. They should be moving cattle at the south end of the ranch. The phone reception is bad there. They live in a small house on the other side of the corral, about a hundred yards from our house. I'd appreciate hearing if they're okay."

"I'll see what we can do."

When Linda hung up, Scott said, "You never told me what the sign on the front door said."

"Spanish. *Un regalo de Francisco y Mateo*." Linda turned to Anna. "You know what that means?"

Anna's eyes grew wide. "It means 'a gift from Francisco and Mateo.' I know a Francisco. He's a murderer."

Linda scrolled through her images to a picture of Francisco on her front porch and handed the phone to Anna, who shuddered in recognition. "It's the same Francisco. Something brought them together. Now they're brothers in crime."

CHAPTER 45

NEW ORLEANS

S cott insisted on following Louie to the hotel, while Linda rode shotgun with Louie. As they entered the parking lot to their hotel, Louie suddenly did a U-turn and exited the way he came. The maneuver caught Linda by surprise and she pulled her gun. Her voice was calm but insistent. "What are you doing?"

Louie spoke hurriedly, in part because of the gun trained on him. "I recognized one of the men in the parking lot. It might be a trap. Does Boss know where you're staying?"

"Don't recall telling him, but it doesn't take a clever person to find out. He knows the names we used. Pull down that side street and park."

Scott pulled in behind her and exited the car quickly, expecting a confrontation with Louie. He wrenched the door open, gun drawn, but Linda calmed him. "Stop. Louie thinks they have a trap set at the hotel. He recognized one of the men."

Louie nodded. "Freddie Shannon, the cop that stopped you, has a partner named Ozzie Beaner. Ozzie was in a black sedan in the parking lot. Don't think he saw me. He was looking at the people entering the hotel. He knows my car, and I thought it best to leave."

Scott was clearly on the fence about whether to believe him, and it showed on his face.

Louie became defensive. "Ozzie works with Freddie sometimes. Freddie could have told them that I'm with you now, so my ass is on the line too. They'd have to conclude I was helping you, since I showed up with Anna and the girls at Freddie's bust and drove off with you."

Scott glanced from Linda to Alvarez and back again. "Do we have anything in the hotel that we can't live without?"

Alvarez winced. "My command center computer following the drones. They could learn just about anything about me from my computer. It's password protected and encrypted, but it doesn't take a genius to work around those issues. You likely have other identifying information you don't normally think about—luggage tags, prescriptions, receipts. Do you want them to know who you are and where you live?"

Linda said, "Freddie has seen my real driver's license, so he knows who I am and where I live."

Louie countered, "I doubt Freddie will admit to anyone that he stopped you and let you go. So your secret is safe with him."

Scott asked, "What about the car rental? You handled that, Alvarez, since you were the chauffeur."

Alvarez spoke proudly. "I used a fake ID and a matching credit card. No paper trail there."

"And the hotel room?" Scott asked Linda.

"I used our WanderLust IDs and paid with cash. Wanted it to match the names we used with Boss in case he wanted to see whether we were legit. He obviously tracked us down."

Scott summed up. "So aside from Freddie, who may not be talking, the only identifying information is in our hotel rooms?"

Linda and Alvarez nodded. Scott continued. "So who wants to remove the identifying information from our rooms?"

Linda and Alvarez raised their hands. Louie said, "Good chance Boss has a man in the lobby too. They generally work in pairs."

"Any idea how we can close things down in our room?"

"Bait and switch," said Alvarez with unusual confidence.

CHAPTER 46

NEW ORLEANS

L inda and Scott took a taxi to the hotel from a restaurant a half-mile away where Louie had just ordered dinner with Anna, Catalina, and the girls. Alvarez left a bit later in a separate cab. It had been an exhausting ordeal to this point, and the dust had not yet settled. The unexpected appearance of Francisco in this country gave me pause. How did he get here? Did he have a passport? Would he hound me until my dying day?

"Louie, would you mind watching the twins while Catalina and I get some fresh air? We'll be right out front, and we'll come back as soon as the food comes."

"My pleasure," said Louie as he tickled Maribel. Guadalupe ran up to him, daring him to do the same. Seemed like he could entertain them for a few minutes.

We stood on the street in front of the restaurant. She held her head low. I asked, "Want to tell me what happened with Boss?"

"He tried to rape me, and would have, except for Scott. That guy was marvelous. I've got to get out of here, but I've run out of places to go. Linda offered to put us up at their ranch for a few days, but now that Francisco has turned up . . ." She began to cry softly.

I put my hand on her shoulder to offer support. I peeked in the restaurant window. Louie was doing a fabulous job entertaining the girls. Guadalupe was on his lap poking at his belly and Maribel was wrapped around his leg. They were laughing as hard as they had the whole trip. I was so confused. Too many new players. Who to trust and who not to?

"Did you happen to mention to Louie how much your girls are worth?"

Catalina shook her head. "I think he genuinely loves them and vice versa. Started on the first day. I'm sure he doesn't know about the money."

I peeked back in the window. Still smiles on everyone's faces. "He's the first big mystery we need to figure out. What's his angle? Why did he suddenly turn from captor to liberator?"

That brought a smile to Catalina's face. "Obvious. He's in love with you. Head over heels. Never seen anything like it. Wish any man would look at me the way he looks at you."

I started to protest. It was Catalina that the men ogled, but, as I thought about it, not Louie. He had become unusually attentive to me. It was me he propositioned. His change of heart seemed to begin in the bayou. I unexpectedly got a warm spot for him yet didn't trust him with our deepest secrets. "I wouldn't mention the thirty million around him. Not sure we can trust him that much."

Catalina nodded in agreement. "Money has a way of turning good people into monsters. What about Scott and Linda and your cousin? Do they know about the money?"

"Not sure. Might have mentioned it to Carlos back in Juarez. Seems like ages ago. I think the Williamses are good people who can be trusted. Carlos likes Linda especially, and he is a good judge of character. Still, let's not bring up the money unless it becomes vital."

Catalina peered in the window and smiled. "The girls are having the best time with Louie. He may be a keeper, Anna. You need to think hard about it."

I put my arm around her waist as I waved at them through the window and shook my head dismissively. "I see what you mean. But it'll be a long time before I forgive him for all the misery he put us through. Moses never got to see the promised land, and I doubt Louie will, either. We do have one more important thing to discuss before we go back in. How did Mateo and Francisco hook up? What brought them together, and to the Williamses' place, no less?"

Catalina shook her head. "No clue."

"They'll be our biggest problem going forward, you know. It was fine when we thought they would stay in Mexico. We had a safety zone. But now, well, they could pop up anywhere, anytime."

A shudder coursed through Catalina's lithe figure as she cast a glance down the street.

CHAPTER 47

NEW ORLEANS

L inda and Scott slipped by Ozzie unnoticed, leaving a single man in the lobby to contend with. They had arranged for the same cabbie to pick up Alvarez from the restaurant, drop him off at the hotel, then wait for the three of them. Linda waved the folders they removed from Boss's safe as bait to the unknown spy. In the center of the lobby, Scott pointed to a cocktail lounge with deliberate sweeping motions that might attract the interest of the spy. Linda countered by pointing up, indicating that she wanted to go to her room. Scott shook his head insistently, again pointing to the cocktail lounge. Linda shook her head again, pointing to the folders and up. Scott grabbed her gently around the waist and directed her into the cocktail lounge. They sat at the far end of the room with their backs against the wall. They had an unobstructed view of anyone who entered the room and took turns watching so as not to be obvious. Linda sat the folders on the table in full view. Scott ordered a beer in a bottle and Linda a glass of wine. It wasn't long before a man sauntered in and took a seat near the doorway facing them.

"We have our mark," Linda whispered. "He's the same man in Alvarez's drone videos from Boss's place. Emile is his name, I believe."

Scott ordered one whiskey, then another, then another. He pretended to chug them with a beer chaser. Instead, he spit the whiskey into the beer bottle. It was an old bar trick. Scott glanced at his phone. "We've been here fifteen minutes. Alvarez should be arriving shortly."

He and Linda opened folders from the stack and began perusing them, confident Emile would be watching but never looking at him.

"I see what you mean about the black book, Scott. You could ruin quite a few careers with this info. I hope the FBI does something with this. Boss seems to have a lock on justice in New Orleans. What a rat."

Linda and Scott had no visual way to keep track of Alvarez, lacking a clear view of the lobby, and they were relegated to communicating by text, when necessary. Alvarez arrived on cue. He had shed his chauffeur's costume and was dressed in contemporary clothes. He combed his hair differently and wore fake glasses. He went directly to the elevator. An elderly couple and a young lady got on with him, but they got off on different floors. He began with Linda and Scott's room where he hastily packed their two small suitcases. He double-checked the drawers and bathroom. He wiped down the surfaces with a cloth to remove fingerprints. Then, he went to his room and repeated the process. Satisfied both rooms were sanitized, he wheeled three suitcases to the elevator and pushed the button. The elevator was empty when it arrived. A young couple with two kids got on at a lower floor. When the elevator door opened on the lobby floor, there were other people waiting to get on, but nothing suspicious. He paused briefly to make sure everyone got on the elevator and no one was following him. Then he muscled the three suitcases to the cab where he texted Scott.

Done.

Scott announced, "Shame to leave all this stuff behind. I mean, we've photographed the documents and sent the pictures to Wilson at FBI headquarters, but these are the originals."

"It's for the best," Linda countered. "That way the FBI can get warrants for the material when they develop their case. These could be thrown out of court because of the way we acquired them."

"We don't know that's true because we aren't FBI agents anymore, just concerned citizens who witnessed the kidnapping of four illegal aliens and attempted to rescue them."

"I don't want to take that chance. I'd like to see Boss go down."

Linda stood and walked to the restroom. Scott staggered to the bar, acting like he had way too much to drink. He paid his tab and slipped his arm in Linda's as they headed to the doorway. They left the folders on the table in plain sight of Emile. When they neared Emile's table, Scott said, "I'm so tired, I'm going to sleep for two days."

Linda replied, "You're certainly going to have a hangover for two days. You drank an awful lot."

They sauntered out of the cocktail lounge, then increased their pace through the lobby and into the waiting cab. Emile had two choices—to follow them and leave the documents unattended or to ignore them and retrieve documents for which he could be paid handsomely. He obviously chose the latter, since he had yet to emerge from the cocktail lounge when they pulled away. Scott gave Alvarez the thumbs-up, and Alvarez returned the gesture.

When they reached the restaurant, Louie and the girls were just finishing dessert. Scott paid the bill. "Okay, let's hit the road. We have reservations at our hotel for another night, so they shouldn't become truly suspicious until we're home."

Linda's phone rang. She put it on speaker so everyone could hear.

"Linda, this is Frank Rafferty with the Hudspeth County Sheriff's department. We found Pedro and Jose. They're fine. They were pushing cattle like you said. They're on their way back to the house now. We have a patrol car on Quitman Pass Road, but so far have noticed nothing suspicious. The burglars tracked mud and paint into the house, but not very far. We found it in the living room, the den, and the kitchen. I doubt if the burglars were in there very long."

"Nine minutes," Linda answered. "I have time stamps on my security cameras. I saw one of them carry off Scott's shotgun. Nothing else."

"Not my favorite shotgun." Scott winced.

"Shush," said Linda, her hand over the phone. "If you're a good boy, Santa may bring you another." Then louder, she said, "Let me ask you this, Frank. How do you think the men got from Mexico to our place?"

"Good question. I would say definitely not by car. There are no fresh tire tracks, though there is a rental car parked next to Scott's truck."

Linda interrupted, "That belongs to our friend Alvarez who is here in New Orleans with us."

Frank continued, "That leaves foot or horseback. There are fresh tracks of both at the hitching post off the front porch. At this point, I can't distinguish theirs from those of your ranch hands. Ten miles over the pass is two hours on horseback or four hours by foot. That's a notable journey. Any idea what they were looking for?"

"Four thousand dollars," Scott spoke up loudly enough to be heard by Frank. "That's what Mateo charged the girls to bring them across the river. That's what I took from Mateo when I caught him in this country."

Frank said, "Probably not enough money to risk hanging around for with the possibility of a breaking and entering charge. I suspect these men are long gone."

Anna cast Catalina an anxious look. "Don't think so," said Anna sheepishly. She bared her soul in case it became important. "Francisco wants me to sign papers that entitle him to thirty million dollars. He wants me to state that he is genetically related to Efrain Hernandez, who died recently. Of course, my genetic tests show that Francisco isn't genetically related to Hernandez, but Catalina's girls are. That would make the twins the rightful heirs to the Hernandez fortune."

Linda turned and gawked at Anna while Scott stared at her in the mirror. They could hear Frank whistle into the phone. "Thirty million. Imagine that. This revelation explains a lot and suggests that Mateo and Francisco haven't gone far."

CHAPTER 48

THE TRIP BACK

I called my folks immediately using Carlos's phone to ease their concerns. Of course they wanted to know where I was and what I was doing. The emotions were too raw, and I couldn't explain everything. Actually, I had a difficult time explaining much of anything, the trip had been so odd. In a few days I went from free woman to captive to slave and back to free woman, and I was no worse for wear. I told them I would call again when we were back in Texas. By then I hoped to be free from Boss. For now, we were running for our lives and did not want to convey anything that might alarm them further. Fortunately, Boss didn't give chase.

For much of the trip, I sat in the back seat of Louie's car listening to Linda. I was astonished at her insightful questions and concise answers. She tried to conceal her smarts, but the wheels moved constantly. Most smart people I know are kind of nerdy, like Carlos. I love him dearly because I understand where he's coming from. But to a casual observer, he is flat and unresponsive to human emotions. Linda was not that way. She came across as warm and endearing in her body language and manner of speaking. I admired her from the start and hoped to become lifelong friends.

Linda spent some time questioning Louie about Boss, our kidnapping, and especially why he changed course and came to our rescue. She seemed particularly suspicious that he might have some hidden motive that could prove costly. Louie was very open about Boss and our kidnapping. He was less forthcoming about the rescue. Linda was relentless in her questions.

"I worked for the FBI for many years. Many perps suffer remorse, but very few risk life and limb to right their wrongs. Could you tell me why you rescued the very girls you kidnapped?"

"I . . . uh . . ." He glanced in the rearview mirror to see if I was paying attention. My eyes were locked on his. He couldn't hold my piercing gaze. "I came to admire Anna's perseverance. She never quit trying to escape. Look at what she did to her hands. She beat off an alligator that was bigger than her. It's remarkable. I thought that having such a woman at my side in a relationship instead of as an adversary would be wonderful. Think of what we could do together."

He gave what sounded like a contented sigh to have it all out in the open. He glanced back at me again. My face blushed. He was a hand-some man, and I was grateful he came to my rescue, but I wasn't the least bit interested in ramping up a romance. A few days ago, I would have run him through with a knife if I had a chance.

Linda mulled this over. "So you what, fell in love with her?"

He nodded.

"So you rescued her out of love and not pity or remorse."

"It's complicated, but more out of love, I think," he answered. "Her and the little girls. They're special to me too."

Linda studied him carefully. He was baring his soul. He clenched the steering wheel much harder than necessary. Beads of sweat formed on his temples. He turned on the AC. I sat in stunned silence.

"So where do you go from here?" inquired Linda in a casual tone.

"I'm moving to California. I'll change my name, go back to being an auto mechanic. Maybe I'll open my own garage."

"No, I mean in your relationship with Anna."

He glanced at the mirror again and cleared his throat. "I hope she'll want to go with me, but I don't blame her if she doesn't. I was horrible to her. I'm not really like that, but it takes a while to mend fences. If she wants to visit me when I'm settled, that would be a fine place to start."

I was not the least bit interested in going with him to California. I wanted to see my family again. We had a lot to talk about. They must have been worried sick about me despite Carlos's assurances. We were planning a happy reunion. Then there was the matter of their safety.

We were all fugitives in a country that didn't want us. As long as Francisco was alive, all our lives were in jeopardy, especially now that he could cross the border at will.

Linda cleared her throat to try and end the subject. "You realize that this is the longest of long shots. You don't go from kidnapper to lover in a few days."

"I know," he answered glumly. "But you have to start somewhere. Thank you for helping me work my way through this."

Jose called Linda. The phone was loud and I overheard the conversation. "We boarded up the broken window and turned off the burglar alarm. No sign of Mateo and Francisco. Deputy Rafferty stops by periodically to check on things. He seems concerned that patrol cars didn't find them on Quitman Pass Road. It's not a mystery. There's open desert for miles along both sides of the road. Border Patrol thinks two men fitting that description were repairing fences along Quitman Pass Road the day of the break-in. Haven't seen the men since."

Linda was concerned. "Call me immediately with anything suspicious. I'm not convinced they're gone. We just hit the road. We'll be back in the morning. And we have two beautiful young ladies with us, about your age. One has three-year-old twin girls that are so cute. I'll pick up some groceries on our way back. We'll have a nice dinner to celebrate."

To tell the truth, I was more intrigued by Jose than Louie. There was clearly an affectionate bond between him and Linda. I needed some affection, but Louie was a man of contradictions. On the way east, he had been arrogant and demanding. On the way west, he was kind. His language was rough and his demeanor coarse, but he spoke of things that appealed to me. He wanted a house and two children. He was good with kids. He spoiled Maribel and Guadalupe. I could use a little spoiling myself, but I didn't let down my guard. Louie was not my dream guy. I wanted someone who listened. Louie was more of a talker. I wanted someone who would turn heads wherever we went. Louie was more of a hulk. He had a lovely Cajun face with dark hair and fine features, but I favored the slender Latino look because that was the way I was built.

We stopped for breakfast about an hour outside of Sierra Blanca. Linda offered to let Louie stay at Setting Sun Ranch for a couple of days to recover from the drive. The plan was that she would take Catalina and the girls to pick up a few groceries with Louie as their chauffeur. Scott would gas up, then drive Carlos and me directly to Setting Sun Ranch. We were all exhausted. It seemed a good plan at the time.

CHAPTER 49

SETTING SUN RANCH

Scott opened his trunk and grabbed a couple of suitcases. He lugged those up the steps and set them on the front porch. He studied the note on the door while he fumbled for his house key. The boys had done a great job boarding up the broken window, the only source of natural light in the living room. They left the message on the door as a reminder that the perps were still on the loose. Scott pushed the door open for me while I grabbed one of the suitcases and ambled inside. It took my eyes a few seconds to adjust to the darkness, and what I saw gave me pause. Two guns were trained on us, and two bodies lay on the floor.

"Home sweet home, Scott," Mateo taunted. "Isn't that what they say in America? I hope you got our message. Come in and relax with those two." He pointed to the bodies on the floor.

"Are they dead?"

"No," said Mateo. "They'll live. You're another question. I hear you have four thousand dollars of my money. I'd like it back now."

"The money is in my wallet. I'm going to get it with my left hand. Then I hope you'll leave."

Scott moved his hand slowly and retrieved the wallet. Francisco snatched the billfold. He holstered his gun and fastened Scott's arms behind his back with flex cuffs. Then he forced him into a wooden chair from the dining room, and used a pair of flex cuffs to bind each leg to the chair. Francisco turned his gun to the door as Alvarez

195

entered the house with his computer. Before his eyes adjusted to the darkness Alvarez announced, "I left the key in the ignition in case you want to . . ." His voice trailed off at the sight of the bodies.

Francisco motioned us away from the door with his gun and kicked the door shut. "We meet again, lovely Anna. This time you will sign the papers."

Mateo cuffed Alvarez's arms and legs and pushed him to the floor beside Pedro and Jose. "Cuff her hands for now," barked Francisco. Motioning to Scott, he said, "We'll deal with this one first."

For some reason, Mateo didn't cuff my hands but pushed me down on the fireplace hearth. I sat upright and had a clear view of the room. Francisco fumbled through the wallet. He put a few credit cards in his shirt pocket. Then he pulled out the money and counted it.

"There's only a thousand here. Where is the rest?"

"I spent it getting Anna back from Mateo's associates. If it's a question of money, I can get more."

"Do you have it here, or do you mean get it from a bank?"

"A bank," Scott said.

Francisco stared at Scott coldly, his eyes demented and caustic. "We can't wait for that."

Next to the fireplace was a set of cleaning tools. Mateo grabbed the small shovel, then approached Scott with it. "My knee and shoulder are still sore, and I have scars where you dragged me through the cacti. You will pay."

Francisco snickered. "That's the attitude, Mateo. A good trick is to come straight down on his shoulder. That breaks the collarbone. It's very painful. I like toying with my victims. Break this, break that, and pretty soon they're groveling for you to stop. At some point, they'll do anything you ask. You watching this, Anna?"

Mateo reared back with the shovel, intending to hit Scott's head. As the shovel came forward, Scott stood as best he could with his feet bound to the chair. It was only a few inches, but it was enough to prevent a head injury. The shovel struck his upper arm just below the shoulder and the shovel handle wrapped around his arm.

"Nice, Mateo. The bone cracked. I'm afraid the shovel is useless. Let's see what other tools we have over there."

Francisco walked over to the hearth and winked at Anna. "Just a few more minutes, honey. Try to be patient. You'll get your turn. Everyone is a winner today."

He grabbed the Setting Sun branding iron and brandished it in front of Scott. "Found this in the stable, Mateo. Perhaps we should brand him like he does his cattle."

Francisco handed the branding iron to Mateo and pointed toward the kitchen. Mateo carried the iron to the kitchen where he fired up one of the burners. Then he went back to the living room. Mateo slammed his fist into Scott's broken arm. "How's that feel, cowboy?"

Scott did his best to keep his mouth closed, but a small whimper escaped.

"Ah, you like it. Great, here's another."

Mateo reared back and hit him in the arm again. Scott groaned. Mateo snickered. "Not such a brave fellow without your horse and your lariat. We'll see how you take to getting branded."

Mateo went to retrieve the iron. "Oh, it's red-hot." His voice trailed off.

There was some banging of pots and pans. A shot rang out, and there was the thud of a body hitting the floor. Instinctively, Francisco grabbed me by the hair. Using me as a human shield, he made his way to the front door. He grabbed the knob and swung the door open. A gun was pointed at us from the kitchen and Linda spoke.

"Give it up, Francisco. Mateo's dead. Let the girl go."

"No way. I have a gun on her, and I'll kill her. Back off."

Francisco slammed the door behind him as he dragged me across the front porch and down the steps.

CHAPTER 50

SETTING SUN RANCH

L inda barked out commands.

"Louie, get your car and meet me around front. We'll follow them. Anyone in here need an ambulance?"

Alvarez said, "Scott has a broken arm."

Linda got a kitchen knife and cut Alvarez's flex cuffs. "You tend to the rest of them. I'll call the police. Catalina and her girls are out back."

Scott spoke weakly. "I want to go too. Cut me loose."

A honk came from around front. "Nope. You need medical attention."

Linda bounded down the steps and into Louie's car. Louie was in a panic. "I've lost them. I have no idea where they went."

"Calm down. I know exactly where they are. When you get to the stop sign, turn left. The street sign will say Quitman Pass Road."

Linda called 911. "This is Linda Williams at Setting Sun Ranch. I need immediate assistance. I shot an armed intruder in my kitchen and he needs an ambulance. My husband, Scott, also in the house, has a broken arm. I'm in pursuit of an armed male with a female hostage. I have lost sight of them, but I believe they are heading south on Quitman Pass Road and intend to cross the Rio Grande into Mexico."

Louie had turned onto Quitman Pass Road, barely slowing down. He had the pedal to the floor. "I think I see them."

Linda's phone rang. "Linda, this is Deputy Frank Rafferty. We'll dispatch an ambulance and medical team to your house. I'm in Sierra

Blanca and am heading to Quitman Pass Road. Are these the two fugitives who broke into your place yesterday?"

"Yes! Mateo may be dead. I shot him in our kitchen when he tried to pull a gun on me. Francisco fled in Scott's car with a hostage. I'm on Quitman Pass Road and think I see them nearing the summit, though we are at least a mile behind."

"The hostage is—?"

"Another Mexican national named Anna, kin to our friend Alvarez."

"You might want to gain a little ground and let me know whether they turn right or left at the end of the road. He'll try to cross the river soon. I'll call another car, but I doubt if either of us can be there before the river crossing. I know you have a storied career with the FBI, but don't do anything rash. Keep your gun in your purse. You're not FBI anymore."

"I can't let Francisco drag Anna across the river where he's free to do anything to her. No, I have to catch them on this side of the river. And it doesn't sound like you'll be here in time to help."

"Linda, I'm just saying that a rash move can end Anna's life. These are vindictive people."

Linda changed the subject. "We've crested the summit. I see Scott's car below. Louie has halved the distance, but only because he had a straight shot. The curves are coming up." After a moment, she added, "Looks like Scott's car is turning left. Yes, left."

Frank replied, "I expect Francisco to make the very next right. There's no sense in dragging this out. He must know he needs to cross the river ASAP. The next road to the right ends very close to the river. Probably less than a hundred yards to Mexico."

"Good call. That's exactly where he's turning. Probably where he came over in the first place."

CHAPTER 51

RIO GRANDE

F rancisco accelerated down the dirt road and burst through the barricade. The car was airborne for a moment, then hit the mud and plowed to a halt. He dragged me out of the driver's side of the car by my hair. I fell getting out of the car headfirst and was covered with mud. Francisco yanked me up by my arm. I gained my balance with difficulty, struggling to move forward, more from the mud and uneven ground than my resistance. I found it difficult to keep my balance. I fell, and Francisco pulled me up again.

"You will come back to Mexico with me and sign those papers, or I'll shoot you here and now."

I struggled to my feet and jogged to show him that I was cooperating. My feet were caked with mud and I soon wearied.

Louie had slammed his car into park at the end of the road and was on the run with catlike speed. His voice boomed. "Leave my Anna alone."

I could hardly believe my ears, my good fortune. My kidnapper and torturer was again my savior. Francisco pulled his gun and fired. The shot was wild but cautioned Louie to crouch low. Louie continued charging, but at a lesser speed due to his awkward center of gravity. "Leave my Anna alone," he yelled again.

Francisco lined up another shot. I tripped over a branch, and my fall pulled him to the muddy ground on the river's edge. The shot went wide. Louie was now about twenty yards away. Francisco rolled away from me and from a prone position fired continuously until the empty chamber clicked. The first shot was wide, but the next two seemed to connect. Louie staggered momentarily, but continued moving forward like the bull of a man he was.

Louie threw himself on top of me to keep me on this side of the river. Francisco could not wrest me from underneath Louie, and he had no more bullets to keep his promise about ending my life. He turned and fled into the river. Louie had saved me, but at what cost? He wrapped his arms around me and held me tight. I think he thought there might be more gunfire and wanted to protect me from bullets, but Francisco was gone. His sodden form crawled onto the sandy bank across the way and slinked into the cane.

Linda arrived, winded and wary. She kept her gun trained on the opposite bank. "Damn, I really need to get more exercise."

I said, "I think he's out of ammo, but stay down in case."

The whine of a police siren in the distance grew louder, and there was another more distant siren. "Thank you, Louie," I whispered in his ear. He said nothing.

I rolled him on his back and noticed his chest covered in blood. Linda was on her phone immediately. "Bullet to the chest. I need an ambulance immediately. Medevac if possible. I don't think he can hang on much longer."

The first police car pulled up, and Linda walked over to meet Deputy Frank. I used the bottom of Louie's shirt to try to staunch the blood flow. No matter how hard I pushed, the blood kept spurting out. "Please hang on, Louie. Help is on the way. You saved my life. I want to save yours. You were so brave. Thank you."

His eyelids fluttered open. He stared at me with unusual intensity, but his eyes kept drifting in and out of focus. His voice was soft. "Just a little scrape. I'll be fine in a few days. Always have been before."

His body trembled and his eyes closed, but then they opened again. This time there was a calm I hadn't seen before. He said, "I love you, Anna." Then his eyes closed for the final time. My eyes filled with tears, and I let them stream down my cheeks. They dropped onto his face, binding us forever.

CHAPTER 52

SETTING SUN RANCH

The first thing I did was call my parents to let them know Carlos and I were safely back in Texas. They were still in Juarez, awaiting passports to bring them across the border. I cautioned them to lay low, as Francisco was still on the prowl and definitely in Mexico. I wanted to hold them and kiss them and let them know that I may have been damaged but was far from broken. Of course, I had no passport and no way to enter Mexico legally just yet. The passports would be done in the next day or two, and we made plans to meet in old town El Paso for a grand family reunion, as tourists, of course.

The homecoming party Linda planned was relegated to Jose and Pedro's much smaller house and yard because there was a police investigation into Mateo's death. Yellow tape was wrapped around Linda's house. Linda seemed confident she would not be charged with homicide because Mateo had brutally assaulted Scott and drawn a gun on her. Plus, the other witnesses, Mateo and Louie, were both dead.

Linda perceptive nature saved Scott's life. The events leading up to the shooting of Mateo began with Linda noticing that the trunk of Scott's car was open. Apparently, Scott was compulsive about loading and unloading the car. He invariably unloaded the trunk completely and closed it immediately before doing anything else. The open trunk and the absence of activity around the car was the first clue. Then there was the absence of Jake. The loyal dog always came out to greet guests. Turns out he was locked up in the barn with the horses. These two clues prompted Linda to have Louie drive around back, where they unloaded Catalina and the girls. Then, Linda and Louie entered the house through the back door where they surprised Mateo, who was heating the poker. As the story went, Mateo tried to draw his gun, but Linda already had hers out. It was no contest. I have no reason to doubt Linda. She's been perfectly honest about everything else.

Linda and Scott sat next to each other at the corral. I think of them as the real dynamic duo. What clever people they were—quick, insightful, decisive. I could see why Carlos loved to spend time with them. I'd been lacking in those qualities. If only I could absorb them for my next adventure. Sadly, Scott's arm was in a cast and held in place with a sling. No lasting damage, the doctors had said. I could tell he was in considerable pain, even though he tried so hard not to let it show. Still, he and Linda were affectionate. Nothing like coming back from the brink of death to help you appreciate the priorities in your life. If only I could find a long and happy relationship.

Jose and Pedro were college graduates from Texas A&M. They wanted to buy their own ranch someday and were working to pay off their college loans. They were cute but painfully shy. I guessed living on an isolated ranch didn't help them meet other girls. They also seemed embarrassed that Mateo and Francisco so easily apprehended them. It was the nature of the male ego. Fortunately, only their pride was injured. It wasn't long before they had me up on a horse. Horseback riding was fun, but I think I prefer two feet on the ground.

I caught up with Catalina and her girls playing with Jake. I believed it was the first time the twins had played with a dog, and there was pure joy with this soft, loving animal. I asked Catalina about her plans for the future. She understood she was in a precarious situation, trapped in this country as an illegal alien. If she surrendered to the Border Patrol, ICE could separate her from her children like they did to thousands of others. They might even send her back to Mexico without her girls. Then came my big question. "Are you going to try to claim their father's fortune for them?"

She shook her head *no* at first, then shook her fist in the air. "I need to learn to be brave like you, Anna. It is their money. I want that for them. It's just that I am too afraid to go back and collect it."

It was the most passion I had seen from her on the subject. It pushed me to think about the enormity of what needed to be done. I wanted to provide the first step. "You can't do it alone. You need the signed genetic test papers to take to the judge. It's my job to sign them for you. I'll do my job when my passport is ready, if that is what you want."

"What of Francisco? He'll kill you."

"Perhaps I can give him a taste of his own medicine. I'll work on a plan."

The party turned into a wake for Louie. Linda, Scott, and Carlos each found something nice to say. I said I was grateful that he twice rescued me, because it took a great deal of personal courage on both occasions. He seemed to enter his career with Boss for the wrong reason and leave for the right reason. I was truly sorry that he died. He was certainly capable of love. He showed that with Maribel and Guadalupe right from the start. But I wondered if he truly loved me. Maybe it was remorse or embarrassment or infatuation that drove him on his fatal rescue mission. I doubted it was love. And yet, he laid down his life for me, which is the ultimate human sacrifice.

Rather than mixed emotions, I should say I had evolving emotions about him. I started out despising him. He tried to make me a modern-day slave in a country that abolished slavery one hundred and fifty years ago. I found this reprehensible. I slapped him when he asked if he could be my first client as a prostitute, but I was also intrigued. Did he find me hotter than Catalina? Men didn't give me a second glance when I was with her. Louie was the only man who chose in my favor, even if the choice was poorly worded. Though there was constant friction between us, I think deep down he liked me for who I was. At least that was what I chose to believe. I'd seen other people cycle through hate, remorse, and love at regular intervals. I could only assume that there was an imbalance of some critical chemical in the human brain that caused such contradictory oscillations. Perhaps they'd identify a gene for it someday and then a cure.

At the end of the evening, Carlos and I went for a walk around the ranch. We were as different as night and day in that we made nearly opposite decisions on the spectrum of possibilities.

He vented his frustration. "Why do you live your life running against the wind? You make so many poor choices."

"I could just as easily ask you why you measure your life's choices in a decision tree of probabilities that are compounded for several moves into the future. You rarely step outside the bounds of what you consider perfectly safe and even then only under extreme duress. I appreciate that you came to Mexico to save me. That was brave and I love you for it. But you need to understand that we react to our world in different ways that are not necessarily ours to choose. I cannot reduce life to mathematical equations just as you cannot embrace my emotional decisions."

Carlos countered, "You made a poor choice signing the papers that cost Marina her life. You made a poor choice on the GPS transmitter that nearly cost you yours. You can't keep shooting from the hip."

"Not the hip," I corrected, "the heart. I choose from my heart. We each have our own logic board for those decisions. Are we really free to choose a different course? I think it's likely that our major decisions are hardwired by genetics into our personalities. I also think that the consequences of those decisions are difficult to predict. Had I made a different choice when I signed the form, Marina might still be alive. Perhaps the twins would be dead. The consequences create ripples in the lives of others that then affect their decisions. The good news is that I now understand Francisco's logic board, while mine is a mystery to him. Advantage to me."

"You're not honestly thinking of going after Francisco, are you?"

"It has to be done before more innocent blood is shed."

CHAPTER 53

JUAREZ

P assport in hand, I entered Mexico, intent on bringing Francisco down. I wanted desperately to swing by the motel where my family was staying, to tell them I loved them in case this ended badly. In the end, I decided that the visit might tip off Francisco and place everyone's lives in jeopardy. There would be time enough for a reunion later in the day if I was still alive. Carlos called my journey madness and tried desperately to change my mind. I wouldn't listen. Carlos pointed out examples from the past few days where he provided sound advice and I made rash and costly decisions to the contrary. He was, of course, right. Was I crazy to enter the lion's den? I didn't think so. I was intent on completing the task that started this messy affair, submitting to the legal authorities the genetic test results and documents that would prove that the twins were the rightful heirs to the Hernandez fortune. But first, I had to deal with Francisco.

I sat in the shade of a small tree outside Misión de Nuestra Señora de Guadalupe, fuming about a lack of justice in this world. Even though the genetic tests showed that Francisco had a false claim on thirty million, he wouldn't let it go. He'd crossed the border illegally in pursuit of a signature falsifying my data and killed Louie in the process. Surely there was a solution that rewarded the two innocent girls who were the real heirs. Why must the good suffer at the hands of the evil?

The sound of a car engine broke my musing. I peered around the tree. Francisco pulled through the parking lot and stopped by the church entrance. My stomach churned. I was here because this was the time of day he normally retrieved his mother from church. Mustering all my courage, I rose on shaky legs. I sashayed past his car, swinging my hips nonchalantly. My walk seemed too forced, given the tremble in my legs. I didn't look at him or let him know that I recognized him. I wanted to make this seem like a chance encounter. I made my way toward the church door, hoping he wouldn't follow just yet. I was relieved when the door opened and his mother emerged. She recognized me with a smile. "Nice to see you again, dear. Say, would you like to meet my son? He's right here in the car. He needs to find a nice girl like you and settle down. He's always been a restless child."

I smiled politely, but the words came out hurried and nervous. "Next time, señora. I have a lot on my mind today."

The old lady's smile faded as she nodded in empathy. "I know what you mean. The church is my refuge. I've always found peace in prayer. It's that young man of yours, isn't it? He didn't seem to amount to much. Not the type of person to build a future with, if you know what I mean. You can do better."

She hobbled by me as I tugged open the large wooden door and entered the church.

I thought, *Carlos traveled two thousand miles to save my life while I fought his sound advice at every turn. I can only hope to find a husband who loves me that much.*

I knew Francisco would drop his mama off at home and return for the big showdown. It was time to make my peace with God. The interior of the church was dark, and I had trouble seeing at first. I focused my attention on a set of votive candles burning near the altar. I placed a few pesos in the metal box and lit a candle. I knelt in front of dozens of flickering candles, each broadcasting a message to the Savior for hope against all odds. My own message was one of despair. My thoughts were so jumbled about right and wrong. The past cannot be mended, but I was young enough to believe that past injustices awaited remedy. What was the remedy that had no detrimental consequences? What act did not assume a future that became unpredictable? Someone always seemed to suffer needlessly. Perhaps it should be me? Then the words of the Lord's Prayer jumped into my mind. *Forgive us our trespasses, as we forgive those who trespass against us.*

I ran the words through my mind over and over again, but couldn't make them apply. The words only seem to work if everyone adheres to them to the same degree. I filled to near bursting with despair and indecision. There was still time to leave, but that wouldn't solve any problems.

You ask more of me than I can give. Someone will die, maybe me. Please forgive me.

I stood and made my way to the back of the church. I sat in a pew in the only lit part of the church. The sun caught a small stained glass window high on the church wall and cast rainbow-tinted hues on the pews around me. My favorite colors, deep blues and reds, surrounded me. On either side, the bright colors faded into inky blackness. I mused on this. Most times I preferred to sit in the shadows, unnoticed and forgotten. I did my part to make the world a better place, unbidden and unseen. It's not because I was afraid of what lurked in the karmic shadows of this world or the next. I derived an immediate sense of peace and self-worth from helping the less fortunate. Was that God in me, or was that a collection of genes firing willy-nilly? I guess I'd never know, at least in this life.

CHAPTER 54

MISIÓN DE NUESTRA SEÑORA DE
GUADALUPE

I shuddered when the large wooden door opened behind me. A spray of white light washed across the church interior, then extinguished as the door swung shut with a thud. I concentrated on keeping my face pointed toward the altar and tried to remain calm. There were a few footsteps and then a loud bang as a kneeler in the pew behind me came down hard on the floor.

"Forgive us our trespasses," I prayed more fervently.

In an empty church, this person sought me out and knelt directly behind me where I couldn't see him. My throat tightened. I started to finish the prayer. "As we forgive . . ." But try as I might, the rest would not come out. Warm breath on the back of my neck with the acrid odor of cigarettes and sweat made my skin crawl. I wanted to run out of the church screaming. I must've been mad to be here.

A cold, raspy voice whispered just inches from the back of my head. "I didn't expect to see you here. Where expectations are low, disappointments are rare. You have raised my expectations. Don't disappoint me. You want to end my pursuit. Enough people have died."

I refused to turn around and face my tormentor. I faced forward, praying in muted tones. "Forgive us our trespasses, forgive us our trespasses, forgive us our trespasses."

Francisco snickered. "Don't worry. I'll forgive you. I'll give you another chance. The killing can end."

My voice morphed into a trembling whisper as I picked up the pace despite my best effort to remain clam. Tears welled up in my eyes. Then, an arm reached around me and dropped some papers into my lap. A cold hand brushed my cheek with slow deliberation as it pulled back toward its owner. It lingered there longer than necessary, then firmly pulled my hair behind my ear.

The voice was louder now as it commanded into my exposed ear. "Sign the papers, and I'll be gone from your life forever, unless you want to start dating." He emitted a demonic, throaty chuckle. "My mother seems to think we would make the perfect couple. Isn't that a laugh? You with one foot in heaven and me with one in hell."

His hand brushed my cheek again, and I jerked away reflexively. Tears began to cleanse the cheek he defiled. A shudder coursed through my body. These papers had already cost two lives, four if you counted Louie and the coyote. Where would it end? Seemed likely that one more death was inevitable. Mine? I plucked the papers from my lap and leafed through forms I knew by heart, pausing on the paragraph that mattered.

In a voice that wavered despite my bidding, I tried to speak my mind. My tone was mousy. "Says here that you are the sole relative. You will be heir to the entire fortune. Are you deliberately excluding the two little girls who are his daughters?"

Francisco brushed my request away casually. "That's right." The demented laugh began again, deep and raspy. "Now sign the papers," he said firmly as a hand reached around me again and dropped a pen into my lap.

"Can't you open your heart and share with them? They have no father."

As the hand drew back, it stopped on my shoulder where it pressed firmly into the side of my neck. "No."

The pressure of his hand hurt, but I resisted the impulse to pull away. "Please. Give them something."

"No. The money is mine." His long fingers moved forward and pressed against my throat to quell my defiance. He could easily snap my neck. I scribbled on the paper, then stood abruptly and faced him. I scrambled the order of the papers, then handed the lot back to him. I flipped the pen to him as I inched toward the aisle.

"There, you have it. I'll be going now."

I exited the pew with dignity that I hoped would hide my haste and was several steps into the aisle when he finished sorting through the papers and stared at my writing. To my surprise, he let out a hearty laugh.

"Mama might have been right about us being a perfect couple. Not one in a thousand people would have dared write 'go to hell' instead of signing their name. But every action has an opposing reaction. Isn't that an unalterable law of physics? It'll cost you dearly."

Then he became more somber and his eyes filled with hate. The words of the padres rose up in my head. *We are all made in the image and likeness of God.* I fought the words back. Not this guy. He was a godless mutant.

I mustered my most defiant voice. "It won't. I have GOD on my side."

Francisco rolled his eyes and shook his head in disbelief. "Are you some kind of religious lunatic? The only gods that rule this world are guns and money. Those are the gods I worship. You can't honestly believe the Almighty will save you."

I studied his posture. It became threatening as he pulled himself up on the kneeler. He inched his way across the kneeler toward the aisle. I took an involuntary step back. I didn't mean to, it just happened. He must have noticed my retreat. He became bolder and picked up his speed toward the aisle. A sudden calm overtook me. This was the way it would end. There was no other possibility. I did everything I could to resolve the impasse peacefully. I took a step toward him. My sudden boldness froze him as he cast a confused look my way.

"Not the Almighty," I said demurely.

"Then what god are you talking about? You're not making any sense."

Evil has a thousand faces. Was I one of them? Could I throw away a life so callously? "I mean Alejandro's brothers—Gabriel, Orlando, and Diego. GOD."

I gave a nervous laugh, hoping they heard their cues. The brothers had been lying under pews, hidden in the deep shadow. They stood as their names were called, one to the right of Francisco, one to the left, and one barring passage to the exit. Each held a pistol. They inched toward him with menacing faces.

As I moved toward the exit, I called out to Francisco in a spiteful voice that belied the raw nerves in the pit of my stomach. "I hear you were boyhood friends. Went to the same school. I'll leave you to reminisce about the good old days."

I burst through the front door, carelessly missing the step down. I sought purchase with broad steps and stabilized my stumble. As my dilated pupils adjusted to a world too bright for their girth, I noticed Carlos about ten feet in front of me, surrounded by a halo of light that seemed divine. "You're a rose among thorns, Anna. I find it gratifying that God would use one of His most innocent lambs to mete out justice and mercy."

A cry inside the church became muffled as the door creaked shut. "Mercy?" I asked incredulously.

He answered matter-of-factly with words I suspected were true. "Francisco would have killed you and the twins unless he got what he wanted. Maybe your family too."

In a world with more perfect beings, there might be no need for consequences. But not in this world. Down the street, a dog barked at some unseen annoyance and then whined as if corrected by his master. Further away, a car accelerated, then shifted gears, linking past and future as surely as the rising sun chases shadows from the valley.

AUTHOR'S NOTE

The evil and illegal enterprise of human trafficking is a $150 billion industry with 25 million victims worldwide. Human trafficking crimes are distinguished by the use of force, fraud, or coercion to ensure victim compliance. Some types of human trafficking involve forced labor in otherwise legal professions, but the vast majority of the cases in the US involve sex trafficking. Common types of sex trafficking involve escort services, pornography, illicit massage businesses, brothels, and outdoor solicitation.

According to the watchdog organization Polaris, California and Texas are the two most notorious US states for human trafficking. I selected Texas for this novel because the most troubled city of the last two decades seems to be the cartel-ridden border town of Juarez, Mexico, sister city to El Paso, Texas. Thought of as replaceable laborers, young women go missing regularly in Juarez. This unmerited aura of dispensability makes women especially vulnerable, and I hope this book leads to a better appreciation of their plight. Young women, mostly under the age of eighteen, are often placed unwillingly into a system of trafficking when their parents are unable to pay a ransom to the cartel. The women continue to be held in the sex trade against their will with threats of violence against them, their parents, or their children. They are often transported to distant cities in the US.

I continue to be a strong proponent of social justice for women, children, and minorities. Anna is based on a collection of characteristics from the many strong and selfless women in my life related by blood, marriage, or adoption. The collective image is one of grace, guile, and perseverance.

There is a human trafficking corridor heading east out of El Paso along I-10 that passes through some of the cities mentioned in this novel. There really is a checkpoint near Sierra Blanca for illegal refugees and drugs that has received notoriety for the arrests of Willie Nelson, Snoop Dogg, and Armie Hammer. Hudspeth County is occasionally patrolled by movie star and deputy Steven Seagal. The trafficking corridors branch out along I-75, I-85, and I-95, among others, to highly populated cities. According to the National Human Trafficking Hotline, statistics for 2007–2016 show that Atlanta, Georgia, the site of the 2019 Super Bowl, ranks second only to Washington, DC, for the number of calls per capita. New Orleans ranks twenty-third.

I-10 passes through the Louisiana bayou at Lake Charles, and the area to the south is a lowland of meandering stream channels. Though not as wild as portrayed in this novel, it is nevertheless rife with gators and snakes. There are stories of bull sharks entering Calcasieu Lake from the Gulf of Mexico. Fishing stories being what they are, I hesitate to confirm them.

Finally, President Trump's "zero tolerance" immigration policy has made America's weak anti-trafficking efforts even weaker as the Department of Homeland Security Immigration and Customs Enforcement (ICE) has shifted money and manpower away from trafficking investigations in order to arrest, detain, and deport illegal immigrants who, like Anna, Catalina, and the twins, are fleeing for their lives. Willful denial of basic human rights to immigrants apprehended at the border and detained in concentration camps is a crime against humanity. Separation of illegal immigrant parents from children who are lawful US citizens is shameful behavior from a nation that has for over two centuries welcomed immigrants regardless of race or religion. One quote on the pedestal of the Statue of Liberty, "Give me your tired, your poor, your huddled masses yearning to breathe free," is from Emma Lazarus's sonnet "The New Colossus." Comprehensive immigration reform is truly needed to protect the innocent and secure the border.

ACKNOWLEDGMENTS

I am indebted to the many people who offered praise for my first novel, *Malice in the Palace*, and encouraged me to write a sequel. Some put their encouragement to words in public reviews (such as on Amazon and Goodreads), which are very much appreciated (and help spread the word). Others did so in private. All helped me push forward in this new effort. Writers, like children, are raised by a village. Love you!

Logan Shimkets is my youngest fan and has been demanding a sequel for over a year. Hope you enjoy.

Caroline Tolley was my line editor and taught me about point of view issues. This was particularly challenging for me since I wanted to write Anna's perspective in first person. Thank you for your sound advice and patience with my first person experiment. Only time will tell whether Anna is conveyed in a sense of intimacy to the readers.

Christi Martin was my copy editor and did a superb job keeping me firmly in the *Chicago Manual of Style*. She went above and beyond the usual to help me understand the rationale for each suggested edit. That Christi hails from Texas and enjoyed the southern camaraderie in the book was a happy accident.

I would like to thank Amber Helt of Rooted in Writing for her thoughtful guidance during the formatting and proofreading.

My beta readers provided invaluable advice about scenes that didn't work for them, which I subsequently modified or deleted.

Writing a book is like living in a tunnel. You get so used to your own perspective that you fail to realize that others can have vastly different perceptions of your storyline until you exit the tunnel. I am grateful you helped smooth the rough edges. My beta readers include my lovely wife Diane Shimkets and my mother Dorothy "Dotte" Salvemini. They also include two of my closest scientific colleagues, William "Barny" Whitman and Marcus Fechheimer, who have become superb friends.

Finally, I'd like to thank Val M. Mathews for graciously providing me with practical advice for contemporary prose and dialog. Also, I recommend you catch her Break Writer's Block workshop (The Exit 271 Studio), which introduced me to her and Christi Martin.

Made in the USA
Columbia, SC
15 June 2020